L.A. Egerbladh is a genderfluid queer author. They were born in 1995 in Sweden. They have been telling stories since they were a small child and fantasy has always been close to their heart. Representation has always been incredibly important part of story-telling to them and they want people to be able to recognise themselves in their characters.

To my mother who always believed in me, especially when I couldn't believe in myself.

L.A. Egerbladh

FEED THE FIRE

AUSTIN MACAULEY PUBLISHERS™
LONDON * CAMBRIDGE * NEW YORK * SHARJAH

Copyright © L.A. Egerbladh 2023

The right of L.A. Egerbladh to be identified as author of this work has been asserted by the author in accordance with sections 77 and 78 of the Copyright, Designs and Patents Act 1988.

All rights reserved. No part of this publication may be reproduced, stored in a retrieval system, or transmitted in any form or by any means, electronic, mechanical, photocopying, recording, or otherwise, without the prior permission of the publishers.

Any person who commits any unauthorised act in relation to this publication may be liable to criminal prosecution and civil claims for damages.

This is a work of fiction. Names, characters, businesses, places, events, locales, and incidents are either the products of the author's imagination or used in a fictitious manner. Any resemblance to actual persons, living or dead, or actual events is purely coincidental.

A CIP catalogue record for this title is available from the British Library.

ISBN 9781035824083 (Paperback)
ISBN 9781035824090 (ePub e-book)

www.austinmacauley.com

First Published 2023
Austin Macauley Publishers Ltd®
1 Canada Square
Canary Wharf
London
E14 5AA

Thank you to Love, Albin and Erika who through our adventures in roleplaying re-awakened my love and passion for story-telling and fantasy.

Thank you to Josefine and Caroline who are always my biggest supporters and read everything I write. Your feedback and support keeps me going.

Thank you to my father who financially helped sponsor this book, it means the world.

And thank you to AM publishing for taking a chance on me and my first book.

Prologue

RUNA

The sun was shining and the breeze warmed Runa's dark skin, her eyes were closed and she took a deep breath. The scent of flowers and fresh grass filled her lungs as she laid on her back in the field. Runa quickly opened her eyes as she heard a rustle mere feet away from her but she relaxed immediately when she saw who it was.

"Anya," Runa almost whispered, her name had slipped past her lips without Runa even noticing. Anya with her dark brown hair, always pulled up into a tight bun, Anya with her soft eyes and thin mouth that almost never turned into a smile. Runa couldn't help but feel the corners of her mouth twitch into a small smile as Anya was returning the same expression. Neither of them smiled a lot these days, they were almost exclusively for each other.

"What are you doing?" Anya asked.

Before Runa could answer, Anya laid down next to her on the grass. Runa slowly looked over at her and realised she hadn't answered when Anya looked back at her with a raised eyebrow. "Just…taking advantage of days like these, I suppose," Runa said and turned her gaze back up into the bright blue sky, feeling her cheeks flush.

It was true, most days weren't this pleasant and the days that were, they were often busy and didn't have time to just relax and exist. There was always something to do, something to stress over to stay alive another day. But today, they could just exist, at least for a little while.

Runa dared a quick glance back over at Anya, who in turn had closed her eyes. Her breathing was slow and relaxed, and Runa couldn't help but to think that the way the sun was bouncing off her pale, reddened face was one of the most beautiful things she'd ever seen.

"It is a nice day," Anya almost whispered.

Anya speaking snapped Runa out of her thoughts and she cleared her throat and turned her gaze back to the sky once again.

"I'm…I'm glad you decided to join us," Runa said.

"It beats working at…" Anya stopped mid-sentence. Runa knew the wound was still fresh, still ached a little too much. "The last place," Anya finally finished saying.

"Still…" Runa said. "It feels good to have you around again."

"You're just saying that because now you're not the newest member anymore," Anya said with a laugh.

Runa smiled at that and slowly moved her hand towards Anya's, only slightly grazing against her pinky finger. Anya flinched at the touch and looked over at Runa, there was worry in her eyes but also shame. Runa just kept her hand close to hers but making sure they weren't touching. An invitation but not a demand. Slowly, Anya intertwined her fingers with Runa's.

They said nothing more, just exchanged another of their rare smiles and Runa could have sworn Anya was blushing. Runa felt like her face was ablaze from just looking at her, like there was nothing and no one else in the world except the two of them at this precise moment. Finally, they turned their heads back to the sky, a content sigh slipping from Runa's lips.

Runa could feel her heart beat hard in her chest, but for once it wasn't out of fear for her own life. It wasn't because she was running from the guards or fighting another gang to protect their turf. It was because of Anya. Anya, who let her hold her hand even after everything she'd been through. It was trust in a gesture, no words needed.

This was something new, something she couldn't quite place but wanted to keep forever. Runa never wanted to let go of Anya's hand.

Chapter 1

A N Y A

4 Years Later

Lightning struck a tree and the sound of crackling wood being split echoed through air, the ground was muddy and the puddles made it a treacherous obstacle to get through. Anya felt her feet slide across a particularly wet patch and just managed to catch herself on a branch near her head.

"Shit," Anya muttered to herself and tried to look up at the sky but the rain was pouring so intensely, she had to evade her gaze almost immediately. The sky was just darkness, sometimes being illuminated by the beautiful yet dangerous lightning travelling across it. Anya knew she should never have gone out today and she could hear James' words of warning earlier that day: "A storm is coming, you should stay in the city today."

But had she listened? Of course not, she never had so why would she start today? Though she did not look forward to getting back home and seeing him look at her with that stare that just yelled 'I told you so', even if he never would actually utter the words, which almost made it worse.

Anya knew these woods better than the back of her hands but it was hard to see anything that was more than five feet in front of her and she was starting to shiver from the cold. The rain hammering down on her hard, combined with the intense wind, made it feel like her bones were turning to ice. Her clothes had been soaking wet for the last 20 minutes and she just prayed she wouldn't catch a cold, being sick wasn't something she could afford to be.

Being sick meant not making any money or going out and trying anyway but being sloppy, which increased the chances of getting arrested or hurt. Anya could not afford to be sick.

Anya let her hands trace the sides of the trees she passed, trying desperately to find any of the markings she'd made in cases like this where she couldn't strictly find her way back by sight alone. Another crack of lightning, even closer than the one before and Anya's whole body tensed for a second before she continued to run, a renewed fire lit inside of her.

She'd been chased plenty of times but never by lightning, and right now it felt like it was trying to hunt her down specifically. She knew it was impossible but every time the sky lit up, she couldn't help but doubt.

The few coins Anya had managed to gather during the day clinked in the pouch that hung on her hip, a sore reminder that it had not been worth going outside today. Robbing people was a harsh term, she preferred calling it relieving people of some of their heavy weight on their travels. Besides, Anya never took enough to put anyone in any real trouble; she took what she thought they could live without.

Two silver coins could be nothing but a small loss to them but it could mean that Anya would be able to eat for the next two days. It wasn't the most glamorous job but it beat begging on the streets or working in brothels—two jobs she'd already done and planned on never doing again. Anya hoped that James had a better day than her even though she doubted it. He was too kind, too generous.

She kept telling him it would come back to bite him in the ass but he always repeated the same thing to her, that it would pay off to be kind in the long run. Well, if they didn't live long enough to see it pay off because they didn't have enough money to survive, what good does being kind do? They couldn't live on kindness.

Anya's legs started to ache from the constant running and the muddy ground put even more strain on her legs than usual. She was already wet from the rain but she did not want to return home completely covered in mud because she'd fallen. She was supposed to be fast and sure footed, at least she knew that was part of her reputation. What little reputation she had.

Anya thought she could finally see the looming dark shape of the Castle that stood in the middle of the city and a rush of relief ran through her, at least she hadn't been running in the completely wrong direction. She took one more step and then the sky turned bright, and for a second, she could see nothing, and before she knew it, she was no longer on her feet but laying on the cold wet ground.

Her head was spinning; the air had been knocked out of her lungs and for a few seconds she felt nothing, her entire body just felt numb. Anya tried to sit up but felt a pain shoot through her left side, her hands shot to the place of the pain and when she looked at them, they were covered in warm, red blood mixed with cold dark mud.

"Shit..." She whispered to herself and tried to keep herself from seeing double or throwing up the little food she'd had that day.

Anya noticed a sharp rock beneath her, she must have hit that when she lost her footing and slashed open her side. Not ideal at this moment. When she finally managed to get into a sitting position, she looked forward and saw a scorch mark a few metres from where she'd just been standing. Lightning must have struck right by her and sent her flying off her feet because of the wet mud. Anya grunted, more in annoyance than in pain, and she slowly stood up. She leaned on a tree to keep her shaking legs from buckling beneath her weight.

She took a deep breath, put one of her hands over the wound on her side to try and stop some of the bleeding. At least, the wound didn't seem very deep or serious but it did hurt; though she knew it would hurt a lot more in a little while when the adrenaline left her body, something she didn't look forward to. Anya took one step and froze in place. The cold rain was still hammering down on her but for this short moment, she barely noticed it or the thunder roaring above her.

Not far in front of her lay what looked like a body. Anya could have sworn it was not there before she was almost struck by lightning. She shook her head, almost thinking she was seeing things but when she returned her gaze the body was still there. It didn't seem to be moving at all and after a few seconds, she shook off the shock and slowly made her way towards the body.

It was in the direction of the city and she was curious, she couldn't help it. Besides, if she was really lucky it was just a dead body and it had some valuables on it, that could help ease the pain of the disaster that had been today.

Anya almost stumbled closer and it seemed to be a masculine shape laying in the dirt. The clothes seemed to be of quite fine quality and it seemed as if he'd just started to get wet. She frowned deeply, this didn't make any sense, but as the body was still not moving, she made her way closer than she would have done normally. He was lying on his stomach and she wasn't very keen on touching him with her bare hands when she had no idea what had killed him, so she simply took the tip of her boot and turned him around.

He weighed almost nothing and flopped over on his back more easily than she would have thought. The person was nothing special, very generic features and build but perhaps on the scrawnier side. He didn't seem to have any visible wounds but she knew better than most that that only meant whoever killed him knew what they were doing.

Anya's eyes spotted what looked like a pouch on his hips and with her eyes trained on the man at all times, her hand reached for it. The moment her fingertips touched the leather, the man shot up and grabbed her arms. Anya recoiled but he was too fast, his eyes were trained on her with a mania she had never seen before and the grip he had on her was almost painfully strong, nothing she would have expected from this scrawny man.

He was also shaking something awfully and his hands on her felt like they were ablaze; he had to be running a very high fever.

Anya tried to fight him off but as her eyes met his frantic blue eyes she almost stopped and something close to fear entered her body. He too was afraid, that much she could see beyond his crazed look. No, he wasn't just afraid, what she saw in his eyes was deep desperation, and for a moment, it was like she was almost drowning in his eyes, like they were an ocean pulling her in.

"P-Please." His voice was raspy, like he hadn't spoken in days.

Anya snapped out of whatever had held her and she felt that his grip on her was almost like he was trying to either drag her down to him or drag himself up to her, and her wounded side shot pain through her body, making her head feel light and making it hard for her to see straight. Anya wasn't a saint or saviour, she was only here to take stuff off a dead body; had she known he was alive she'd...she would have just left.

She was wounded and the storm was treacherous; she couldn't think about anyone else but herself right now. It wasn't a noble thing but it was what it took to stay alive.

"What?" Anya almost whispered, her voice feeling weaker than usual.

"F-Find...Find her..." The man was struggling to get the words out. His breathing was becoming more erratic by the second and it was obvious that he was starting to panic, which only made Anya start to panic.

"What are you talking about?" Anya asked with a hiss. She should have kicked him off herself. He was holding a hard grip on her but she knew that if she really wanted to she could have pushed him away, but there was...something stopping her and making her listen.

"M-Moira Sto..." he stammered. Anya couldn't hear the end of whatever name he was saying which just made her irritated.

"Moira who?" She asked, trying to keep any anger out of her voice.

"Trust…Trust no one…" The man said desperately.

A sudden almost deafening crack of lightning lit up the sky and for a moment, Anya saw nothing but white. When she found his eyes again, something in them had changed.

It had gone from mania to something calmer, like he finally understood or accepted something, and Anya didn't know if that calmed her down or made her more afraid. His left hand released its grip on her but before she could do anything, he gripped her left hand as if he was trying to shake it.

"I…I am sorry," he whispered, and there was genuine remorse in his voice that almost made her heart ache.

"Wha…" that's all she managed to get out.

A searing pain surged through the hand he was holding and Anya glanced down at it. She hadn't noticed it until now but he had some strange marking or symbol carved into the back of his hand. She was just about to speak again when the Mark lit up and the searing pain turned almost unbearable.

Anya couldn't scream, she couldn't even breathe, it felt as if her whole body was ablaze and she could do nothing except try and not be completely swallowed by the flame. The only thought running through her head, the only thought she could manage to have was a simple, basic instinct.

I am not going to die here.

Chapter 2

JAMES

James groaned as he stretched out his bad leg, propped it up on a chair and tried to rub it to get some circulation going, but quickly gave up and just leaned back in his chair. The storm was raging outside, he could hear the thunder and the lightning and from time to time, even some frightened scream coming from someone caught outside or perhaps a scared child. His bad leg always got worse during storms and this one was particularly bad.

It was starting to get late and he could not help but feel a slight pang of worry that Anya had not gotten back yet. He had warned her about the storm, he had felt it in his leg in the morning when there had been nothing but sunshine. She hadn't listened, which wasn't very surprising at this point; she usually did whatever she wanted which only made James worry more. He scratched his head and pulled his hand through his salt and pepper hair that was due for a good cut.

James looked around his apartment and the makeshift doctor's office. It wasn't much but it was better than what the people on the east side could get anywhere else. He was the only person who he knew about that had actual medical education that helped anyone, no matter if they could pay or not. He knew it would come back to him, to show kindness. It always paid off in the end.

They might not be able to pay in money but later they would come by with a pie as gratitude, or when he was really lucky, some of them had gotten hold of disinfectant or clean rags to use. He was always grateful for the help the people he tried to help could give him.

Another loud thunder roared through the sky and James couldn't help but twitch at the loud sound; he couldn't stand loud sudden noises anymore. He'd had more than enough of that for a lifetime.

James decided after another half hour of just staring out the window that it wasn't helping anyone and he grabbed one of the few books he owned. It was starting to fall apart at the bindings but it was one of his favourites. A simple but old children's story that perhaps was a little too dark for actual children. It held a very special place in his heart and he'd carried it around with him for almost two decades.

He managed to get his thoughts on something other than Anya in the storm, so when there were rapid and almost violent knocks on his door, he almost fell out of his chair. He hadn't expected anyone to come by, unless someone had been struck by lightning or similar. He knew Anya would have just climbed into her room by the window and then taken some loud stomps to tell him she was home.

James grabbed his cane and with a groan, he managed to get himself up from his chair and walked slower than usual over to the door. He simply cracked it open a little. He would never turn anyone away but he also knew there were people living here that did not have the best intentions. People who just thought about their own survival in the short run and not thinking about the bigger picture. He knew how desperate people could get and there was nothing more dangerous than a desperate person.

James frowned in confusion as he saw Anya standing outside the door. She was standing under the little roof so no rain got on her but she was bone dry. It was like no part of her had been out in the rain but behind her it was pouring down more than ever.

"Anya?" He asked carefully.

Her gaze was empty and she stood completely still, almost like her body was locked in place, but the moment he said her name, it was like something was released and she tipped forward and collapsed in his arms. James instinctually dropped his cane to catch her, pain shooting through his leg but he was a lot more concerned about Anya, his bad leg be damned. Anya's body was completely limp and James got the uncomfortable feeling that it was almost like holding a corpse.

James managed to carefully put her down on the floor, he then quickly closed the door and went back to her. He knelt beside her and put his hand on her cheek, he almost recoiled as he touched her skin. He hadn't realised when he'd caught her how extremely warm she was. It was like she was burning up from the inside.

"Anya," he said with as much calm as he could muster, but he could feel the panic start to rise inside of him. That was when he glimpsed a tear in her shirt and it was stained with blood. With quick fingers, he checked the tear but found no open wound. Only what seemed like an almost healed cauterised scar. James' frown deepened and he swallowed and forced himself to take a deep breath.

Anya had a pulse and she was breathing, both were incredibly steady; a little too steady for what seemed like a life threateningly high fever. For a few seconds, it was like he was stuck and could only stare at Anya's unmoving body before he snapped back into himself. This was not going to happen, he refused. He needed to cool her down before her body shut down from the extreme fever.

He didn't really know how, it was almost like he was moving on autopilot but somehow he managed to get Anya up into her room and put her down on her bed. He knew his bad leg would need multiple days for it to recover from this strenuous moving about, but right now, he didn't care. He could deal with his bad leg later, right now, Anya was all that mattered. As he moved through the apartment, gathering anything and everything he thought could be of use there was an uncomfortable feeling in his stomach.

The feeling that came with years of experience, of years of seeing high fevers like this and he knew that if he didn't get it down soon, Anya would not make it more than twenty-four hours.

The thought terrified him more than he would ever admit to anyone or even himself.

Chapter 3

ANYA

Interesting. So much rage, so much spite in such a small body. I think you'll do. Feed the fire or the fire will feed on you.

Anya woke up with a gasp and shot up from where she was laying. Her heart was beating so hard in her chest she thought it might explode. A rag she must have had on her head fell off and for a second, she couldn't remember what had happened or where she was, but as she looked around the small room, she realised she was in James' upper room or what had technically become her room.

She blinked in confusion and tried to calm down her almost hysteric breathing. Her mouth felt like it was as dry as the desert and all she could think about was to get a glass of cold water.

It was almost like he must have known because when Anya looked on the table next to the bed, she saw a tall glass of water. She almost fell out of the bed as she quickly reached for the glass and just poured it into her mouth, not caring that some of it spilled down her chin. She drank it all within seconds and yet she still felt an incredible thirst but at least it wasn't as desperate as it had been a minute ago. Finally, she managed to gather her thoughts a little and thought back to what had happened.

Had it all been a dream? Anya quickly checked her left side where she'd ripped open a small wound and found that it was healed. It almost looked like someone had cauterised it. James must have done that as she'd been unconscious to stop the bleeding. As she was staring at the small scar forming, she heard the door open and she looked up with haste.

In the doorway stood James, his normally cheery exterior was exchanged with a tired and worried one and he looked like he hadn't slept in days. But when he saw her, his eyes lit up and he smiled.

The sound of his cane hitting the hardwood floor as he walked closer to her always brought her some comfort, it was a sound that meant she wasn't alone.

"Anya," he said and looked at her with worry clear in his eyes. "How are you feeling?" She cleared her throat and tried to laugh a little but it turned into somewhat of a coughing fit instead.

"I'm fine," she finally managed to say.

"What happened to you?" James asked and sat down on the side of the bed.

Anya just shook my head. "I'm…Not entirely sure. It feels more like a dream than anything else."

James reached over slowly and put his hand on her forehead; his hand felt unusually cold against her skin.

"You're still running a fever," he said seriously.

"Still?" Anya asked, confused.

He frowned slightly. "What do you remember?"

Anya scoffed and averted her gaze down onto her lap. Her eyes caught sight of her left hand and the strange Mark that was now carved into it. The same Mark she had seen on that man in the woods before she'd passed out. Anya froze and she could feel all colour leave her face. So it hadn't been a dream after all.

"I…I…" she stammered, not really managing to get any proper words out.

"Hey," James said and put a reassuring hand on her shoulder. "It's okay, you're okay. Just tell me what happened."

"The storm," Anya slowly said. "I got caught out in it. I know you said I should have stayed home and I should have listened but…"

"It's okay, it doesn't matter," James said with a small smile that was supposed to be reassuring.

"What do you remember after that?"

She closed her eyes for a brief second and tried to calm down her breathing which had once again started to exhilarate.

"A lightning bolt almost hit me and I cut open my side," Anya said and gestured to the now cauterised wound. "Then I saw…" She slowly tapered off, lost in her own memories.

"You saw?" James said, obviously just trying to help her keep going.

"A man," Anya said and looked straight into James' eyes. "I thought he was dead."

James frowned slightly and leaned back a little bit, almost like he was thinking. He raised an eyebrow as a sign for her to go on.

Anya cleared her throat.

"I went up to him to…" She stopped herself, not entirely sure if she wanted to say that she went up to him to just take a dead man's possessions instead of checking if he was okay. It would sound worse said out loud, and even though James knew she stole for a living, he wasn't like her. He would always help someone in need while Anya had been taught growing up to always put herself first if she wanted to survive.

"To see if he was alive or not," Anya finally said. "He grabbed me."

James frown only grew with every word she spoke. The man's warning echoed through Anya's head 'trust no one', but she trusted James with her life. She knew he would never betray her and she would never betray him either; he'd done too much for her for that thought to even cross her mind. So ignoring the man's warning she continued. Besides, James must have already seen the Mark on her hand while she was asleep.

Anya raised her left hand and showed him the Mark.

"He had this Mark on his hand and he tried to tell me something but I could barely make out what he was saying. He was hysterical."

"Did he hurt you?" James asked.

Anya frowned slightly; it was hard to explain the searing pain she had felt once he grabbed her hand but she didn't think he ever intended to hurt her. It felt more like it was just a by-product of something else. He really did seem full of remorse for what was about to happen.

"No," she said low. "But after he grabbed me, I…I must have passed out. Then I woke up here." James reached out for her left hand and she instinctually flinched away from his touch, but he was used to this and just kept his hand reaching out and waited for her to let him touch her. Anya took a deep breath and put her left hand in his. His fingers slowly went over the Mark now carved into the back of her hand.

"You don't remember how you got here?" James asked, still keeping his eyes on the Mark. Anya just shook her head. James was silent for a moment before he let go of her hand and looked up at her with a calm expression, or at least the pretence of one.

"You came home later than usual," James said. "I was starting to worry as the storm only seemed to get worse, even though I know you can take care of yourself."

He sighed lightly.

"Then there was a knock on my door and there you were. You weren't even wet, every part of you was bone dry and when I tried to talk to you, I got no response. You took one step into the house before you collapsed. I noticed the blood on your side but the wound seemed to have been cauterised."

Anya was staring at him with large eyes and she tried to keep her heart from beating out of her chest. How could she possibly have been dry? The last thing she remembered she'd been soaking wet from the storm and she had no recollection of walking all the way back into the city.

"When I checked on you, I noticed that you had a fever," James continued and something very serious fell over his eyes for a split second. "The kind of fever I know a body isn't meant to survive for any longer period of time. I was afraid that you…" He stopped himself and cleared his throat.

"You've been unconscious for three days," he said. "That fever not wavering for a single moment, it was like you were burning up from the inside. I've never seen anything like it."

"Three days?" Anya asked low.

He only nodded.

"This morning, you were finally feeling a little cooler but you still have a high fever. Honestly…I'm not sure how you survived." There was a hint of fear in his voice, something Anya wasn't used to hearing.

Anya frowned, she felt fine. A little thirsty sure and confused from what had happened but not sick. She'd had high fevers before and this was not how it felt.

"I feel fine," she said. "You know, considering," she added with a weak laugh.

James sighed slightly.

"I'm just afraid of what happened between you falling unconscious in the woods and you reaching my door. You weren't yourself and you say you don't remember any of it. Then who cauterised your wound and why were you bone dry?"

"I don't know," she said. She hadn't really thought about it like that but she guessed James had three days thinking about this.

James forced a smile on his face; it wasn't his normal smile that came with ease, it was obvious. "I'm just glad you're back and that you're awake. Though I suggest you should continue resting until your fever goes down completely."

Anya nodded but all she could think about was how she wanted to go back into the woods and try and find the man's body, perhaps that would hold some of the answers she was seeking.

Perhaps he was dead or perhaps he was alive and had also made his way back into the city.

There was just a strong feeling, almost like a pull, that she had to find that man no matter what.

Chapter 4

RUNA

Runa slowly walked down the large wooden stairs, her feet feeling unusually heavy and clumsy. The moment she stepped down onto the bottom floor, it was like she was being assaulted by noises and smells. The noise of drunken laughter and fighting, the smell of alcohol and cigarette smoke heavy in the air. Runa looked around the Keg. It wasn't a large bar by any means but it was home to her and the Silver Swans.

She glimpsed the few members who weren't out in the same corner they always sat in, laughing and playing cards, but the place was mostly filled with paying customers just looking for cheap alcohol and no questions asked. Runa made her way straight to the bar counter. She hadn't slept well in days and was in dire need of a drink. The tall and slightly ominous shape of Egil appeared in front of her.

They were muscular with almost onyx black skin and small eyes that were so dark, they almost seemed like black holes. They smiled gently as they cleaned the glasses.

"What can I get you, R?" They asked, their voice deep and gravelly.

"Anything strong but that won't knock me out," Runa answered.

Egil frowned slightly and glanced up towards the stairs.

"Bad day?" Egil asked and they poured Runa a glass of something dark brown and murky.

"More like days," Runa said and in one swoop, she downed the drink.

"You want to talk about it?" Egil asked even though they knew what she was going to answer.

"I'm good," Runa said with a fake smile and a wink. "Any fun news?"

"Just the same as last time," Egil said.

"The Rusty Coffins aren't standing down?" Runa asked with a slight frown.

"Doesn't seem like it. The boss isn't happy about it," Egil said.

When is the boss ever happy, was Runa's immediate thought but said nothing.

"Watch out when you're out there, R," Egil said. "It could get ugly."

"I can take care of myself," Runa said but quickly added. "But thank you."

Egil nodded and turned back to stacking glasses and fixing behind the bar. Runa cleared her throat.

"If you hear anything about Anya, would you let me know?" Runa said, her voice a lot lower than before.

Egil frowned deeply.

"Anya?" They said, slightly confused. "Why?"

Runa shrugged.

"No one has seen her for a couple of days," Runa simply said.

"You're worried," Egil said.

If it had been anyone other than Egil, Runa would have bit back with some smart remark but with them, she just sighed lightly.

"That's one way of looking at it," Runa said and looked around the bar again, making sure no one was paying attention to them. "If you hear anything, tell me first, okay?"

"The boss won't be happy that you're looking for her again," Egil said. "He doesn't look kindly on people who leave the Silver Swans or on those who keep in contact with them either."

"I know, okay?" Runa said, not being able to keep all the irritation from her voice. "I know what I'm doing. So if you hear anything, tell me, no one else, alright?"

Egil slowly nodded.

"Thank you, Egil," Runa said slowly. "And I'm heading out, so if anyone wants anything, just tell them to leave you a message, you know the drill."

"Be careful, R," Egil said and returned to cleaning the glasses.

"I always am," Runa said, trying her best to make the smile on her face as believable as possible and from Egil's reaction, she was successful. If anything, Runa was a great liar.

Runa was just about to step outside the Keg when she was stopped by Irena, a middle aged woman with the first hints of grey in her otherwise black hair. Irena's amber eyes were shining with excitement.

"Have you heard?" Irena asked.

"Heard what?" Runa answered.

"The princess turns 20 in a couple of weeks and is supposedly having a grand party in the Castle," Irena said.

"So?" Runa said.

"So?" Irena said with disbelief. "Do you realise how many duke, duchesses and whatever other titles there are, are going to come here for that? Probably from all around Taurin!" Irena said.

"A lot probably," Runa said.

"Pickpocketing one of them could keep our coffers full for weeks," Irena said.

Runa was silent for a moment. Sometimes she truly felt like she was the only one that actually thought things through here.

"You want to pickpocket them?" Runa asked slowly.

"Or rob the place they stay at while they're at the party!" Irena said.

"They'll likely be staying at the Castle," Runa said.

Irena huffed in annoyance.

"The people coming here for the party are not going to just walk around the city, and even if they do, people like that don't carry money with them, they carry check books. You think you'll be able to cash in a check with a duke's name on it?" Runa said.

Irena said nothing.

"Never go after people that high up without a plan, and saying 'I'm going to pickpocket them' isn't a plan," Runa said. "Remember last time we went in without a plan on a high profile person?"

"We made it out," Irena muttered.

"Because of *me*," Runa said with just the smallest hint of annoyance in her words. She couldn't let Irena think she was losing her cool.

Irena sighed deeply.

"So what, we're just going to let this opportunity slip through our fingers?" Irena asked. Runa rubbed her eyes. She was one of the newest members of the Silver Swans but she'd proven herself useful, and because everyone always seemed to think she had everything in control, a lot of them came to her to talk about plans. They then had to go through Mr Parker to be approved but it all started with gathering people for a job.

"All the Blue Birds are probably going to be focusing on the high profile people in the Castle more than usual, which leaves other rich snobs more vulnerable. Go after them, not people close to royalty," Runa said.

Irena slowly started to smile.

"Will you help?" Irena asked.

Runa sighed and glanced at the stairs leading up.

"I have my own mission to do," Runa said. "I'm sure Trent or Shirley will want to join you."

"Oh right, I heard about your mission," Irena said with a flash of remorse in her eyes.

Runa despised her for it.

"People really can't keep their mouths shut, huh," Runa said with clenched jaws. The mission was supposed to be her secret, at least until it was done, but apparently someone had found out and spread it around, which wasn't ideal.

"Have fun pickpocketing people," Runa said to Irena before she quickly left the Keg.

Runa quickly headed out into the city. She couldn't completely shake her conversation with Irena and the fact that possibly everyone in the Silver Swans knew about her mission now, but she also couldn't focus on that. Runa had other things that were far more urgent. She had her orders from Mr Parker and they were etched into her head but the mere thought of it made her uneasy. The only thing she was sure of was that she had to find Anya and find out where she'd been these past three days.

Runa and Anya almost never spoke or saw each other directly anymore. It could go weeks without them laying their eyes on each other but it was inevitable in a city like this. But Runa almost always had tabs on Anya, she had people keep an eye out and if they saw her, they would report to Runa, and Egil was the Silver Swans' eyes and ears. They heard and saw a lot of things being the bar keep in the Keg, mostly gossip and similar but more often than not they would have a solid lead on a job for them to do.

Runa knew Mr Parker didn't look kindly on the fact that Runa kept a close eye on Anya; ever since she'd left, her mere name would make him turn red with anger. Leaving wasn't something most people did and for him, it was the largest of betrayals. The fact that Runa liked to keep a close eye on Anya to make sure she was okay was the reason she was in this entire mess, but then again, when hadn't Anya been the source of Runa doing something stupid?

As usual, Runa started her search by circling James' house. Anyone who knew anything about Anya knew she lived with him. Runa glanced up at the window on the upper floor, the one she had seen Anya climb out of multiple times but the room was still dark and she could detect no movement. After half an hour, Runa left and searched the rest of the city, or at least the east side but she would sneak her way into the higher districts as well.

She picked some pockets from some people that looked gullible, lost and like they had far too much money in their pockets. Runa was on a mission, but bringing back money to the Keg was always looked at favourably, it meant you put the gang above anything else.

As Runa slowly started to make her way back towards the Keg her eyes caught the movement in the corner of her eyes; a very familiar movement, if only a little more sluggish than normally. Runa quickly followed and to her surprise, she managed to do so without much trouble and without being detected. Finally, she came close enough when the shape stopped to look around a corner and Runa could see Anya's flush face in the low light.

There was something off about her. Runa had stared at her face long enough to notice the smallest change and there was none, not physically at least. But there was something different about her.

Perhaps it was just the lighting and the fact that Runa hadn't seen or heard from her in a long time, but it almost looked like her skin was glowing.

Chapter 5

ANYA

Once James was satisfied that Anya was stable enough and wasn't going to fall unconscious at any moment, he left her to go back to his work. He promised he'd check on her every now and then, and that if she needed anything she just had to call for him. He'd given her cheek a soft stroke that had sent a painful reminder that her own father hadn't wanted her.

Anya knew she was putting that role on James; but he didn't seem to mind. She'd had a suspicion for a while that he might have lost a child, which is why he'd taken her in, but it was pure speculation, it wasn't something they talked about. He didn't ask about her childhood and she didn't ask about his past, it was a silent pact they'd made.

James had told her to stay put and drink more water and just rest until her fever went down completely but Anya had no intention of doing that. The moment he left the room, she threw off the cover and swung her legs over the bed and felt the cold floor boards beneath her feet. Was it just her or did everything feel colder? Maybe she was running a high fever even though she felt fine.

She changed clothes and put on her jacket and threw a scarf over her head to cover most of her head and face. As a last thing, she slipped on a pair of leather gloves, she had a feeling this thing was not something to parade around with in the open. She turned her attention back to the door James had left from and gave it a second to make sure he hadn't heard her move around.

"Sorry James, I'll be back soon," Anya whispered more to herself than anyone else before she pulled open the window and climbed out of it.

His upper room was on the second floor but she'd done this more times than she could keep track of at this point. There was a little part of the roof that stuck out just beneath the window and from there it was an easy jump down to the street. For a moment, she just sat on that small part of the roof, perched almost like a bird scanning her surroundings. The streets were as busy as usual but she did rapidly notice that there was a larger guard presence than before.

Anya quickly slid off the roof and into an alleyway before anyone noticed her. Guards and her had never really been friends, they'd been on her tail for years, ever since she left the Red Rose and then later the Silver Swan gang, but thus far they'd never been able to actually catch her red handed or with any real proof. She would admit that having James as a friend did help quite a bit, and even though he wasn't exactly highly respected in the city, most people liked him. And as he was the only doctor on the east side, he was invaluable and people knew that at least. If he disappeared, the people in charge could almost count on having a small riot on their hands. There was no one else here to help the poor and unfortunate.

Anya pulled her scarf tighter around her head and made her way further into the city with quick and sure steps. She'd grown up here and knew every alley and house by heart. Not a lot went on that she didn't know about and it was something she prided herself on. The atmosphere in the city seemed slightly off; she guessed it had something to do with the increased guards but everyone tried to pretend like they didn't notice.

Anya passed the Red Rose, it was something she always did, even if it wasn't on the path she was going. It had become a habit and a dire reminder of where she'd come from and where she never wanted to end up again. The door suddenly opened and an older man stepped in, which gave Anya a glimpse of the girls in there and her heart sank a little. Every time she saw them, it was like she was looking at a younger version of herself. Sometimes she would have nightmares about entering the Red Rose and all the workers wore her face. There was a deep-seated rage inside of Anya that would flare up at the thought of the Red Rose. At the thought of what they'd taken from her. At the thought of what they'd taken and continued to take from so many other young people. Anya wasn't done with the Red Rose but it was good that they thought she was, it would make things easier later down the line.

She continued down the street, moving between people, making sure she was covered partially by someone at all times when a guard came near, which honestly wasn't particularly hard. She soon made her way to the gate leading out of the city and stopped in her tracks. There were more than double the amount of guards standing there than usual and they stopped everyone coming in and out, something they had never done before.

In particular, Anya quickly noticed that they were asking to see everyone's hands. She cast a quick glance at her left hand and forced herself to take a deep breath, it had to be a coincidence. A weird, unlikely coincidence sure but a coincidence nonetheless. It was impossible that they were looking for the Mark.

Anya turned around on her feet. The large obvious entrance wasn't the only way out of the city but it was the least suspicious one, which is why she liked to use it but there was no way she was getting either out or back in through there. She made her way back towards the east side of the city, where the poorest lived, which meant the guard presence was lower and people tended to mind their business a lot more. But it was also the part of the city you were most likely to get robbed or jumped in.

It wasn't something she particularly worried about, she could take care of herself, but after having been unconscious for three days and still feeling like everything in her surrounding was colder than usual, she wasn't as self-assured as usual. But she had to get back to the forest where she'd found that man. The thought refused to leave her head and she was sure that if she just found him again she would get answers.

"Well, well, isn't this a pleasant surprise," a familiar voice spoke from behind her. She spun around. There were only a handful of people that could sneak up on her, at least when she was at peak performance. It was Runa. Her black thick hair framing her sharp and dark face, her large brown eyes gave her an almost innocent look, but anyone who fell for that would be sorely mistaken.

"Runa," was all Anya said but she straightened her back a little out of reflex.

Runa took a few steps closer to her. Her hands in her pockets and there was a calm and casualty in the way she walked. Runa gave her a good look up and down before a small smile grazed her face.

"Heard you were dead." It was more of a statement than a question.

"Yeah you know, being a ghost makes stealing and getting around much easier so you know, I thought I'd try it out," Anya answered. Runa let out a short laugh.

"No one has seen you in three days. Even James refused to speak. He said he didn't know where you were," Runa said, and there was a glimpse of something serious in her voice when she spoke about James, a threat Anya knew all too well.

"You spoke to James?" She asked, trying to keep her voice as calm as possible.

"Of course," Runa said as if it was obvious but they both knew that wasn't true. "He's not just your friend. He's...a good person. Wouldn't you agree?"

Anya bit her lip and she stared right into her eyes. The challenge was there as clear as day, or maybe it was just because she'd known Runa for so long that she read into every gaze, every twitch of her face. Read into everything she did.

"What do you want?" Anya wasn't in the mood for these fake pleasantries. Runa broke their eye contact but still with that small smile playing on her lips.

"I just saw you on the streets and I wanted to check that everything was alright. As I said, no one has seen you in three days. What have you been up to?" She tilted her head slightly and Anya could see that she tried to scan for any wounds or signs for what she'd been doing. Runa was a perceptive person but Anya didn't think she'd find what she was looking for just by glancing.

"Right, I forget about your good nature, you always just want the best for people," Anya said sarcastically. The moment the words left her mouth, she could see they had struck a chord because the smile was wiped off Runa's face.

"I want what's best for *my* people," she answered low. "You used to be included in that once."

"Once," was all Anya said in reply. The smile crept back on her face but Anya could see it was hollow compared to the one she'd worn before.

"Just wanted to make sure you weren't dead, Anya," Runa said. "I know we have our differences but…"

Anya let out a laugh at that. "I guess you could call drawing the line at murder 'differences', sure," Anya said, interrupting her. Runa just stared at her; her large eyes piercing her and almost made her want to avert her gaze.

"But you can always ask for help if you need it," Runa continued.

"I know who to ask for help from," Anya answered, and for the briefest moment, she could see a flash of hurt in Runa's eyes before they went back to normal. Anya felt a tinge of regret after seeing that.

"I'm not sure you do," Runa said with a scoff.

There was a brief moment of silence before Runa spoke again.

"Give James my best regards, won't you?" Runa said. "And be careful, Anya."

Anya wasn't sure if that last part was meant as a warning or a threat but she just nodded. Runa walked forward until they stood side by side, then she stopped for a moment. Runa didn't look at her, they just stood like that for a second and Anya almost thought she was going to say something before she simply exhaled deeply and continued walking.

Anya turned around and watched her veer off into another street. She rubbed her eyes in annoyance. She knew Runa meant well, at least for the kind of people they were but seeing her was always complicated these days.

It hurt to remember that she'd once used to make Runa laugh but now all she got was that plastered on fake smile she'd almost perfected. Almost.

Chapter 6

ANYA

Anya shook off the lingering feelings from seeing Runa again so out of the blue and continued moving. This really wasn't the time to deal with her, she had a lot of other things on her plate right now. Anya didn't know if it was just her imagination but when she'd gotten annoyed, she could have sworn her left hand had pulsed a little in heat. She clenched her left fist but it felt just like normal again, if it had ever felt different.

She soon found the edge of the eastern part and the wall surrounding the city. It was old and overgrown and it certainly wouldn't survive any sort of attack if the attacker was at least a little competent, but as Taurin hadn't been at war for the past 50 years, it wasn't really a concern. Now it served more as a means for trapping its inhabitants inside, or at least to make sure that they only entered and exited from one place so they could keep tabs on everyone.

Maybe it was supposed to make them feel safe but Anya knew most people felt trapped more than anything, even if you could come and go as you pleased from the main exit.

One piece of the wall had become completely overgrown by vegetation, she looked around and made sure no one was around or paying attention. When she felt sure she was unobserved, she slightly pushed aside the vegetation and slipped behind it. For once, she felt lucky that she was so skinny, being malnourished her entire childhood had made sure of that, as the crack in the wall behind the vegetation was slim and it took even her a couple of carefully manoeuvred minutes to make it through to the other side.

As soon as she made it out on the outside, she took a few deep breaths and felt the sun shine on her face and the breeze rustle her hair. It was always a little claustrophobic to take this route, which is another reason she preferred the main entrance, but it was a good thing to have in a pinch. Most people didn't know it existed and even most of those who did, thought it was too slim of a crack to actually get through.

As she was getting out on the east side, she had a longer way around the city to reach the place in the forest she'd been in last time but she wasn't in any particular hurry. She had to get there, even if it meant getting caught in another storm again.

It took her a little over an hour of carefully walking to make sure no one out and about spotted her to get to the place. Anya saw the tree split in half from the lightning and knew she was close and she soon found the slightly seared spot in the grass where the lightning had almost hit her. She put her hand on her left side where she'd gotten the wound; she wondered who had helped her seal it, but that was a problem for later.

Anya lifted her gaze from the seared spot and looked to where the man had been and she saw no body. She found it unlikely that the animals would have gotten it so fast and even the bones. Perhaps someone had found his body and disposed of it but it also seemed unlikely. The most likely conclusion was that he too had survived and left, either for the city or far away from here.

Anya sighed but for some reason she walked closer, perhaps she would find some tracks or any evidence he'd even been here. The closer she got, the more she saw and where she was pretty sure that man's body had been was also a little scorch mark. Anya turned and looked at the mark the lightning had made on the ground, it looked similar sure but this was smaller and seemed strangely contained.

Anya pulled off the glove on her right hand and then slowly dragged it on the ground and found that it felt a little strange, it almost felt like the scorched earth was coated in something. When she pulled back and looked at her fingers, they were covered in an ashy grey powder substance. She quickly tried to clean her fingers on some of the grass and put on the glove again.

Anya didn't know why, but she just knew, she felt it in her heart, that this was the ashes of the man she had found. Her heart sank in her chest and she collapsed onto the ground and just shook her head.

"Breathe. Breathe," Anya whispered and forced herself to take some deep breaths, but she could feel the panic rise inside of her.

Whoever he had been had burnt to a crisp, to literal ashes after she had left him. It didn't make any sense. If anyone had set fire to him, there should be more marks and clues around, it wouldn't just be this tiny little mark on the ground.

Anya tore off the glove on her left hand and just stared at the Mark. "What the hell are you…"

She shut her eyes hard and she could feel anger filling her instead of the panic and it was a welcome change. Who the hell had that man been and what had he done to her? It wasn't fair; whatever weird crap he was involved in she didn't want any part of. Anya leaned on a tree as she got up and for a moment, she could smell burning.

In a slight panic, she turned around to look for the source of the smell. If there was a fire in the woods, she did not want to be here when it really started spreading. She'd tried to outrun lightning a few days ago, she didn't want to add fire to the list this soon. But the smell quickly dissipated and as she turned back to the tree she'd used as leverage to get up, she saw that there was a perfect handprint burnt into the tree. Her handprint.

Anya slowly reached for it with her right hand that was still gloved and she could feel her hand shaking. She must be losing her mind. That lightning must have struck her directly and now she was going insane, that was the most logical explanation. As her gloved hand touched the burn mark, nothing happened but she could still feel the heat coming from the scorch mark through her glove and she pulled back her hand faster than she would like to admit.

Anya looked back at her left hand, it was perfectly fine. The only thing wrong with it was that strange Mark, almost giving off a low orange glow that was quickly disappearing.

Chapter 7

INARA

Inara made sure the scarf around her head was properly secured before she continued down the streets of the east side. She quickly glanced down at her uniform and the glimmer of the guard badge pinned to it, and with quick hands she dusted off whatever little dust had been on it. Inara took great pride in this uniform and what it stood for, or at least what it was supposed to stand for.

Security, safety and order but she knew most of the time, the rich slipped through the cracks of the system and the poorer got thrown in The Grove for sometimes minor offences. It was what she hated about the guards but if she could climb in ranks, she could do real good in this city. Inara looked around the streets she passed on her patrol.

She knew these neighbourhoods well, she'd grown up in them after all. She knew those few who would recognise her from her childhood did not look kindly upon the fact that she'd become a guard. It was a kind of betrayal to them, which she understood to a certain degree but she was thinking about the future and couldn't be bothered by people's perception of her.

This part of the city had such potential to be a beautiful and happy place but as it was right now, the moment you stepped into the east side, it was almost like a grey filter laid on top of the entire district. She had stopped counting the amount of children running around in dirty and ripped up clothes, sometimes begging for money, sometimes stealing. Inara was very adamant that the law was the law and a crime no matter what had to be punished; it didn't matter if you were rich or poor, popular or hated.

But not all crimes had the same punishments and especially when it came to the children of the east side, Inara often chose to turn her gaze to another place. Almost as if she didn't see the crime, it didn't happen. She knew they were just trying to survive and as she passed the brothel known as the Red Rose, she preferred the children stealing than being lured in there to work. More than once, Inara had seen what looked like kids no more than fourteen standing outside, trying to entice people inside and more than once, she had brought it up with her supervisor but every time she had been shot down.

The Red Rose was a legitimate business, was what they said, they paid their employees and paid taxes, it was all above the board but Inara knew that wasn't true. None of her supervisors had grown up on the east side, they hadn't heard first person accounts of what it was like. How they lured you in with the promise of work, a roof over your head, food and pay.

Then after about a week, they demanded payment for said room and food and of course part of the pay went to them from their work. It meant they quickly got into debt to the Red Rose and had to work even more to try and pay it back, meaning you were stuck there, working until your debt was paid. Which for some would never happen. It was a trap, an evil circle and it made Inara sick to her stomach. It wasn't a legitimate business, it was taking advantage of poor, vulnerable kids for profit.

Inara quickly continued her patrol down the road, trying to stop her hands from shaking slightly. She knew these streets well and knew very well what parts were 'owned' by which gangs; even though it sometimes felt like new gangs sprouted up every other week while old ones died out. It was only the old and really dangerous ones that seemed to stick around; the ones that seemed almost untouchable and they were never able to pin them to a crime directly.

Inara guessed they had something on several people in charge, which gave them some protection but it was mere speculation.

Most of the time, guards were always supposed to patrol in a couple but there weren't many that wanted to patrol the east side. Inara had requested it specifically, even if she had to go alone. She'd been alone most of her childhood and didn't mind it but she knew it left her more vulnerable if someone decided to attack her. Inara put a steady hand on her sword that hung from her hip.

She was strong and capable and not afraid of a little fight, though she hated hurting people but she would do whatever was necessary for justice to be made.

Inara wanted to make a change in this city for the better, even if she knew that the chance of that happening wasn't big, she had to try.

Chapter 8

ANYA

Anya barely remembered anything on the way back to the city. It felt as if her legs were moving on their own and every time she blinked and opened her eyes, she had moved a significant distance. Her feet knew the way around these woods and the city, so she wasn't especially surprised when she found herself inside the walls again and just a few blocks from James' house. Anya didn't feel like herself.

She felt like she was just beneath a watery surface, trying to break through but unable to, no matter how much she kicked her legs and thrashed her arms. She finally regained some control of her body and rapidly veered into an empty alleyway and threw up and as she hadn't had a proper meal in days, it was mostly liquid and bile and it stung as it came up her throat and made her eyes water.

She wiped her mouth with the back of her gloved hand and just leaned against the cold brick wall and forced herself to calm her breathing. "This is a dream," she whispered to herself, her eyes still firmly shut. "I'm just dreaming."

"Quite a realistic dream then wouldn't you say?" A voice appeared out of nowhere and she almost jumped out of her skin; it wasn't a voice she recognised. It was rough and had a crackle to it, which made it a very distinct voice.

Anya looked around the alley with a quick glance but saw no one. She swallowed hard and she could hear her heartbeat drumming hard in her ears, drowning out any other noise from the city. "Great," her voice wavered as she spoke. "Now I'm hearing things as well. Might as well just lock me up in The Chimney right away."

An involuntary chill went down her spine at the thought of The Chimney, or the loony house or the place for mentally insane, whatever they wanted to call it. Anya and most people knew it as The Chimney because people went up in smoke there, never to be seen again. Maybe the people there did get the help they needed and they were just isolated from the rest of the city for everyone's benefit but she'd never heard of anyone returning. She'd take being thrown into The Grove, or the prison any day before going to The Chimney.

Anya couldn't get the horrid taste after throwing up out of her mouth and she just wanted a cold glass of water to drink. Maybe James had been right. Maybe she should have just gone back to sleep and kept resting, she clearly wasn't well. Anya took one step before she felt a searing pain coming from her left hand.

As she looked down at it, she could see that vague orange glow through the glove from the Mark. She flexed her hand and it quickly dissipated but when she glanced up again, her heart dropped.

It was the man. The man she'd seen out in the woods during the storm. He was standing at the end of the alley, his head cocked slightly to the side and he stared at her with a mixture of pity and curiosity. Then, before she had the chance to move or say anything, he stepped outside her view. Anya's legs moved before she could think and she ran towards the end of the alley and looked around the open street.

It was crowded with people but no more than usual. She scanned the street and saw nothing. Unless he was the greatest rogue in the world, there was no way he could have disappeared that fast. And something in her, something she didn't really want to admit, told her that he'd never actually been there, even though she'd seen him.

Maybe it was the way his eyes had shone or the way her left hand had felt as she stared at him. Anya didn't know; all she knew was that she was connected to that man somehow and she didn't like it in the least.

As she managed to calm down a little, she noticed she had attracted some unwanted attention to herself, some people were staring, or rather trying very hard not to stare, which was a dead giveaway she had acted out of the ordinary. She wrapped her scarf tighter around her head and disappeared into another alleyway, and made her way to James' house with quick steps. She didn't want him to know she'd been out, so instead of going through the front door, she climbed up to the small roof that was beneath his second floor window.

From there, it was easy to open up the window and climb inside, she had done it so many times, she could do it in mere seconds and without attracting all too much unwanted attention, but she did feel out of shape as she made the climb. Her fingers didn't find the correct places to grab onto immediately and it took slightly longer than usual, but as she finally stepped inside the room and closed the window behind her, she exhaled a breath she had barely noticed she was holding.

"Was it a nice excursion?" James' smooth voice spoke from the opening of the door. She must really be losing it if she hadn't noticed him immediately. Anya sighed and hung her head, she didn't want to meet his gaze right now. She slowly peeled off her gloves, boots and jacket before she sat down on the bed again.

"When did you notice?" Anya asked.

"You've sneaked out enough times for me to recognise that look on your face before you do it," James said calmly.

She frowned slightly.

"So why did you let me go?" She asked. James sighed and walked over to the bed and sat down next to her.

"Because I know that look," James said with a semblance of a smile. "You were going to do it no matter what and I have never been able to stop you."

That finally made her look up at him and meet his eyes. They were filled with worry and she had to quickly avert her gaze again. She hated that she was the cause of that worry, she couldn't stand it.

"Did you at least find what you were looking for?" James asked carefully.

Anya frowned and looked down at her left hand. Somehow she felt as if she'd received an answer, she just didn't understand what it meant yet.

"I think the man is dead," was all she said instead.

"Okay," James said, not pressing her for any more information on why she thought so. He really was too kind.

"Have you seen the guards? The way they're blocking the entrance?" She asked, trying to keep her voice calm.

James had a slightly surprised look on his face.

"No. What do you mean?" He asked.

"You haven't been out?" She asked.

James shook his head.

"I've had my hands filled with trying to keep you alive for the past three days, I haven't left the house. So what do you mean?" He asked again.

Anya rubbed her eyes.

"The guard presence is at least doubled and they are inspecting everyone coming and leaving the city," she said and then looked into his eyes. "They're inspecting everyone's hands, James." James raised an eyebrow and his eyes shot to the Mark on her hand.

"Must be a coincidence, surely? Perhaps a convict has escaped The Grove and they have a certain hand tattoo or similar?" James said, but she could tell from the tone in his voice that he was trying to calm her down more than anything else.

Anya rose and took a few steps forth and back in the room.

"I think the man I found was burnt to ash," she said, hearing the way her voice sounded. She wondered for a moment if she looked like the man had done when he'd grabbed her, that mania and frantic speaking. That thought frightened her almost more.

"This. This thing." She waved her left hand in front of James. "I burnt a handprint into a tree with this." Anya could see the frown on James' face grow and he couldn't conceal the worry any longer.

"Anya, calm down, it's just a marking," he said slowly.

"Just a marking?" She said and she could see James' flinch as she slammed her left hand, palm first, into the wooden wall next to her.

Unlike the times before, when it had either been a burning sensation in her hand or it had happened in a moment of anger, this time she noticed it in a different way. It was like a small fire had been ignited inside of her and she was throwing wood into the flickering and weak flame. *Feed the fire or the fire feeds on you,* the words she'd thought she'd heard in a dream, came rushing back and she felt the palm of her hand start to heat up but there was no pain this time, just an intense feeling of purpose.

It was almost liberating if it hadn't been so frightening. The sound of searing wood was heard and the smell of burning filled the room and just as she thought James was going to speak, she lifted her hand from the wall and the flickering flame inside of her quieted down until she could no longer detect it. Anya turned her head away from James' almost horrified face and they both stared at the handprint that was now permanently seared into the wall.

"I'm not crazy," she said, her voice no longer filled with doubt. Something had happened, something had changed. James could see what she had done. It wasn't just in her head and even though that sent a wave of relief through her body, the repercussions of this being real; she couldn't even begin to imagine.

Something had changed inside of her. Anya could no longer detect the small flame within herself but it had left a warm, calming sensation in her core, almost like it was congratulating her on feeding the fire.

Chapter 9

ANYA

Anya and James stood in silence for a moment, both of them just staring at her left hand and sometimes glancing at the burnt handprint on the wall. She didn't want to be the first one to speak and when she glanced over at James, she could see that he'd turned slightly grey and clammy and she saw fear in his eyes. Good. That meant she wasn't the only one afraid.

She didn't want to feel like a lost little child, powerless to do anything and letting things spiral out of her hands. Anya had been powerless her entire childhood, it wasn't something she intended to repeat but she could feel her hands shake ever so slightly.

"Okay," James finally said, his voice unusually low.

"Okay?" Anya asked carefully. He looked up at her, the fear was still there but there was something else now in his eyes but she couldn't figure out what it was, determination? A certain calm? Anya couldn't tell.

"What's the plan, Anya?" James asked. She couldn't help but let a laugh slip past her lips, it sounded slightly manic even in her own ears.

"Plan? You think I have a plan?" She said. "I have no idea what's happening."

James' eyes flickered to her left hand then back up to her eyes.

"Then we figure it out," he said as if it was the most obvious thing in the world. She rubbed her eyes, she could feel tears start to form but she refused to cry. Just a few seconds ago, she'd been angry, she'd been determined but now when the fire had gone out, she just felt afraid and wanted someone to tell her how to fix this.

"How?" She asked, clearing her throat.

"We have contacts," James said. "You have a lot of contacts. Let's figure out if the guard presence is because of the Mark or if it's a coincidence. Then we figure out what that Mark is and we move on from there," he spoke so matter of factly and calmly, it was his physician voice, the voice he used on patients who had been badly hurt and he wasn't sure they were going to make it. She'd heard it a hundred times before; James just refused to think negatively or not even try.

He was too kind.

Anya sighed and then only nodded as an answer.

"The man I met said that I should trust no one," she slowly said. "I have a bad feeling this Mark isn't anything good." James nodded slightly.

"So no mentioning that you have that Mark to anyone," James said. She stared at him for a brief second. James had taken her in, he'd cleared her debt to the Red Rose and he'd treated her as if she'd been his own child. Anya owed him her life, she owed him everything. She couldn't bear to think of anything happening to him, especially because of her.

"I'll go ask around," she said, clearing her throat. "You stay here and..." She stopped briefly and the silence hung heavy in the air. "I'll let you know what I find. It's less suspicious if I ask around than if you start." James glared at her; it felt like he was looking through her, like he knew exactly what she was thinking. Then his facial expression softened and he gripped his cane and started to make his way out of the room.

"I'm here if you need anything," he simply said with a soft smile.

James really was too kind, it would kill him one day. Anya just prayed it wouldn't be because of her. She could live with a lot of things, but she didn't think she could live with that.

Trust no one, she remembered those words as clear as day but she hadn't forgotten the other part, when he'd tried to say a name. Moira Sto...Moira something. He'd wanted her to find her for some reason, perhaps she held answers that he couldn't give anymore or she could help, but Anya didn't feel too optimistic about it. Strangers rarely did anything good without anything in exchange, James excluded.

She shook her head. First thing first, she had things to figure out without directing too much attention to herself. She knew a few people in the city that could help but that she certainly did not trust to either keep this secret or to not pry into it more. Runa was the last person that could hear about this, because if there was one thing Runa was, it was stubborn and she would not give up until she found your answer satisfying.

Anya knew one person who wasn't loose lipped and wouldn't pry. Maybe it was time she went to Mara and paid her a visit, it had been a while. She decided to go out through the front door this time instead of the window, but she made sure to put on the leather gloves again before she left. James had returned back to work, she could hear him speak low from further back in the house, he must have a patient in right now. She didn't bother to say anything, he knew she was leaving.

Mara's shop, The Fantastical Page Turner was slightly to the east but closer to the middle of the city than anything else. A poorer neighbourhood but with a better reputation that further east. Anya was more alert than ever as she made her way through the streets and alleys. Everywhere she went, it felt as if people were staring at her but they clearly weren't when she actually checked.

She simply had the feeling of eyes watching her constantly even though no one paid her more attention than usual. Perhaps she was getting paranoid, or rather more paranoid and she wouldn't be surprised. She had barely any idea of what was happening to herself and she realised it was bad; she was scared to know how she'd feel when she knew the whole picture. If she ever would know the whole picture.

Finally, she saw the front door of the shop. The trip had felt at least twice as long but she was just glad to be there.

One step in front of the other, one thing at a time, that was how she was going to figure this thing out.

Chapter 10

ANYA

Anya opened the door to the shop and it slammed shut behind her. It currently looked empty and it was a small, cramped space, filled to the brim with books of all types, qualities and sizes. She'd learnt quickly that there was no better place to go to if you were looking for something specific and perhaps obscure. Mara dealt in things perhaps not the everyday person would find interesting or useful, and just like James, she was liked for being kind and helpful, but also like James, not a lot of people visited her unless they had to.

Anya's kind of people. Being inside the shop made her feel a little calmer and she walked up to the counter, slowly eyeing the rows of books reaching the ceiling. She knew a lot of these books were in languages she'd never even heard of and perhaps even languages long dead but she guessed that if nothing else, perhaps some rich man would buy them as collectibles, to show how worldly he was. Anya stopped in front of the counter and simply waited.

After a brief moment, a head popped out from the back room. Mara's bright red curls bounced as she moved and her freckled face lit up when she saw her. Anya couldn't help but smile back at her.

Anya signed the word for "Hello." Her sign language skills had become rusty in the last few years she had to admit, she had used them a lot more when she'd been part of the Silver Swans and when Mara had helped her learn the basics. But that had been a while now, ever since she'd split from the Silver Swans she hadn't really come by and seen Mara either.

Anya knew she liked Runa and she just hadn't been in the headspace to deal with that, but as she was looking at Mara's bright grey eyes now, she wondered why she'd stayed away for so long.

"Anya! It's so nice to see you!" Mara's hands moved a lot faster than Anya's. Every movement came as natural to her as speaking came to Anya and there was something special in seeing her so excited.

"How are you?" Mara continued signing. "What have you been doing?"

Anya was sure she was going to continue but she could barely follow as she was signing so fast and finally Anya just held up her hands in a show of stop, but made sure to have a small smile on her face. Mara understood and she looked a little embarrassed but it quickly disappeared.

"It's nice seeing you too," Anya signed. "I know it's been a while but I could use some help." Mara's face lit up the second she understood that she wanted her help and she couldn't help but to bask in Mara's excitement and...goodness for a moment.

"Of course!" She signed. "I'd love to help! It's what I'm here for."

Anya knew she should just ask what she was here for, she should keep it brief and professional but she couldn't help it. Anya liked Mara, she couldn't deny it and she had missed her more than she realised now that she was so close to her.

"First," Anya signed slowly and took a deep breath. "Have you talked with Runa?" Mara frowned in confusion at the question.

"Is she in trouble?" Mara asked. Anya shook her head. She should change the subject, she shouldn't bring this back up but she couldn't help herself.

"I just wondered if you'd spoken," Anya signed.

Mara nodded.

"She came by a few days ago and asked if I'd heard from you," Mara signed. For a moment, Anya's heart dropped in her chest until she realised Runa had simply come by to see if Mara knew anything as she'd been gone for three days. Runa was just trying to gather information as usual.

"I said no," Mara continued. "Are you two still..." Mara's hands stopped mid-sentence, and Anya could tell on her facial expression and wiggling fingers that her friend was looking for the correct word to use, since she knew whatever was going on between Runa and Anya was a sensitive subject. "Arguing?" She finally finished.

Anya chuckled low.

"A little maybe," she answered.

Mara smiled softly at her and there was a flash of something close to sadness in her eyes.

"I've missed you," Mara signed.

Anya looked away, pretending like her shoes had become incredibly interesting all of a sudden, she just didn't want her to look at her like that.

"Sorry," was all she signed before she looked up again.

"You're here now," Mara signed. "So what can I help you with?"

Anya cleared her throat as she tried to figure out how she was going to sign this without giving away too much.

"Do you have books about…Symbols? Or Markings?" Anya signed, trying to keep her hands from shaking, trying to feign slight disinterest. Mara raised an eyebrow at the request.

"What kind of symbols or markings?" She asked. "From any special religion, cult or country? What is it that you're looking for?" Anya frowned in confusion at her questions, she really had no idea did she? She had no leads of where this thing could come from except…Except its connection to fire and burning.

"Any markings revolving around…Fire perhaps?" Anya signed, feeling suddenly her heart beating hard in her chest. Mara scratched the back of her neck and she could see the cogs turn in her head; it was adorable.

"Fire?" She signed, making sure Anya hadn't miss signed anything. Anya nodded what she hoped was a calm nod and not panicked.

"When do you need it?" Mara asked. She pretended to think, pretended that she didn't want anything that could give her answers this very second. She didn't want to get Mara more involved in this than necessary. James was already involved and that was bad enough.

"Whenever you can," Anya signed and tried to smile a reassuring smile. Mara squinted for a second. Anya could see that she knew something was up but she had bet on the fact that she didn't pry and she hoped she'd been right in that.

"Okay," Mara signed. "I'll see what I can find. I'm guessing you're still staying at James' if I need to find you?" Anya nodded.

"I can come back later, so you don't have to come by," Anya signed. Mara simply shook her head with a small smile on her lips.

"It's been a while since I was outside this place, I tend to get lost in books," Mara signed and laughed. "I could use the fresh air and besides, I haven't seen James in ages. He's doing well I hope?"

"Yeah, he's good," Anya signed. "And if you're sure."

Mara simply nodded. "So is there anything else I can help you with while you're here?" She signed.

Anya bit her lip and hesitated for a moment. She'd just said she hadn't been outside the shop in a while, would she know anything about the increased guard presence? In for a penny, in for a pound, she might as well ask.

"Have you noticed the amount of new guards walking around?" Anya asked and made sure her face portrayed how crazy she thought it was.

"You're not the first to complain about that," Mara signed. "I've had a couple of customers saying the same thing but I haven't actually seen it myself yet. Why do you ask?"

Anya just shook her head and shrugged.

"Just wanted to check, it just seems weird. Don't you think?" She signed. Mara was silent for a moment. Anya could see she was considering telling her something or not.

"I have a guard friend you could ask," Mara said. "If it's important."

Anya scratched her head and smiled awkwardly. "Guards and I aren't exactly friends," she signed.

Mara smiled.

"I am aware. But she's a good one, she grew up on the east side," Mara signed.

"And she became a guard?" Anya signed.

"Through hard work and a fair share of luck I suppose," Mara signed. "She wants to help, actually help and she won't arrest you unless you actually do something illegal." There was a pause. "You can do that right? Not do something illegal for a little while?"

Anya could see the teasing look in her eyes as she signed that last part.

"There's a first time for everything," Anya signed back.

Like speaking with a guard apparently, but she knew Mara wouldn't send her into the arms of a guard just to get her arrested. She could have done it a thousand times over and this would be the most lazy and stupid trick to do so.

"Will she tell me anything?" Anya signed. "I'm just a civilian after all."

Mara smiled softly.

"Say that I sent you, that should get you a foot in at least. Then it's up to you to just be your charming self." Anya chuckled at that.

"Thank you," she signed.

Mara took up a piece of paper and quickly scribbled something on it before she handed it over to Anya folded in two. She opened it and it simply said 'Guard

Inara Justifa.' Mara's handwriting was prettier than any handwriting Anya had ever seen, it was in cursive with a little extra flare.

Mara pointed to the name.

"Ask for her and you should be fine," Mara signed. "She's usually stationed on the east side. Shouldn't be too hard to miss as there are almost no guards there."

Anya slipped the piece of paper into her pocket and nodded appreciatively towards Mara. "Thank you," she signed once again.

Just as she was about to walk away, Mara grabbed her arm and for a split second she was back in the forest, rain hammering down on her as the man had grabbed her. The feeling quickly vanished, but not without leaving her feeling slightly nauseous. Mara let go of her and with a furrowed brow she simply signed, "Be careful."

Chapter 11

ANYA

Anya exited Mara's shop, her last words playing in front of her eyes over and over. Mara knew something was off, she wasn't sure how, except the fact that she suddenly came talking to her asking weird questions. Maybe it wasn't so weird. Mara was a master at reading body language and facial expressions and Anya knew she hadn't been able to hide how she was feeling entirely.

To someone less perceptive, she might have seemed fine but that was not Mara. She sighed and rubbed her eyes and when she looked forward, she saw a familiar face. Runa was standing a few feet away from her, half obscured by the shadow from the alley she was in, but even from here, Anya could see the smirk on her face. She gave a quick nod towards further into the alley, a signal that she wanted Anya to follow her.

Runa quickly disappeared into the darkness of the alley and Anya just stood still for a moment. She really didn't have time for whatever game Runa was playing right now and she didn't like the fact that she'd seen her twice in the same day, usually they could go weeks without laying eyes on each other. Finally, Anya decided to follow her. She obviously wanted something and she might as well find out what it was. Not that she wasn't thrilled to go search for a guard to talk to.

Anya gave a quick glance around herself but found the street quite empty and then with light feet, she ran after Runa into the alley. At first, she couldn't see her but she quickly came into view. She was leaning against the brick wall, looking as relaxed as ever.

"What do you want?" Anya asked. Runa looked over at her, almost like she'd forgotten she'd asked Anya to follow her but she knew it was one of the games she liked to play, nothing more.

"What are you up to, Anya?" Runa asked and there was a dangerous edge to her voice.

"What are you talking about?" She shot back, trying to keep her voice from wavering. Runa took a few steps closer to Anya, her large eyes had an intensity in them she hadn't seen in a while.

"Don't play with me. I've followed you around the entire day and you've been behaving beyond erratic, even for you," Runa said. "The fact that you didn't even notice me at any point is only further proof." It almost felt like she'd punched Anya in the stomach. She'd followed her this entire time? Even outside the city? Had she seen what she'd done in the forest with the tree?

How much did she know?

"You followed me outside the city?" Was all Anya managed to ask.

Runa rolled her eyes.

"No, that's the only point I lost sight of you," she admitted. "I can't squeeze through that tiny little gap like yourself and I didn't feel like talking to a bunch of guards just to follow you." Anya couldn't help but let out a small sigh of relief at that. So she'd just seen her run around, which admittedly was a little weird but nothing she couldn't explain away.

"I'm just trying to get my bearings after…being gone for three days," Anya said. "I wasn't expecting the amount of guards walking around, so I panicked a little, sue me." Runa narrowed her eyes and Anya could tell she didn't believe her, which wasn't good for her.

"You left the city only for a few hours and when you came back…" Runa said then paused for a second. "What is going on?"

"Nothing," Anya said. "I'm just a little rattled."

"From what?" Runa asked. "Where were you those three days?"

Damn it. "I was sick, okay?" Anya said honestly. "That's it, I was just really sick." Runa scanned her face for any sign of a lie but her face softened when she didn't find any.

"Why didn't you just say so?" Runa asked. Anya shrugged.

"Weakness is easily taken advantage of here. I'm still…recovering from it," Anya said, and it wasn't a lie, it just wasn't the complete truth either.

"You think I'd take advantage of that information?" Runa asked.

"You might give it to someone else who might," Anya answered. "Word tends to spread fast." Runa shook her head in disbelief.

"What did you want with Mara then?" She changed the subject. "You haven't been to see her since you left the gang. What changed?"

"Almost dying clears your head a little," Anya simply said. "I missed her so I went to talk to her."

"You know I can walk in there right now and ask what you talked about and she'd tell me," Runa said, challenging.

"She's not a snitch," Anya said. Runa raised an eyebrow at that.

"You're right at that, but if she's worried about you, she might let it slide if I say that I want to help you."

Anya bit her lower lip. She knew Mara wasn't loose lipped but she cared way too much and she wasn't sure she wouldn't tell Runa.

"What do you want, Runa?" Anya said, irritation creeping into her voice.

"Is it so impossible for you to imagine that I want to help you?" Runa answered with the same kind of irritation in her voice.

"Yes, it is!" Anya answered a little too quickly and a little too harshly. Runa flinched back at that, almost like she'd been struck.

"Fine, fine!" She said, her voice filled with a mixture of hurt and annoyance. "Forget I said anything! Stupid me for thinking our…" She stopped herself mid-sentence and Anya could see Runa's eyes flicker from her eyes to her lips before she continued. "Our friendship meant anything. Maybe you can throw away years of loyalty like it's nothing but I'm not that cold,"

"Cold?" Anya repeated. She could feel that small flame inside of her ignite. "I'm not the one who killed a man in cold blood for no reason and acted like it was nothing."

Runa stepped even closer to her. Anya could see the hurt but also the anger that mirrored back to her in Runa's large eyes. They were so close, Anya could feel her breath on her face and if one of them had moved just a little, their bodies would have touched.

"I did what had to be done to protect the people I cared about," Runa said. She spoke low and slow and there was something dangerous creeping into her voice. "I killed one man to save everyone in my gang. You would have let us all hang to save one idiotic rich man! Who of us is cold?"

Anya straightened her back and did not break eye contact with her. Runa did not frighten her and they'd had this argument a thousand times before in a thousand different ways and it always ended the same way. Simply because Anya refused to budge and neither did Runa, none of them were willing to compromise so this is where it left them.

The little flame inside of Anya went out as fast as it had arrived and she felt her heart slow down and she unclenched her fists, she hadn't even noticed closing them.

"I would have figured something out, Runa," Anya said as calmly as possible. "My biggest problem is that your first instinct was to kill him, like it was the easiest choice in the world to you."

"Figured something out," Runa repeated, her voice filled with bitterness. "One day you won't have time to 'figure something out' later, Anya. You'll have to act on instinct or someone else's instinct will get you instead."

"So far, so good," Anya said. "That day that sorrow but I think I'll keep doing my thing until then."

Runa shook her head and finally took a few steps back from Anya.

"I did it for you," Runa said, her voice suddenly filled with raw honesty. "I did it for all of you. Can't you see that?"

Anya did. She did see it. She knew why Runa had done it but she couldn't forget the look in her eyes as she'd done it. There had been no hesitation and it had never seemed to bother her since, that was what really frightened Anya. She hadn't thought Runa was capable of that kind of thing and it had changed how she'd looked at her.

It had changed every smile, every glance and every scowl. Anya had second guessed everything Runa had done until she couldn't stand it anymore and left.

"Don't help me, Runa," Anya finally said. "Stop following me. Stop asking around for me." Runa's face turned to stone as she said those words and Anya knew she'd taken them the wrong way but she couldn't blame her.

"Right," Runa almost spat out. "You won't have to worry about me watching your back anymore. You've made it clear you like to live your life without any kind of safety net."

Runa stormed past her, knocking into her shoulder and kept walking. Anya's shoulder didn't physically hurt but it did hurt in some strange way. Anya sighed, she should get some rest, the other things could wait until tomorrow. Anya was simply too exhausted to keep going right now.

Chapter 12

ANYA

Anya stood at the end of a steep cliff. The harsh breeze tugged at her hair and it was almost like it was pushing her towards the edge even more. As she stared down into the abyss, she realised there was nothing but darkness, not a single light or shape moved in the deep. It felt infinite, like if she stepped off the cliff, she'd fall forever. Yet she was not afraid as she stared down into the nothingness, a strange calm had her in its grips.

Suddenly, she saw something in the darkness, a spark of light, gone as fast as it had appeared. Then again, brighter this time. And again, stronger each time until she could see the small flickering flame so far down there. Anya didn't think it was at the bottom, if there even was a bottom, it felt like it was just floating in the darkness. Bringing some illumination to an otherwise clouded space.

"Anya." Her name was spoken like a whisper, or rather it almost sounded like the crackling of fire. She felt it. The push, the pull towards the flame so far down in the darkness. It called for her and she wanted to answer.

"We can help you. If you help us," the voice spoke again, it came from nowhere and everywhere all at once. It was calm and focused, it sounded ancient. She knew that whoever was speaking was telling the truth, she didn't know how she knew it but it didn't matter to her at this moment.

"Okay." Her voice was barely audible; she sounded like a child in her own ears.

"Take a step. Fall. Answer the call of the flame."

It sounded so easy, so obvious once the voice had spoken. Of course, all she had to do was step off the edge. Go towards the flame, it would catch her, it would not let her fall into nothingness.

Not if she answered its call.

Anya's eyes were focused on the flickering flame down below and without hesitation she took a leap forward, off the edge of the cliff. There was no fear as she fell, it barely felt like falling at all. It was as if she was gliding towards her goal and she rapidly came closer to the fire. It was growing exponentially by the second, almost like it was meeting her halfway. She reached out her left hand to touch it.

"Good," the voice spoke as she was a mere breath away from the flame.

Anya woke up as she felt her body hit the cold floor. Her breathing was heavy and she was soaked by her own sweat and she looked around herself in confusion. Right. She was back at James'; that had just been a very vivid dream. She glanced down at her left hand and its orange glow was slowly fading. Perhaps not just a vivid dream.

She rubbed her eyes and as she tried to get off the floor, she could feel how tired and worn out her body was. She had hoped a long rest would have helped with the exhaustion she was feeling but in a way it seemed to have gotten worse, at least her mind felt clearer than yesterday.

She washed up to the best of her ability but no matter what she did, the water felt ice cold against her skin and she gave up when she had at least gotten presentable and wasn't covered in her own sweat from head to toe. Just as she was putting on the last of her clothes, she heard a knock on the door. Anya couldn't lie, it still startled her to a certain extent. She was still not used to really having her own room and when she did, people would just barge in as they pleased.

"James?" Anya asked. She knew it was silly, the chance that it wasn't him was very low but she couldn't stop herself from asking.

"It's me. Can I come on?" He asked. Always so polite and considerate.

"Yeah."

The door opened and James smiled gently towards her as he carried a bowl into the room.

"I thought you might be hungry," he said and put down the bowl of porridge on the side of her bed. Anya nodded to him in gratitude and ate it all in a matter of seconds, food was never something she took for granted or would waste. It was too much of a precious resource to not enjoy to its full extent.

"How are you feeling?" James asked. She cleared her throat as she finished the last piece of the porridge.

"Okay, I think," she said vaguely. "Had a crazy dream but that's about it." She tried to laugh but it sounded false even to herself. James stared at her for a moment, she hated when he did that.

"Did you find anything useful yesterday? You seemed very tired when you got back," James said, that hint of worry creeping into his voice.

"I don't know, maybe," she answered. "And yeah, I suppose having a fever coma for three days took a little more out of me than I thought." To that she actually managed to smile a little and James seemed to appreciate that.

"Maybe you should take it a little easy," James said.

Anya sighed. "I'm trying," she said.

He gave her a sceptical look. "I am!" She answered. "While I also do other stuff."

"Just be careful," James said.

Wasn't that what everyone she'd met in the last days had said to her? Be careful. It was as if James, Runa, Mara, all of them could sense that something was off. That she was off. She didn't like to think that it was that obvious because how long would it take for others that didn't know her to figure it out?

"Mara gave her regards by the way," she said, changing the subject slightly.

"Is she well?" James asked, obviously trying to hide his surprise. He knew better than anyone that Anya hadn't seen her in a while. She simply nodded. She was quiet for a moment before she spoke again.

"Runa came and asked for me, didn't she, while I was sick," Anya said, more like a statement than a question.

James looked at her, checking to see what he should say no doubt.

"Yes," he simply answered.

"Why didn't you tell her anything?" Anya asked.

"It was none of her business," James said. "I knew…you wouldn't have wanted me to tell her. And as I had no idea what was wrong with you, I simply didn't want to spread any false information."

"How did she take your refusal to talk?" She asked carefully.

James frowned slightly.

"She took it fine." Anya could tell he wasn't telling the entire truth and it was almost like he was challenging her to call him out on it.

"Did she now?" Was finally all she said.

"She's not a bad person. She cares about you," James said, but there was a hint of something in his voice, something that sounded awfully close to resentment.

"Do you like her?" Anya asked, keeping her eyes focused on him to see his every reaction. He laughed a low laugh and looked slightly surprised by the question.

"Does it matter?" He asked.

"I simply asked if you liked her or not," she pressed. James hand clenched around his cane handle before he relaxed again. Anya was sure he hadn't even noticed doing it himself.

"As I said, she's not a bad person and she cares about you. That's good enough for me." He was being vague on purpose.

"Fine," she said but she held his gaze for a few seconds too long. "Just be careful around her."

James raised an eyebrow in slight disbelief at that.

"I know what she's capable of," James said. "I've treated her wounds and wounds made by her hand multiple times."

Anya wanted to ask why; why he treated anyone who managed to crawl their way to his front door. No matter if they were a thief, a murderer, a noble or the poorest man in the city. She had never seen him reject anyone. She'd seen him more or less happy while helping someone but he'd never once complained or said anything.

She knew he always said it would come back in his favour to do good but there had to be another reason why he did this? She just couldn't fathom what it would be. Perhaps that was what really separated the two of them at the end of the day.

"I'm going out again. I don't know when I'll be back," she said and just as she was about to leave, she turned back and continued. "Mara might come by with some books I asked about as well."

"About the Mark?" James asked.

Anya nodded.

"Do you want me to do some research if she comes by with books? So I can make myself useful?" James' voice was calm and his eyes were scanning Anya's face for a reaction.

She wanted to say no, absolutely not. The less he knew the better she had a feeling. He wanted to help so badly, she could see it in his eyes. But she also knew she couldn't do this alone. She knew the man had said to trust no one but if she trusted no one she would be fumbling in the dark.

Anya did not only need this flame inside of her to grow, she needed to trust that when it went out that she would have someone to hold her hand in the darkness. Runa's words rang in her head as she thought this. Runa was wrong.

Anya did want a safety net, she needed one, she just didn't trust Runa to be that for her anymore.

Chapter 13

ANYA

Anya walked towards the east district, that was where Mara had told her she would find her friend if she was out on patrol and she didn't exactly plan on going to a guard station and asking around. Anya wasn't exactly wanted at this point; she was smart when she worked and always wore a scarf around her face and her clothes were nondescript and she worked fast.

But still, she looked like an orphan from the east district, which technically was true and guards didn't often have any respect for people like her, criminal or not. The new heightened guard presence still made her uneasy as she made her way through the city, but from her observation they weren't checking everyone's hands they were passing, perhaps trying to keep it on the down low as much as possible.

She knew that it was improbable that she was going to get any answers from Mara's friend but it was worth a try at least. If nothing else, if she played her cards right, she might gain something of an ally inside the guards which would be of great use. The further into the east district she came, the less guards she saw, as usual. Anya didn't know why it still made her angry even after all this time.

Crime ran rampant here, much more than anywhere else in the city yet no guards were ever seen here. But then again, she had learnt a long time ago that the King and the nobility didn't care about some lowly poor people trying to survive. The guards were a sham, they were nothing more than pretence of civilisation and law and order but all they ever did was punish people who didn't deserve it, while the rich bastards who did, they went walking.

They didn't care what happened in the east district, as long as it stayed there and didn't cause too much of a ruckus, but Gods help the poor idiot who ventured further into the city and tried to pickpocket someone wealthy. Those poor idiots often didn't return. Which was why Anya had settled to do most of her business outside the walls of the city. Those people coming and going, they had money and as they were outside the city's protection, the guards had no real power and it was easier to disappear on the road, close to the forest. Out there, she was just another anonymous bandit.

Anya knew her way around the entire city at this point. She'd lived here her entire life after all and she'd had plenty of time just roaming around, getting familiar with all the shortcuts and what walls were climbable or not, and to a certain degree, who would open the door to help and who would simply shout for the guards attention. As she passed through the alleys, she couldn't help but look behind herself more often than usual and she was surprised every time when she didn't see Runa's face there.

Anya tried to shake off that feeling; she wouldn't bother her anymore and that was the best for both of them. Then her eyes caught the glimmer of a guards badge, a woman, her hair was wrapped in a tight scarf and framed her quite severe face. She was tall with light brown skin, narrow amber eyes and Anya thought she could see some freckles speckled over her face.

No, she wasn't just tall, she was large; there was a looming presence over her that intimidated even Anya a little at first glance. If this was Mara's friend, she was surely screwed. That did not look like anyone who would answer questions from someone like her but she'd come this far, she might as well try.

"Excuse me!" Anya said, trying to keep her voice calm and pleasant.

The woman snapped her head towards her and a small frown formed on her face and her amber eyes looked Anya up and down, as if she was contemplating whether she was a danger or not. Anya's eyes couldn't help but drift for a quick second towards the sharp blade that hung around her hip. She was sure it was for more than just decoration and this woman sure looked like she knew how to use it.

"Can I help you?" She said, her voice a lot deeper and raspier than Anya would have expected.

"This might sound weird, but are you Inara?" She asked, faking a small kind smile.

The woman's eyes narrowed even further. "Who's asking?" Was all she said.

Anya cleared her throat, here it goes.

"I got your name from a common friend of ours, she said you might be able to help me," she said, trying to keep her heart from beating too fast in her chest. She wasn't sure why she was so nervous. "Mara?" She added.

The woman's face instantly softened and she had a look of mild surprise on her face for a short second.

"Mara said we were friends?" She asked.

Anya froze in place but tried to keep that same smile still on her face, that wasn't a good sign.

Had Mara lied to her? Exactly what had Mara sent her into?

"Yes," Anya simply said and swallowed.

Inara looked her up and down once again, clearing thinking about what to say next.

"I suppose that's one way of saying it," Inara finally said with a sigh and her whole demeanour relaxed a little, but only a little. "So you're a friend of Mara as well?"

"I am," Anya said, feeling a little better once she'd relaxed. "My name is…" For a split second she thought about using a fake name but quickly realised there was no point. If Inara went to Mara and asked about her, she'd figure out real fast that she'd lied about her name and that was no way of building trust. "I'm Anya," she finally said.

Inara raised an eyebrow, clearly having noticed the small pause.

"Are you a criminal?" She asked, her voice devoid of feeling.

Anya chuckled a little at that.

"Most guards think that when they see someone like me, don't they?" She answered and looked challengingly into her eyes. "Someone from the east side."

Inara's eyes darkened and she held her gaze.

"I am from the east side," was all she said.

"Mara said as much," Anya said. "Doesn't mean you're not a guard now though, am I right?" Anya knew she was pushing her buttons but she needed to see if she truly cared about the wellbeing of someone like her or felt anything except distain for the east side and its residences. Anya needed to see if she could be trusted even a little. She trusted Mara's judgment to a certain degree but she saw good in people, people who might not always deserve it. Inara took a deep breath before she spoke again.

"I am stationed here by request for a reason, Anya," she said, putting a lot of emphasis on the name. "I know how guards view the east side."

"So you're here to be its saviour?" Anya asked. "A daughter of the east side made guard, now back to change everything, is that it?"

Anya knew she was going too far, she knew she was making it personal even if she pretended otherwise. Guards had never done anything for her except made her already hard life harder. They were supposed to help those in need but she'd only found them paying her any kind of attention when they paid for her company at the Red Rose.

She just couldn't stop the words from spilling from her mouth once she'd started. She couldn't help it, she was bitter and angry, not at Inara but at the bright, shining badge and what it symbolised. It was a joke, a cruel joke, laughing her directly in the face every time she saw it.

Inara cocked her head to the side slightly and surprisingly, a small smile creeped onto her face.

"I can tell you don't especially care for guards," Inara said. "Me neither."

Anya stared at her for a brief moment.

"But you are a guard," Anya said.

"Correct," she answered.

"So why…?" Anya started to speak.

Inara looked around herself for a brief moment.

"There's no better way to change things than from the inside. I don't see myself as a saviour and I don't think I can change how things are run around here but I'd hate myself forever if I didn't try."

Anya was taken aback by the raw honesty and the passion in her voice, there was no doubt that she fully believed in what she was saying and finding someone like that was rare these days. She must have seen the slightly stunned expression on her face because her smile grew a little bigger.

"So, Anya, friend of Mara," she said. "What can I help you with?"

Chapter 14

ANYA

Anya took a look around them, it wasn't a crowded street they were standing on but she wasn't sure if what she wanted to discuss was something to talk about so openly about, and maybe Inara wouldn't answer as truthfully as she would in private.

"Do you want to go somewhere to talk?" Anya asked. "I'd suggest your place but I'm sure you don't want-…"

"My place works fine, if that's what you want," Inara said, interrupting her. "I am supposed to go on break now anyway, so as long as we make it quick."

"Oh," Anya said, a little surprised. "You're not afraid I'm going to do something?"

Inara's eyes went up and down Anya's body and with a self-assured smile she spoke again.

"I can handle myself." Pause. "And you're a friend of Mara so you can't be too bad."

You have no idea, was Anya's first thought but she just smiled at that.

"Lead the way," Anya said and made a gesture for her.

Inara simply nodded and started walking. They walked in relative silence for no longer than ten minutes and they ended up right on the edge of the east district, just where it started to get a little more fancy. They stopped in front of a brick red three storey house and Inara walked inside. "Nice place," Anya said as she looked around the inside, they walked up two stairs, she assumed Inara's apartment was there.

Inara didn't say anything in response and Anya got a sudden chill running through her body. Inara was a guard but was Anya absolutely sure that she wouldn't close the door behind them and then attack her. She could easily say Anya had broken in and that she'd taken her down in self-defence, something like that would land her in The Grove for a good while. Attacking a guard always ended in long and painful punishments.

Inara unlocked the fourth door on the second floor and went inside, not even looking behind her to see that Anya was following her. Carefully and now a lot more aware of every movement she was making, Anya made her way into the apartment. It was quite a small apartment but bigger than a lot she'd seen. It was one larger room with a small stove and a sofa and a poorly filled bookshelf.

Anya saw two other doors and assumed they led to the bathroom and to the bedroom. It was a very impersonal space, either like she'd just moved here and was still putting her touches to the place or she simply didn't own things.

Inara gestured to the small sofa for Anya to sit but she cleared her throat and simply shook her head in reply. Inara raised an eyebrow but then went over to the sink.

"You want a glass of water? Some tea?" She asked.

"I'm good," Anya said politely. She'd learnt to never take a drink or food from someone you weren't completely sure weren't going to poison or drug them. It was a security precaution she couldn't shake.

Inara poured a glass of water and downed it quickly, before she filled it again and downed that one as well. Anya guessed they didn't have the best opportunities to drink when they were out patrolling. As she was drinking, Anya strolled over to the bookshelf and took a look at the few books there. There was one on the history of the city, not her thing at all.

Another seemed to be a hand manual for guards, that could be of interest depending what information it contained. The last three books were instructions on how to learn sign language. Interesting.

"Do you find my reading habits interesting?" Inara asked.

"Some of them," Anya answered shortly.

"But I assume that's not why you're here," Inara said. "So what can I do for you? Has a guard been treating you badly? Or has someone threatened you?"

Anya laughed low. Of course that's what Inara thought she was going to talk about. Made sense why she invited her into her apartment then.

"No," Anya said. "I was wondering about the sudden heightened guard presence? Especially stationed at the entrance? And they seem to be checking people?"

Inara's face dropped a little, her back straightened and she frowned slightly.

"Why does that concern you?"

"Because as we established earlier I don't care much for guards and they don't care for me either, or anyone from the east side to be precise," Anya said. "You don't think this will hurt people like me more than anyone else? People just trying to survive? I was wondering if anything has happened, if I should stay away from certain places or similar."

Anya licked her lips and took a stab in the dark. "Mara was concerned about my safety, which is why she gave me your name."

At the mention of Mara's name, Inara's face once again softened. There was something there between them, Inara couldn't help showing it all over her face. Inara took a deep breath and was silent for a moment, clearly weighing over her options.

"I am not supposed to discuss things like this with civilians," Inara finally said but Anya could hear the uncertainty in her voice.

"Please," Anya said.

Inara licked her lips and shook her head.

"If I tell you anything, you cannot repeat it to anyone. Do you understand me? It will get me in immense trouble and I will have you arrested."

Her amber eyes found Anya's and she could see she meant every word she said. Anya had no doubt she would throw her into The Grove with little regret if she crossed her. Anya simply nodded.

"I don't know all the details," Inara started. "But something was apparently stolen from the Castle."

"When?" Anya asked, her voice wavering slightly as she spoke.

Inara stared at her intensely for a short second.

"About four days ago, I think."

Anya bit her lower lip. The same day she'd found that man out in the rain, the same day he'd forced the Mark onto her.

"So…So why are they checking people's hands when they're entering and exiting the city?"

Anya asked, trying to keep my voice from shaking.

Inara shrugged.

"Those were the instructions and if we saw anything out of the ordinary, we are supposed to get them into questioning."

"Out of the ordinary…" Anya repeated, low as a whisper.

"Are you alright?" Inara asked and she gave her a weird look.

Anya nodded but she felt nauseous.

"What was stolen?" She asked.

"They wouldn't say. It has to be important though if it was kept in the Castle," Inara answered. "And to be fair, even if I did know, I wouldn't tell you."

"Fair," Anya said and tried to smile.

"So as long as you haven't been in the Castle and stolen something, you're fine," Inara said.

"You've got nothing to worry about."

Anya wanted to laugh at that but managed to stop herself, Inara was already finding her strange and suspicious, she could tell. She didn't have to make it even more obvious.

"Good," Anya said. "Well, that was it. Sorry to have wasted your time."

Anya started to make her way towards the door but Inara stepped in front of her, out of reflex she took a large step backwards, making space between them.

"Wait," Inara said.

"What?" Anya asked, feeling her heart beating hard in her chest. She'd almost entered a fight or flight mode but she'd managed to calm down at the last second. There was no need to panic, yet. "How well do you know Mara?" Inara asked and her whole face had softened, she almost looked a little embarrassed.

Anya frowned, that was not exactly what she had expected.

"Pretty well," Anya answered slowly.

"You can...talk with her?" Inara asked slowly.

Anya's eyes flashed back to the sign language books in her bookshelf.

"If you're asking if I know sign language, then yes," Anya said.

Inara was silent for a moment and something clicked inside Anya's head.

"You don't know sign language, do you?" She asked.

Inara looked away. "I'm...I'm learning," she answered.

"You're learning for Mara?" Anya asked.

"I was wondering if in exchange for the information I gave you, if you could think about teaching me...a little sign language?" Inara said, her voice filled with uncertainty as she completely ignored what Anya had last said.

"Oh," Anya said. "Yeah, sure."

Inara looked back at her, almost a little surprised.

"You will?" She asked.

"Seems only fair, right?" Anya said and smiled. "Besides, it helps Mara. I know...she can be lonely sometimes. Not a lot of people know sign language and that..."

"Ostracises her," Inara filled in.

Anya looked at Inara for a second; her large and tall frame, her severe face that seemed to soften any time at the mention of Mara's name. Anya had no doubt she would cut someone down if needed but there was a softness inside her that almost reminded her of James.

"Alright, what do you say about this?" Anya said, feeling a little braver with this new information. "I give you some lessons in sign language and you give me any new information you get on this thing that's going on in the city?"

Inara frowned a little; it was obvious this was testing her limits.

"Nothing too confidential of course," Anya added. "Simply if you find any suspects or anything else. Deal?"

Anya put out her hand, touching people or having people touch her wasn't her favourite thing since her time in the Red Rose but it was something she was actively working on. Anya wouldn't let that place take more of her than it already had. She would still flinch from time to time, especially if people moved fast or unpredictably but every soft touch or gentle hug helped. James had helped so much. Inara took her hand, her grip strong and sure.

"Deal," she said.

Chapter 15

INARA

The moment Inara shook hands with Anya, there was something inside of her telling her that something was wrong. Even through the gloves Anya was wearing, she could feel heat radiating from her. And her eyes, there was something behind them that Inara couldn't place, but whatever it was it sent alarm bells through her head.

She had to remind herself that Mara trusted this person, had even recommended that Anya come and speak to her and she had to keep that in consideration. Inara wanted nothing more than to have a better relationship with Mara and doing this could go a long way in making that happen. Inara had to prove herself to Mara, not the other way around, and if Anya could teach her sign language as well, that was just an added bonus.

Half the times Inara had gone to Mara's shop, she had chickened out and left even before entering and the other half she always left feeling embarrassed and disappointed in herself. Inara had tried to teach herself sign language but it just seemed she wasn't apt for it naturally, and not being able to talk with Mara in her own language but instead having to write everything out made her feel awful. Inara couldn't imagine the struggles Mara had to go through daily when barely anyone could communicate properly with her in her own way.

Inara took her job extremely seriously. Being a guard was something she had worked hard for and she truly did believe in equality and that through reforms, the east side could become a better place to live and get more job opportunities, to keep kids out of crime. She also knew that most other guards laughed at her and called her an idealist and told her to just stay away from the east side like the rest of them, let the east side deal with itself like it had done for so many years. Inara couldn't listen to them.

She was from the east side, she had seen the crime up close, the gang wars going on but also how people went out of their way to help others in need. It was two sides of the same coin. The most hostile part of the city but also the most close knit community.

***

After having made the deal with Anya, life for Inara continued as usual, except she no longer had any free time left in the day. When she wasn't on patrol or helping at the guard station, she was with Anya, trying to get a grip on sign language. Even when Anya left, Inara forced herself to stay up and continue her reading.

She was really trying but it mostly ended up in her not getting enough sleep, though she was good at hiding it and she would take micro naps during the day at any given opportunity when no one was around to chastise her for it. Anya wasn't the best teacher and Inara certainly wasn't the best student, which resulted in a lot of frustration for her. Anya would explain something multiple times in a row but the exact same way, and it did not matter how many times she repeated it, Inara did not understand.

Most days, she sent Anya home with a scowl but still a 'thank you'. She might be frustrated but she was appreciative nonetheless and it wasn't Anya's fault. Inara would offer her tea every time Anya and it took a long time for her to accept, which Inara found strange and slightly insulting. Inara was very proud of her tea collection and her tea making skills. It was something she had perfected over the years as she had found nothing calmed her down better than a scalding hot cup of tea.

Inara also noticed Anya always wore those leather gloves she'd worn the first time they'd met. She had asked her about them but the answer she'd gotten had been very unsatisfying and there was always a hint of panic in Anya's eyes when she asked.

After seven days of rigorously working her job and practicing her sign language, she and the entire guard presence were told to gather at their different guard stations. It wasn't anything unusual, it often meant they had new instructions to give out that would affect the city more than usual.

"As you all know, our efforts to retrieve the culprit who stole from the Castle has been…unsuccessful. And the people at the top are growing restless and think it's time to increase the search," the commanding officer at Inara's guard station said. His name was Dante if she remembered correctly; she barely saw him as she was nothing more than a low standing patrol guard.

"They think that trying to keep it as low profile as possible has been a waste of time and that the culprit has to be apprehended immediately," he continued. "Whoever catches the culprit will be rewarded handsomely."

Whispers of excitement started to go through the room. Inara rolled her eyes, of course that was all they cared about, not the fact that a crime had been committed, a seemingly serious one for that matter.

"Silence," Dante continued. "From tomorrow, we are going to search through every home, starting on the east side. Every home is to be searched, every person on the street is to be searched, no one is above this, understood?"

"And what, we're still just looking for some mark on a left hand?" A voice spoke up from the crowd. "What if they no longer have what was stolen?"

"Then at least they will have information about it. Finding the person with the Mark is all the instructions we've got. Use force if needed, most people are not going to enjoy having their houses searched. Also when approaching the different gangs, make sure you are a large group of guards and take care, they will most certainly not go down without a fight."

The excited murmur turned colder and more serious. No one wanted to be in the group that went from gang to gang, demanding to check their left hands and their places. Even the gangs were careful to not harm or kill an officer, it would send you straight to The Grove with little chance of getting out but Inara knew Dante was correct, this could get ugly and messy really fast. Inara didn't want to see that happen, not if she could stop it.

Chapter 16

A N Y A

The next few days passed in a bit of a blur. Mara came over with all the books she'd found that she thought could be of help after three days and there were quite a few of them, more than Anya would have thought. She once again realised how lucky she was to have James by her side because without even saying anything, he dove headfirst into the pile of books.

Anya tried to help as much as possible but she couldn't manage to keep her concentration for more than a few minutes, so she mostly flipped through the books, trying to see if they had any pictures or drawings of the Mark or anything similar. She didn't have much luck.

Anya kept her promise to Inara and every day, after she'd finished her guard shift, Anya went over to her apartment and they sat for hours studying sign language. It was actually good for Anya too as she'd become rusty over the years and getting back to the basics really helped. Inara wasn't a fast learner and she easily became frustrated when she got something wrong but Anya couldn't blame her, she didn't like not being good at something either.

It had taken Anya five days of going to Inara to accept a glass of water and she then accepted her tea as well. It seemed like she was something of a tea fanatic, her cupboard was stocked with more flavours of tea than Anya even thought possible and she was terrific at preparing it. Anya had never had better tea, normally she thought it tasted like lightly flavoured water but the depth Inara had in her tea made her feel warm and safe. It was like a hug in a cup but without any of the human contact.

On the seventh day, Inara really seemed to struggle, she seemed distracted.

"I'm never gonna get this," she said, annoyance clear in her voice and she slammed shut the book.

"Don't be so dramatic," Anya said, trying not to smile. "You are showing progress."

"You're just saying that because you want information," Inara muttered.

"I mean partly," she said jokingly but there was certainly truth behind it. Even though Inara was a guard, Anya found she did enjoy her company more than she would have thought. Sure, she was a little hot headed from time to time and could be stubborn like nothing else but she was also calm and patient when it counted. She was much more of a listener than a talker, at least what Anya could tell.

Inara took a deep breath and stretched her back. They had gone from sitting on her sofa to slowly migrating down onto the floor and taking up more and more space. Inara looked at Anya with her amber eyes and there was something there but she couldn't pinpoint it. Anya cleared her throat.

"You still haven't really told me why you're so interested in learning sign language," Anya said and picked up one of the books she'd gotten on the subject.

"I said…" Inara started.

"Yeah, because of Mara," Anya said, interrupting her. "Do you have a crush on her?" Inara looked taken aback by the question, almost a look of horror flashing over her face for a second.

"Oh God, no, no, no," Inara said and shook her head.

Anya tensed and felt a sudden anger rise inside of her.

"Why? Because she's a girl? Because she's deaf?" Anya started, the venom clear in her voice.

Inara almost looked like she'd been slapped and she then quickly glanced down, away from Anya's gaze. Anya thought it was the first time she'd ever seen her properly avoid eye contact.

"No…No, it's not that," Inara said low.

"Then what?" Anya asked. She had relaxed a little but was still on edge.

Inara bit her lower lip and she looked out through the window.

"If…It's not my place to talk about, I don't think so at least," Inara said uncertainty.

Anya frowned; what was she talking about? She would have bet money that Inara had a crush on Mara because there was certainly something there, at least from Inara's side. Perhaps she'd mistaken the affection for something romantic when that wasn't the case.

"You don't have to tell me," Anya said. "But I could ask Mara."

Inara twitched a little at that but just nodded.

"Perhaps it's better that way," Inara said. "If…if she didn't tell you when she sent you to me, I don't think it's my place to talk about it."

Now that made Anya ten times more curious about what was going on than before but she just made the mental note to talk to Mara about it later. She could probably swing by her shop after this on her way home.

"You care for her though," Anya said, as a fact, not a question. "I can see it in your eyes." Inara's eyes shot back at her and she looked a little surprised but it quickly turned into a soft smile.

"Our eyes give away more than our words ever could," Inara said.

"Our eyes are really snitching on us, huh?" Anya said jokingly. "What bastards." Inara let out a small laugh at that then she turned back a little more serious to Anya.

"We should probably stop for today," she said.

Anya looked out the window and noticed that the sun was about to go down, she'd been here longer than she'd thought. She nodded and slowly made her way to get up, her left leg had fallen asleep and that weird static pain shot through it as it was waking up.

"Anya," Inara said seriously.

She turned back to Inara with a questioning look on her face.

"The guards are supposed to start going from home to home, looking for whatever was stolen. Everyone is to be searched, starting with the east side," Inara said, her voice heavy.

Anya felt a sudden nausea hit her and she had to resist the urge to throw up.

"Oh," was all she managed to say.

"It's going to get messy. A lot of people are not going to like it and I'm afraid there is going to be violence and…worse," Inara said. "The people at the top wanted to keep it as discreet as possible but as we've found nothing. We're going to start having to get a little rough," Inara said.

"Is what was stolen really so important?" Anya asked, her voice shaking slightly.

"For them it is," Inara said.

Her eyes suddenly shot to Anya's gloved hands hanging by her sides. She almost felt her heart stop beating for a brief second. Anya hadn't taken them off at any point when she'd been with Inara for obvious reasons. She'd asked once and Anya had just shrugged it off.

The left leg that had fallen asleep refused to wake up, it just continued shooting that static pain through her body and it almost felt like it was spreading but it had to just be because she was panicking. Inara rose from where she was sitting and Anya was reminded how imposing she could be.

"Could you please take off your gloves, Anya," she said, her voice as cold as stone but Anya thought she could hear a small crack in it.

Anya shook her head, she felt like she couldn't speak.

"Please," Inara said, her face unmoving but her eyes. Anya saw the pain this was causing her screaming through her eyes. "Take off your gloves. If you're innocent, you have nothing to fear and I apologise for…"

Inara's glance went to Anya's empty tea cup. Anya's legs betrayed her and she collapsed onto the floor as she realised what had just happened. Inara had drugged the tea, Anya couldn't believe she'd been this reckless. She couldn't believe she'd trusted a guard for even a second. She'd let her guard down and it might cost her everything.

Anya's eyes were starting to get heavy as Inara slowly walked closer to her. Inara ripped off Anya's gloves, she tried to struggle but her body wasn't responding. When she saw the Mark on Anya's left hand, a small gasp escaped her mouth, as if she'd hoped she wouldn't find anything. She frowned deeply before her face turned to stone again.

"I am sorry, Anya," Inara said. "But at least now the people on the east side won't have to suffer."

Anya wanted to laugh, she wanted to cry, she wanted to scream. She wanted to do anything at all but she just laid on the floor, staring up into the ceiling. She could feel the flickering flame inside her ignite as she lost consciousness.

Chapter 17

ANYA

"Anya."

Her eyes shot open at the soft mention of her name, but her eyes were met only with complete darkness. It felt as if she was floating. When she looked down, she saw nothing but the empty darkness continuing for what seemed like forever. But when she glanced up, she could just barely make out a little glint of sunlight and what looked like a cliff? Anya knew it was the same cliff she'd stepped off the last time. She wasn't scared, there was only a calm inside of her.

A bright, searing light emerged in front of her and Anya had to close her eyes, the sudden light hurt her eyes after having stared into the darkness for what felt like such a long time. When she finally managed to pry her eyes open and squint at whatever was emanating that light, all she saw was the same man she'd seen in the storm. The same man who had given the Mark to her, or rather forced it onto her. It had not been given to her, she had not willingly accepted it but here she was all the same.

For a short moment, they just stared at each other. The man looked over Anya like he was inspecting her and she was just staring at him, not entirely sure what she wanted to say or where she wanted to start.

"Who are you?" Anya's voice echoed in the darkness and she barely recognised it as her own voice.

"Me?" The man asked with a raised eyebrow. "Or ME?"

The man in front of her changed into a woman with small angular eyes and bronze skin, then changed again into a pale white man who reminded her of a skeleton. It started to switch between people faster. Finally, it was so fast that Anya couldn't even take in any features of the people, it was nothing more than a constant moving static. Anya closed her eyes, it was too much to take in and she couldn't bear to look at all the different people. They shared one thing as far as Anya could tell. They all had the same dead, calm expression on their face.

"Stop," Anya whispered low.

She could almost feel it slow down until it was calm; she hadn't realised it but the static had vibrated through her entire body. Slowly, she once again opened her eyes and the same man stood in front of her.

"So?" He asked calmly.

Anya swallowed hard. "Both?" She finally answered. She wanted to know who that man who had forced the Mark on her was, she just needed to know. Then she could ask other questions. The man lifted his left hand and looked at it, which did not bear the Mark anymore. "Of course not," Anya thought. "I have it."

"He was a scientist," the man spoke. "His name was Andrew."

Silence.

"Now, he's just another part of me," it continued. Anya realised that what stood before her wasn't a man, nor a woman or person of any gender. It was something else entirely.

"And who are you?" She asked.

It smiled gently and put its hands behind its back.

"Wrong question," it simply said.

Anya frowned.

"I am not a person. I am so much more, I exist everywhere and nowhere," it continued. "There have been many names for me over the centuries. I do not particularly care what you call me, it doesn't mean anything to me or change what I am."

Another short pause, it almost felt as if the air had gotten thicker with every word it spoke.

"But I would assume the easiest name to use for me would be Fire," it continued.

Anya just stared at it for a moment. "Fire," she said and finally glanced down at her left hand.

The Mark was glowing just the slightest.

"Yes, Fire," it said. "You must have felt it. The call."

Anya simply nodded; she'd felt it pulling at her almost as if she had no choice but to answer it.

"You're the Mark on my hand," Anya said, not a question in the slightest.

"In a manner of speaking, I suppose," it said. "I simply am Fire in its purest magical form." Anya was silent for a second, trying to take in the last part it had said, surely she must have misheard?

"Magic?" Anya said with a frown. "Magic isn't real."

It laughed but it was hollow, like it was trying to replicate someone laughing without ever having done it itself.

"I have been away for some time but magic, as you call it, is very much real," it said. "It exists all around you at all times. Just because humans have lost the ability to see and use it, doesn't mean it's gone."

Anya tried to take it all in. It was like everything it said was obvious as soon as it had spoken but not a second before. She couldn't see any reason why it would lie to her as it was as dependent on her as she was on it if she understood correctly.

"Are there more Marks?" Anya asked. She couldn't stop the thought from entering her head.

"One? Ten? A hundred? A million? Unlimited?" It said. "I do not know. Humans often try to get rid of us every time we re-emerge; they seem to think that they can kill us so it is hard to know how many of us exist at any one point."

It took a pause, looking directly into Anya's eyes.

"We are forever. We existed long before man and will outlive them as well. When there is nothing but darkness, we will still persist."

Anya was silent for a moment. She was starting to feel slightly nauseous but this place, whatever it was, had such a calming effect. She wasn't even sure she could panic here if she even wanted to. After what felt like minutes of long silence, Anya spoke again.

"Why me?" Her voice was low and childlike.

It shrugged. "You were there. Call it luck or bad luck, it all depends on how you look at it." It slowly started to move closer to Anya. She had the instinct to back away but she felt stuck in place. It stopped just in front of her and grasped her left hand.

The fire inside of her ignited almost a little too violently; pain shot through her veins but it also felt strangely good, it felt like power. It released her and it went out as fast as it had ignited.

"But you survived," it continued. "The last three before you didn't last more than twelve hours."

"And why did I survive?" Her voice was hoarse, almost like she hadn't spoken in years.

It smiled. "Because you already had a fire burning inside of you, Anya."

Anya frowned slightly, not entirely sure on what it meant with that. "Now, we can work together and there will be no limits to what we can achieve," it said. "Or you can ignore me, reject the call and live in fear that someone will discover me."

"Doesn't sound like much of a choice," she said. The last sentence it had spoken sent a shiver down her spine, a warning.

"You always have a choice," it said. "But if you do not feed the flame, it will flicker and finally go out and you will grow old and sickly, and die like any other human. Feed the flame and I will keep you alive for as long as we work together. I will heal you, just like I did before." Anya remembered the wound she'd suffered during the storm, that miraculously had been cauterised and healed.

"I will make you strong. Strong enough to burn all those who oppose you to the ground. Strong enough to protect everyone you care about," it continued.

"How...how do I feed the flame?" She asked carefully.

The smile on its face grew wider.

"It is simple. Life feeds it, makes it burn brighter and stronger than ever before," it said.

"Life?" Anya asked with a frown.

"You must shed blood or take a life to properly feed the flame. Humans are the best kindling but other animals will suffice in a pinch," it said.

Anya just stared at it. She almost wanted to laugh because surely it was joking? But the smile on its face didn't waver and Anya felt her heart drop in her chest.

"I'm not a killer," she answered, trying to sound braver than she felt.

It tilted its head slightly to the left. It sighed and looked up, towards the glimmer of light.

"Your friend betrayed you," it said.

The memory of the last minutes at Inara's place rushed through her head and anger took hold of her. It must have seen it on her face, because its smile grew impossibly bigger.

"They have you," it continued. "If you are lucky, they will kill you because they fear you but I think their curiosity will outweigh their fear this time. I cannot *think they have anything good in store for you. Humans want power beyond anything else."*

Fear suddenly mixed in with the rage.

"I...I don't want to die," Anya stammered. "I don't want..." She stopped herself, she didn't want any of this but didn't know how to articulate it.

It leaned in closer, and the little kindling inside of her ignited. It was barely anything more than a spark.

"Then feed the flame, Anya," it said. "Feed it and I promise to give you whatever your heart desires."

Chapter 18

R U N A

Like it was nothing. The sentence Anya had spoken went around in Runa's head on repeat, no matter how much she wanted to stop it. *Like it was nothing*; Runa wanted to laugh. Like she didn't see the faces of the people she'd killed every time she closed her eyes. Like it didn't haunt her to see the light go out in their eyes and feel something dying inside of herself as well.

Like she didn't remember their names. Like she sometimes didn't sneak away to the graveyard and stood in the shadows of their tombstones, just staring for hours. Runa really did think if anyone would have understood it would have been Anya, but apparently she couldn't have been more wrong. The way Anya had looked at her when she'd killed that noble, Runa thought she might never forget that face.

Runa had seen it all unravel from there, one action to save them all from the noose had cost her Anya. Runa knew she was a good actress, a master of disguising her emotions but so often she had just wished someone would see through it. Or, not just anyone, just one person really. Showing weakness on the east side was a dangerous thing, especially if you were part of a gang.

Runa had gained a reputation of being calm, relaxed and a little cocky at all times, like she always had the upper hand in a discussion but often she felt as if she was out of her depth.

Runa let out a frustrated groan and kicked a stone before she took a deep breath and forced her shoulders to relax and pushed down all her irritation and anger. There was no time for emotions right now, not as she was entering the bar, the Keg, her gang owned. As she opened the door, she was immediately hit by the smell of alcohol and cigarette smoke; it was a rowdy crowd there tonight.

As Runa scanned the people, she saw a few customers but she also saw her gang members sitting by their usual table. Runa intended to ignore them but when Trent, a large dumb bald man shouted over to her.

"How are you, you little love bird?" A roar of laughter broke out and Runa saw red and marched over to them. After everything that had happened today, she was not in the mood; calm, relaxed Runa be damned. She couldn't let them walk all over her or laugh at her; she could not let them think she was weaker than any of them.

Runa unsheathed one of her knives, hidden behind her jacket and pointed it towards Trent. The laughter stopped and the entire bar suddenly changed its atmosphere.

"What did you say?" Runa asked challengingly.

Trent didn't look scared by any means but he had a much more serious look on his face now. "We know you haven't done it," he said with a scorn. "We know you followed her like a lost puppy all day lo…"

Runa moved faster than any of the people around the table and before they could react, she was in front of Trent with her knife up against his throat.

"You should choose your next words very carefully," Runa hissed. "Or the next sound coming out of your mouth will be a scream."

Runa could hear shuffling behind her and she knew the rest of the gang was slowly moving towards their own weapons. Scuffles within the gang were nothing new or surprising but if you actually killed one of your own, the price on your head would be high. Before Trent could speak again, another voice, coming from the stairs, spoke out.

"R, Mr Parker wants to speak with you." Runa recognised it as Tamara's voice, a new addition to the gang and she worked mostly as Mr Parker's secretary. Runa felt sorry for her and couldn't imagine how awful it had to be for Tamara to be that close to him and at his beck and call at all times. Tamara was a sweet young girl, barely out of her teenage years and she still had some semblance of innocence in her eyes. Runa slowly moved her hand away from Trent's throat; his face had a distinctly smug look on his face that she couldn't stand. He thought he'd won this argument.

With a quick jab, she slammed the handle of the dagger into Trent's nose. He let out a surprised scream as blood started to pour from his face. Then Runa left the table and went towards the stairs. She could hear the other people around the table laugh but now they were laughing at Trent and not her. They knew as well as she did, that he'd earned that broken nose and as he didn't go after her, so did he on some level. Violence was respected in this place, if you had the stomach to do it.

Runa passed Tamara on the staircase but could hear her scrambling to follow her upstairs.

"What mood should I expect from him?" Runa asked.

Tamara cleared her throat. "He's in a pretty good mood."

Runa shot her a quick glance but Tamara avoided her gaze. Runa didn't say anything to that, she knew better than most that look on Tamara's face. Runa would not pry into that unless Tamara wanted to speak about it with her, but she doubted she ever would. They passed the first floor where everyone in the gang had their own rooms to sleep in or use however they pleased. It wasn't much, a small rectangle filled with nothing but an uncomfortable bed but it was home. It was better than sleeping on the street in the cold and rain and being extremely vulnerable. Here, at least she had a roof over her head.

The top floor had a few doors as well but not nearly as many. The largest one was Mr Parker's office, the other rooms were for…for people they needed to interrogate or talk some sense into. They were almost completely soundproof, courtesy of Mr Parker. Runa stopped in front of Mr Parker's door and took a deep breath.

She shot Tamara one last glance who looked at Runa with a sad smile before she scurried back down. So he didn't want anyone listening in on their conversation. Runa knocked, put her hands behind her back and waited. It barely took a moment before she heard Mr Parker's rough voice through the door.

"Come in."

Runa took one last deep breath, shook loose the tension in her body and put on her best charming smile before she opened the door.

Mr Parker's office was about twice the size of their bedrooms and it was decorated with bookshelves, a large wooden desk and pretty curtains framing a large window. It was clean and professional but not braggy. He wanted to keep the pretence that he was just another person in the gang, no one bought it but they let him believe it, whatever kept him happy. As Runa entered, Mr Parker's grey eyes shot up from where he'd been looking at his desk and he smiled. Runa had always hated that smile.

"Runa, please sit down," he said and gestured to the seat in front of his desk and he leaned back in his own chair.

Runa sat down in the chair. It was just a few inches shorter than normal chairs, a trick they used to make people feel inferior and that the other person towered over them without it being too obvious. Mr Parker folded his hands over his lap and then there was silence. Runa knew better than to talk before spoken to.

"How's your day been?" Mr Parker asked.

"I would rather you just get to the point than talk pleasantries," Runa said and she did realise the irony in saying that because talking around people was all she did. Anya had always been annoyed with that about her. Mr Parker scoffed and leaned forward.

"Someone's had a bad day," Mr Parker said. "Very well, straight to business then."

Runa knew what was coming next.

"Anya still lives. Why?" Mr Parker asked and there it was, that dangerous glint in his eyes that showed the real him. The person who really was controlling this gang.

"I haven't had a good time…" Runa started.

"I don't have time for lies," Mr Parker interrupted her. His voice was already running out of patience and Runa knew that wasn't good for her.

Mr Parker sighed deeply and when he looked back at Runa, he had that disguise of a kind old man again.

"I know this is hard for you," Mr Parker said, trying to sound understanding but just coming off as degrading.

Runa straightened her back in her seat, she didn't want his pity.

"But you know why this is necessary," Mr Parker continued.

Runa nodded.

"I want to hear you say it," Mr Parker said, that edge back in his voice.

Runa bit her lip and swallowed before she spoke again, trying to keep her voice calm and steady.

"Because she betrayed us by leaving," Runa said.

"And?" Mr Parker said.

Runa looked straight into his eyes.

"Because…because she was my friend and I can't have two loyalties," Runa said.

"Exactly," he said. "Loyalty. Nothing is more important than that."

Runa didn't say anything, she didn't have anything to say to that.

"Feelings are good and all," Mr Parker continued. "If you can keep them in check and you've proven time and time again that you cannot do that around Anya."

Runa wanted to protest but she knew he would just call her lie and it would just make him angrier, so she stayed silent.

"How long have you been with us now?" Mr Parker asked.

"Five years," Runa answered.

"Five long years," Mr Parker said. "And yet with the exception of Tamara, you are one of the newest members and one of the youngest."

Runa was very aware of both these facts, most people in the gang were over 25 and had been around way longer than her. Mr Parker kept everyone in check and they knew there was no leaving, and why would they? They got paid, they got somewhere to sleep and they got a freedom they could never get living on the street. It wasn't a hard choice to make.

"You have proven yourself useful and ruthless when needed," he continued. "And I appreciate that, you are a quick learner and are good at following orders." Pause.

"Except when it comes to this apparently," Mr Parker said.

"I'm going to do it," Runa said, hoping her voice was as convincing as usual. "Just give me more time."

"More time?" Mr Parker asked as he stood up from his chair.

Runa forced herself to keep her eyes looking forward and not following his every move but she could feel when he stopped behind her. His bony hands gripped her shoulders, almost like he was going to give her a massage but he pressed down in a painfully tight grip. A grip that said, you are mine and you are not going anywhere.

"You've caught me in a good mood," he said and Runa could smell the alcohol on his breath.

"You'll have two more weeks."

"Thank you," Runa forced herself to say.

"But," he said and he pressed his fingers deeper into her flesh for just a brief second. "If she still lives after two weeks, I know where your loyalties truly lie. I will throw you to the boys and the girls of the gang and they will get to do whatever they please with you before throwing you out on the street. Am I making myself understood?"

Runa felt the slightest crack in her facade as her lip trembled but she managed to push it down before it could escalate and truly show on her face. Show no weakness.

"Understood," Runa said, her voice void of any feeling.

Runa could almost feel him smiling from behind her and his grip on her shoulders changed from painful to a much lighter touch but he did not let go.

"Good girl," Mr Parker said.

Runa felt a calm overtake her. *I am going to kill him one day,* she thought. And she knew his face would never haunt her whenever she closed her eyes. It would put a smile on her face instead.

Chapter 19

INARA

As soon as Anya had fallen unconscious, Inara had moved and tied her hands behind her back and also tied her ankles together just to be extra safe. Inara also searched Anya's clothes for weapons and as she had suspected, she found three daggers hidden in different places. After Inara had made sure that Anya would not be able to get loose or had any weapons to use, she sat down in the same place she'd sat when they had been studying.

She released a breath she hadn't noticed she'd been holding and out of pure habit, made sure her scarf covering her hair was secured properly. If she was being honest with herself, she hadn't really thought this far ahead. Or she had but now when she was actually here and it wasn't just a theoretical thing, it felt different. The absolute fear and betrayal Inara had seen in Anya's eyes hurt more than she would like to admit; she did not enjoy betraying people.

Inara rubbed her eyes and glanced over to her bedroom door where she knew her uniform laid out properly on her bed, ready to be worn tomorrow. Inara shook her head in frustration. She just had to calm down a little and think this through, then everything would surely work out. Inara looked out the window, the sun was slowly setting in the distance, leaving the sky in a haze of red and orange.

"If I turn her in," Inara said to herself, she found that speaking out loud even if no one else was there sometimes helped. "I would be rewarded."

Inara knew that the chance of multiple people having a mark or tattoo on their left hand was not impossibly low. Tattoos were a popular thing to get after all. But the moment Inara had laid her eyes on that strange Mark on Anya's hand, she just knew this was what everyone was looking for. There was something about it, something that almost made her nauseous and sent an unpleasant feeling through her body.

It wasn't just a normal tattoo, it almost seemed carved into her skin, fully healed yet still like a wound somehow. And if she was rewarded, perhaps she could choose the reward or she could at least have a guess at what it could be. Inara wasn't interested in money; she had enough to get by with the guard salary and she had never been one to spend money lavishly. What Inara wanted was a promotion.

If she rose in rank, if turning in the thief everyone had been looking for gave her a reputation of someone that could be trusted, someone who could get the job done then perhaps, maybe she could use that to help others. As a patrolling guard now, she had no authority or leverage to get any of her ideas into motion, but if she rose in rank, then maybe people would listen to her. The King was even involved, perhaps she could even get an audience with him and explain her ideas and everything good that would come with it in time.

Inara had heard rumours about the King and the royal family, mostly bad rumours but as the King surely he would be excited to hear a suggestion about how to make this city better, it would only reflect well on him. Then another, less exciting idea filled Inara's head. "If I turn her in," Inara continued to herself. "Mara will be angry with me. Probably beyond angry."

That thought made her even more nauseous. Inara closed her eyes tightly and took a deep breath. If Anya was the culprit, she had committed a crime, she had stolen something from the Castle, something that apparently was incredibly valuable to them. Could Inara truly look the other way knowing this fact? Could she turn a blind eye because she didn't want one person to be upset with her? Even if that person was someone she was desperately trying to get a better relationship with?

Inara opened her eyes and stared at Anya's unconscious body. A thief or not, she had been of help for Inara. For a price she had to remind herself, not out of the goodness of her heart. Inara liked Anya, but she liked a lot of people but that didn't mean she would let them get away with doing crimes. Being a good friend and being a good guard could not always coexist.

Inara could simply pick up Anya's body and carry her to the guard station right now and if she was wrong about this, if Anya was innocent then she had nothing to worry about. Then Inara would simply have made a fool out of herself and lost the person teaching her sign language and probably get on even worse terms with Mara, but it wasn't the end of the world. It wouldn't be the end of the world, she reminded herself yet she didn't move from where she was sitting.

Inara sighed deeply as she realised that she wasn't going to do that, not at least right away. Even if it wasn't the end of the world for her, if she accused Anya of being the thief, even if she was innocent, the chance that she would not get hurt or punished before they realised she was innocent was low. She would suffer, there was no way around it even if Inara didn't want to think about it.

Innocent people got blamed every day and some even got convicted and hung for the offences. Sometimes, people don't really want to catch the person who committed the crime, they simply want to close the case, even if someone innocent has to suffer for it and the criminal gets away scot free.

So before Inara made this decision, before she accused Anya of a crime that had led to the whole city being searched, a crime committed towards the Castle, The King himself, Inara had to know what Anya had to say in her defence. She knew that the chance of Anya lying was high but Inara wasn't a naive little kid and she wasn't in any position to do anything. Inara held all the cards, she held Anya's freedom in her hands, not something she particularly liked but it could be useful in getting the truth.

Inara did not enjoy the feeling of standing above someone, of holding someone's life in her hands and threatening to take it away unless she got what she wanted. But it was this or it was turn Anya in immediately and Inara thought that she at least owed her to listen to what she had to say. If she tried anything, Inara would not hesitate to punch her unconscious and turn her in; this was a one-time offer Inara was offering her. If she didn't want to take it, that was on her.

Inara also thought she at least owed Mara to listen to the friend she had sent to her. Inara knew she would blame herself if she found out that she had put her friend in this situation and Inara wanted to avoid that if possible.

So Inara made herself a new cup of tea, sat down on the same spot and waited for Anya to wake up.

Chapter 20

RUNA

Ever since Runa's talk with Mr Parker, she had been on edge, for numerous reasons but the number one reason was as always Anya. A week had passed since the talk and all Runa had done was follow Anya around. She had noticed that Anya left James' place and went somewhere, Runa lost her every time after a while. Apparently, whatever sickness that had made her sluggish earlier had completely vanished because she was as elusive as ever, which both made Runa proud but also annoyed her somewhat.

For seven days, Runa stalked Anya as much as possible without making herself known, her head spinning with what she was supposed to do. The simple answer was of course to just do what she was told, kill Anya and be done with it. Sever that last connection outside the Silver Swans, sever whatever mercy still remained inside of her.

In theory, it was easy; in practice, not so much. Runa had planned to speak with Anya every day she'd followed her but in the end, she had either lost her or watched her go back into James' house where she couldn't follow. Besides, she had no idea what she would tell Anya if she spoke to her. "Hey, you remember Mr Parker right? The dude that hates your guts since you left, you know! Yeah, he wants me to kill you and he's given me a time limit or I'm done for."

Runa thought it sounded insane even in her own head, she couldn't imagine how insane it would sound said out loud. What was even the point in telling Anya any of this? It wasn't like she could help Runa in this, it would probably only end in them fighting as they usually did nowadays. Runa knew that Anya would throw this order in her face as she did with everything Runa did wrong.

Anya would probably yell at her and in the worst case, Anya would say that she always knew Runa would do this to her. That would break Runa's heart. Runa wouldn't be in this situation if she didn't care, if she was a merciless, careless killer who could throw anyone away like trash. Runa's own life was on the line in this but Anya would never accept that as an answer, she would only see it as a poor excuse.

Whenever Runa saw Anya slide from shadow to shadow, her heart ached in a weird way. Maybe it was the fact that she was just watching Anya from a distance, like she was nothing but another shadow in Anya's life that she just passed through without another thought. But Runa thought about Anya every day.

There was no one there for Runa to talk to; she didn't have anyone close to her that she trusted enough to spill her secrets. Anya had been that person but that was a long time ago now. So Runa had to deal with this alone, as she dealt with everything. This city, this place was Runa's home. She'd lived here her entire life and even if she didn't have entirely good memories, it was still home.

She didn't want to run out of the city with her tail between her legs. She wanted to be someone in this city. She wanted to take down Mr Parker and lead the Silver Swans, to finally have something for herself and be feared and respected. Runa had thought many times about trying to change Mr Parker's mind, to ask if she could do anything else to prove her loyalty but she knew what his answer would be.

He would see that question as the answer he sought, he would see that as Runa choosing Anya. Runa's hands were tied and she was slowly sinking in cement, yet instead of simply removing the ties and crawling out, she kept waiting, feeling herself sink deeper and deeper. There wasn't much time left until she would be completely engulfed.

Runa couldn't help but let her mind drift to things she didn't want to think about. What would the rest of the people in the Silver Swans do to her before throwing her out on the street? She would be beaten senseless but that was a given. That kind of violence didn't scare her anymore, there were way worse things to experience in this world.

Runa hoped that because they knew her, because they had fought side by side, that they would simply rough her up a little and then throw her out on the street to fend for herself again. Runa hoped but there was a nauseating feeling deep inside her that they would be even crueller because they had known her.

Runa needed to speak with Anya. She hadn't come to any decision, but either way, it might be the last time either of them saw each other. In seven days, either Anya would be dead or Runa would be…something. Dead if she was lucky, she thought bitterly. There was one place, one person who always at least had an inclination of where Anya was and that was James. Runa didn't particularly like James but then again, she had a hard time trusting any man that broke her trust even a little bit.

She'd found that no matter how kind or gentle a man was, violence was just a second away if the wrong word was said or the wrong look was exchanged. But what made her truly angry was the fact that no one else seemed to be able to see through his 'kind man' exterior. That Anya refused to see beyond it. James had helped Runa multiple times, he had brought her back from death even and never charged a penny. Runa knew he was kind, he was helpful but all she could see when she looked at him was that one time he hadn't been.

Runa made her way to James' house. It was getting late, the sun had started to set and the sky was looking spectacular. It was red and orange, almost like the sky was on fire. The lights were on inside the house and she knew better than to try and sneak inside. James was a lot of things but not an idiot and certainly not helpless.

A straightforward approach was always the best with him. Runa took a deep breath and then knocked gently on the door. She could hear the muffled sound of what she assumed was his cane hitting the hard wooden floor coming closer to the door before it opened. James opened with a smile but the moment he set eyes on Runa, his face turned a lot sterner.

"Hello, James," Runa said, trying to keep a balance between how serious she was and her normal relaxed persona. She wasn't sure it was working this time.

"Runa," he said and he made sure that the door was not entirely open, it was more like it was cracked open. Enough space for Runa to shove her way through if needed but she really didn't want to do that.

"I need to speak with Anya," Runa said. "Is she inside?"

James didn't answer for a moment, just looked at her.

"I don't know where she is," James answered.

"This again?" Runa asked; she remembered when she'd asked where Anya had been when she'd been gone for three days. Obviously she had been laying sick upstairs in her room, yet he had given her the same answer as now.

"I don't know what you want me to say," James said. "I don't know where she is."

Runa took a deep breath. She didn't want to explode, she wanted to stay calm and collected but the weight on her shoulders were really starting to pile on and James lying was the last thing she needed right now.

"Let me inside," Runa said. "Let me talk to her."

"She's not inside," James said and shuffled a little so he completely covered the crack of the door.

"Sure she's not. Just like last time, right?" Runa said sarcastically.

"You have no business here, Runa. Leave," James said, his voice stern.

"You have no idea what I'm here for, so I suggest you let me inside. It's important," Runa said, feeling anger mix into her voice.

"It's always important with you," James said bitterly. "Anya doesn't want anything to do with you anymore, I thought she made that clear."

Runa clenched her jaw and she remembered the last conversation she'd had with Anya. Runa had said she would stay away and yet here she was.

"Just because you bought her from the Red Rose doesn't mean she's your property," Runa said, her voice filled with venom. "You can't control who she meets and not."

Runa saw that her comment hit its mark as most colour was drained from James' face.

"I didn't buy…" James started, his voice shaking.

"Whatever makes you sleep at night, old man," Runa said. "We can stand here and argue all damn night. Please let me inside, I just want to talk to her. It'll only be a few minutes."

James was silent for a moment.

"No," James finally said.

Runa sighed deeply, she'd had enough of this. She was done playing, she was done trying to be polite, she was done with his lies. She was just going to force her way inside if he refused to listen to her, if he wanted to continue to be unreasonable. But as Runa started to move, James slammed his cane in front of her, stopping her in her tracks and startling her with the loud sound.

"The only way you're getting inside is if you're hurt," James said. "And as you're not, I suggest you leave."

Without thinking or hesitating, Runa unsheathed one of her many blades and ran its razor sharp edge over her arm. It cut deeper than she had intended and the sharp and throbbing pain shot through her. The blood poured out of her arm at an alarming rate and it was like the entire world got quiet, the only sound was the rapid dripping of Runa's blood on the ground. Even through the pain, Runa looked up at James who had lost all colour in his face and looked like he was almost going to be sick.

"I'm hurt. Let me in," Runa said, trying to keep her voice steady.

James just stared at her in slight shock for a moment, like he couldn't believe what he'd just witnessed. He thought he knew what desperate people could do, Runa knew he was wrong. He knew nothing of true desperation.

"I know you're not going to let me bleed to death on your front step," Runa said, even though there was a small part of her that wondered if he would. "So help me."

Finally, almost defeatedly, James stepped aside and ushered Runa inside without saying a word to her. Runa could already feel that she had lost a considerable amount of blood, the trail of crimson behind her confirmed her suspicion. Her head started to feel light and her feet felt heavy as she managed to sit down in a chair while James hurried around the room, getting the things he needed. Runa could hear him muttering to himself.

"Idiotic," James muttered. "How stupid can you be…"

Runa almost smiled at that. She was stupid, she was an idiot but she did what it took to get things done. James placed a chair in front of Runa and quickly started to try and stop the bleeding. Runa's entire arm was now coated in red, warm blood. It was getting everywhere but she couldn't really find it in herself to care.

Her clothes had been covered in blood before, there were stains she'd never been able to get out and the tear she'd made in her sleeve was nothing she couldn't fix. As long as she didn't die, this was just another scar, another day.

"You could have killed yourself," James said, his voice shaking but if it was by anger or something else Runa didn't know.

"Well, it was the only way to get you to let me in. You didn't give me a choice," Runa said and then glanced down at the gash in her arm. "Though, I might have gone a little deeper than I had intended."

Runa glanced towards the stairs, up to where she knew Anya's room was.

"Anya?" Runa shouted but there was no real force in her voice, she was getting a little tired.

"She isn't home," James said and it was definitely anger in his voice. "As I told you before."

"Oh," Runa said dumbstruck.

"So you did this for nothing," James continued. "I can't believe…"

"Stop with the dad routine," Runa said. "I don't want nor need it."

James froze as she said that and he gave her a gaze that was filled with a warning to not go there. Then he continued with trying to patch her up, she wasn't paying any attention to what he was doing to her. It hurt from time to time but she was used to that by now. As things were right now between them, Runa doubted that he would do anything to get her killed.

After all, James was kind unless you crossed him. Instead her eyes went over the absurd amount of books that laid on the table beside them, most of them opened and with stray papers with random scribbles on them.

"What are you reading?" Runa asked.

"Nothing of interest to you," James quickly.

"That's a lot of books," Runa continued, ignoring him.

"What, you suddenly developed a mind for reading, have you?" James said and gave her a knowing look.

Runa clenched her jaw. She hated that he knew she couldn't read. It wasn't something a lot of people knew about, most of the time she could get away with it. Most instructions in the Silver Swans were by word and there was always someone else there that could read a note if needed. She could easily talk herself out of reading something, talk she could do. But it was still a big shame for Runa, that shame was seared into her very bone marrow.

"I'm going to stay here until Anya comes back," Runa said, not a question but a statement.

James sighed deeply but for once didn't argue with her. He had been reminded of the extremes Runa could take to get what she wanted. After a short period of silence, James spoke again but without looking at Runa in the face, wholly concentrated on her wound.

"You won't mention…?" James said, his voice low and fragile.

"I won't spill your damn secret if that's what you're worrying about," Runa said exasperated.

"You made it clear what could happen to me if I said anything."

Runa stared at him even when he purposefully avoided her gaze but she could see that there was almost a look of shame flashing over his face as she said it. So he felt shame for what he'd done, it didn't matter to Runa really. She had a lot of shame over things she'd done, but she'd still done them. People had still gotten hurt, a simple sorry wouldn't change a thing.

The rest of the time, they sat in silence. Neither of them had anything to say to the other but they both kept a close eye on each other, knowing what they both were capable of.

Chapter 21

ANYA

Anya slowly opened her eyes, trying to blink away the blurriness that obscured her sight. Her head was throbbing and her mouth felt like the desert. She tried to look around, to try and gather where she was. The first thing that came into view without any of the blurriness was Inara sitting across from her, her legs crossed and with a cup of tea in her hands.

Anya made to sit up but quickly found that she could barely move, her hands were tied behind her back and her legs were tied together as well. The knots were tight and had already started to chafe against her skin. "What?" Was all Anya managed to get out at first, she swallowed hard, trying to get her voice back.

"I apologise for..." Inara started.

"For what? For drugging me?" Anya interrupted, feeling almost immediately more like herself and she was pissed.

Anya struggled against the ties but Inara knew what she was doing, these were good knots.

"You'll only hurt yourself if you struggle," Inara said.

Anya shot her an angry glance. Then Anya really looked around the room; she was still in Inara's apartment and there were no other guards around. Did that mean she hadn't told them about her yet? And in that case why? Why drug her and do all of this? Anya just couldn't figure it out.

"Talk," Inara said coldly.

"What?" Anya said with a frown.

"Don't," Inara said, a very real warning.

Anya swallowed and tried to take a deep breath but she could feel herself start to panic. Being trapped like this, not being able to move, having no control over her body, it usually spiralled into a panic attack. It was not the time for that right now.

"What do you want me to say?" Anya asked, her voice shaking.

Inara frowned, she must have noticed the shift in Anya, the panic starting to rise beneath the surface. *Don't think about it. Don't think about it. Focus on Inara. Focus on talking. Focus on anything else but the knots restraining you,* Anya thought to herself over and over.

"The Mark," Inara said. "What is it?"

"I don't know," Anya said lowly and shook her head. Not a complete lie but certainly not the entire truth. There was still so much she didn't know.

Inara's face hardened and she looked tired and almost frustrated, like during their lessons.

"P-Please. Can you release me?" Anya asked, trying not to sound too pathetic.

"I'll do it if you answer my questions," Inara said.

Anya could feel the chafing wounds starting to form on her wrists from tensing and wriggling. She couldn't help it but she would lose both hands if it meant getting out of these restraints. "Just…Just the feet then if you don't trust me," Anya said, she was close to begging.

She didn't want to black out; she didn't want to be reminded of how she'd been treated at the Red Rose. She wanted to be in control but it was slipping away from her and she had no way of reeling it back.

Inara sighed and Anya could feel herself starting to shake slightly, even if she tried to stay still. The only thing she was focusing on now was breathing; breathing was the key. As long as she was breathing, she wasn't dying; as long as she was breathing, she was here in this room, at this moment. Nowhere else. Anya didn't even notice when Inara cut off the ties to her ankles until she felt that she could move them.

Getting control back over her feet and legs managed to drag Anya back from the brink of panic. These bonds were temporary, they were not going to hold her forever. She could survive this. Anya took a deep but shaky breath and stretched her legs and even managed to get into a sitting position after some wriggling. She could feel her wrist burning but she didn't care about that kind of pain.

When Anya looked back at Inara, there was a genuine look of worry on her face. Anya didn't want it, not from her.

"What do you want?" Anya said, her voice low and bitter but under a certain control.

"What happened just now?" Inara asked.

"You drugged and tied me up to ask about my trauma?" Anya said sarcastically. "What do you want?"

Inara stared at Anya. It was obvious that she was thinking about whether she was going to push her on this or not.

"The Mark," Inara said. "What did you steal from the Castle?"

Anya let out a laugh, it sounded close to hysterical.

"I haven't stolen anything," Anya said.

"So you're saying you're not the one we're looking for?" Inara asked.

Anya shook her head. "I haven't done anything. Not anything related to this," she said. Inara clenched her jaw. The question was if she was going to believe what Anya told her or not and Anya had simply no idea. This could go either way and Anya hated it.

"You're telling me that Mark is nothing? Just another tattoo?" Inara asked and Anya could hear it in her voice, she knew. She didn't know everything but Inara certainly knew something was special about it. That did not bode well for Anya.

Anya continued to carefully struggle behind her back, she wanted out of these restraints, she didn't care if they cut into her flesh or left scars.

"I haven't stolen anything from the Castle," Anya repeated.

"So if I turned you in, would they let you go?" Inara said with a raised eyebrow.

Fear flashed over Anya's face.

"I thought so," Inara said seriously.

"I don't know! Okay? I don't know! I promise!" Anya said, she had to make Inara let her go. "I didn't have this Mark two weeks ago okay? All I know is that I got it the day something was stolen from the Castle during the storm but I was out in the forest, trying to get back home. Please."

Inara frowned.

"How did you get it?" Inara asked.

Anya dropped her head to her chest. *"Don't tell her,"* a familiar voice whispered in her head.

That made Anya snap back into attention.

"I've never been in the Castle," Anya said. "So I can't be the thief. You have to believe me."

"I…" Inara started, her voice uncertain. "I do believe that. But I do not believe you when you say that Mark is nothing. It's…it's wrong, somehow it's wrong."

"*I can easily get you out of those bindings if you wish,*" the same voice whispered to Anya. Anya tried to not let it show on her face but she accepted the help. In a second, Anya could feel the restraints behind her back fall off her raw wrists, like they'd been snapped off as easily as a twig. Anya kept her arms behind her back, she didn't want to let Inara know she was free and she didn't seem to have noticed anything.

"If you didn't have it two weeks ago and if you weren't in the Castle and if you haven't stolen anything, I promise you, Anya, you will be released," Inara said. "I will make sure of it."

"Your words mean nothing after you drugged and tied me up," Anya spat out.

A flash of hurt went over Inara's face but then she was back to the same stone face she'd almost had the entire time.

"I'm going to turn you in," Inara said and got up from the floor. "Whether you believe me or not is up to you but I am not dirty. I just want justice to be done when a crime has been committed."

Something snapped inside of Anya, there was no way she was going to let Inara turn her in, at least not without a fight. Anya's eyes flashed towards her knives that laid on the counter behind Inara. If Anya surprised her and moved fast, she could get past her and to her knives before Inara had even moved.

"*Do it,*" the voice spurred her on and without thinking Anya moved.

Anya had been correct, Inara was not expecting it and Anya managed to quickly spin past her, almost like a ballerina, and grabbed her sharpest knife. The door was behind her. She could bolt for it but she knew it would be locked and Inara would get to her before she got out. The element of surprise was gone, now it was just going to be a straight up fight if Inara didn't let her go.

"Let me go," Anya said, holding her blade in front of her in a defensive stance.

Inara straightened her back and there it was again, that looming, intimidating woman that Anya had first met. Anya saw in Inara's eyes that she would never let her go.

"Drop the knife, Anya," Inara said, her voice stone. "I don't want to hurt you. But you will come with me."

Anya shook her head violently. Inara took a fast step forward, faster than Anya had imagined and she just managed to duck just seconds before Inara's fist would have connected with her face. Inara almost stumbled a little after missing her target. So she wasn't an agile fighter, she was all brute force, Anya filed that away for later use. Later as in, probably ten seconds.

The knife in Anya's hand felt heavy and warm. She didn't want to use it on Inara, she didn't want to kill her or even seriously harm her, she simply wanted to get out of here.

"She's going to be your undoing."

Inara regained her composure and instead charged at Anya, once again, she just managed to jump out of the way but she crashed into the small table by the sofa. A grunt of pain left Anya, her hip would be sorely bruised tomorrow from that.

"Get up."

When Anya opened her eyes and looked up, she saw Inara swinging back her right hand for another punch. This time, Anya knew she had been too slow, she would not have the time to roll out of the way.

"Protect yourself."

Instead out of pure desperation, Anya slashed out her knife towards Inara and surprisingly, connected. Inara hissed in pain and retreated a few steps, it was barely more than a scratch but Anya saw blood on the edge of her blade. The moment her blade had connected with Inara and drawn blood, Anya had felt a surge of energy run through her. Her hip didn't hurt at all and her rope burnt wrists were healed, like she'd never even been hurt.

"You fed the fire. The fire protects you."

Anya moved, faster than she'd ever moved before and in the blink of an eye, she was up in Inara's face. Anya could barely register the look of surprise on Inara's face before she slammed the blunt edge of her blade onto the side of

Inara's face. There was a nasty crack at the impact and Inara wobbled a little on her legs and leaned against a wall, but turned back towards Anya with unsteady yet determined eyes.

"Kill her."

The words went through Anya like a shock wave and Inara managed to get in a hard punch to her gut. Anya gasped in pain and doubled over for a second but managed to stay on her feet.

"Kill her."

Anya shook her head, shedding blood was one thing, murder was another. Anya wasn't that kind of person, no matter how good that rush of energy had felt. Another punch connected with Anya's face and she could feel something warm trickling down her forehead.
"If you do not kill her, she will tell everyone. Your life will be ruined. Kill her. Save yourself." Anger filled Anya and she screamed, a horrifying sound coming out of her mouth as she slammed the blunt edge of her knife in Inara's face once again. This time, Inara tumbled to the floor almost as if she no longer had any bones in her body. Anya knew she wasn't particularly strong, but the power that had gone into that punch had been monumental.

"Kill her."

Anya straddled Inara, placing her knees on her arms and placing her whole weight on her chest. Inara was bleeding from somewhere on the side of her face, Anya couldn't see the wound but she could see that her scarf had become wet at the same place Anya had hit her on. She was also bleeding from her nose, and she looked disoriented.

"Kill her."

Anya closed her eyes and took a deep breath. She felt it, the fire burning inside of her, the extra power she had gotten from that little slash she had made on Inara and then again after every hit that drew blood. It was kindling and it almost felt like the fire was getting out of her control, like there was nothing else but the fire.

"Kill her!"

Anya slammed her knife down on the floor next to Inara's face, she barely seemed to register it. "I am not a murderer," Anya said, her voice low and uncertain. This was not the person she wanted to be. She would not be like Runa and kill because it was easier. She would find another way out of this, like she always did.

Inara seemed to finally regain some of her consciousness because her eyes sharpened and she noticed the knife next to her head. Anya still felt the power of the flame run through her veins and she couldn't lie, it felt electrifying. Inara tried to struggle against Anya and in any other scenario, she would have easily gotten out of Anya's grip. But now? With Inara's blood as the kindling for the fire, Anya sat on top of Inara like she was made of iron made to keep her down.

There was no way for Inara to get out unless Anya let her.

"D-Don't do this," Inara stammered, her eyes almost pleading.

Anya clenched her jaw and tore her knife from the floor, Inara flinched a little at that.

"Don't follow me," Anya said. She barely recognised her own voice, the strength it possessed.

"Let me go and pretend this never happened."

Inara shook her head. What a stupid woman.

"I don't want to kill you," Anya continued. "I am not a killer. But I will not be punished for something I had no choice in."

Inara frowned slightly.

"I am going to leave this city. I won't be your problem any more, okay? So just let me go," Anya continued.

Anya wasn't sure of what she was saying but she knew that if she let Inara live, she could not stay in the city. She would tell everyone, of that Anya was certain and there would be no place to hide for her here. Anya had to get out as fast as possible.

"If you come with me, I can help you," Inara said.

Anya believed her, she believed that she would try and help her. Anya just didn't think she would succeed. Inara was making a promise she couldn't keep because she had no idea what she was dealing with and Anya couldn't blame her for that, not really.

"I am only going to say this one more time," Anya hissed. "Let me go. Or next time it will get ugly."

Inara closed her eyes with a frown. It almost looked like she was accepting defeat but Anya wasn't certain if it was from failing to convince Anya to turn herself in or losing the fight.

Perhaps it was both.

Anya had to buy herself some time to get out of the city before Inara could get the word out to everyone, so Anya slammed her fist into Inara's face and she felt her go limp beneath her.

Anya drew back her hand and saw that her knuckles were bloody; it felt good in the most horrifying way and she wasn't sure she wanted it to ever stop.

Chapter 22

JAMES

As soon as James had gotten Runa's wound cleaned and wrapped, he had picked up one of the books on the table and started reading again. He glanced over at Runa from time to time and he noticed she was doing the same, not very surprising. But mostly, Runa just sat in her chair with closed eyes in silence but it was obvious she wasn't sleeping. James knew she wouldn't sleep where she didn't feel safe.

Though as James observed her and let his eyes wander to the bloody mess she had left all over the floor, she had lost quite a lot of blood. It shouldn't be enough to cause any long term problems but she would certainly feel it in the coming days. With a sigh, James rose from his seat, grabbed his cane and went over to his stock of medicine. He did have an iron pill he sometimes gave patients that had lost a lot of blood, it was dissolved in water to then either be drunk all in one or over the course of an hour.

Most people didn't manage to drink it all in one go, it didn't taste very good and blood loss had a tendency to make people nauseous as it was. He wasn't even sure Runa would accept it. She didn't trust him and he couldn't completely blame her. James glanced back at Runa and her carefully wrapped arm, blood had already started to seep through; it would have to be changed regularly. He felt a sort of shame because even if he wasn't responsible for her actions, she was partly correct that he had forced her hand a little.

This wasn't the first time Runa had shown up, claiming that she had something important to talk with Anya about. James wasn't even sure why he hadn't let her in this time; she had seemed almost desperate, not something she usually showed. He guessed it was pride in some way and the fact that he wanted to protect Anya. He didn't want to set a precedent that Runa could come around any time she felt like it just because she missed Anya. If Anya wanted anything to do with Runa, she would come and find her, not the other way around.

James took out a pill and put it in a glass before he filled it with water, he then slowly walked back to his seat and planted the glass in front of Runa. She opened one eyelid to see what was happening and frowned when she saw the glass with some white-ish foaming liquid in it.

"Drink it. It'll help," James said.

"I'm not drinking that," Runa said and closed her eyes again.

"You lost a lot of blood, you know how that feels like already, this helps so you won't feel as bad," James said. "So drink it."

Runa slowly opened her eyes again and just stared at James for a moment. He sighed heavily and picked up the glass and took a sip from it before he put it down again.

"It's not poison or drugged," James said. "So please."

Runa hesitated for another moment but then slowly took the glass. She first smelled it and she wrinkled her nose and James had to keep himself from chuckling. Then in one go, Runa downed the entire drink and then made a noise that could be nothing else than a noise of disgust.

"I almost wish it was poison, that tasted awful," Runa said and cleared her throat.

James said nothing at that and turned back to the book he'd been reading. He wasn't going to converse with her, he was going to make sure she didn't die right here and now, that was it. In any other case, he would have tried to put away the books and notes he'd made but because it was Runa, he knew it didn't matter. She couldn't read so they could be anything to her, medical books or novels.

Whenever James glanced over at Runa, his eyes would drift to the place Anya usually would sit when she tried to help him look through the books. He tried to repress a soft smile as he thought of her changing sitting position every five minutes, flipping through pages obviously without taking in any of the information on the pages. Anya wanted to help, he knew she didn't want to put this on him but he was happy to do it.

Sitting in silence, in peace and quiet to read and try and find answers, it was perfect for him. Anya wasn't built to sit and read and research like this, she always needed to be moving.

After a decent amount of silence, it was broken by Runa speaking. "How is Anya doing?" She said low.

James sighed but didn't look away from the book. "Let's not do this," James answered.

"What? I'm not allowed to ask how she's doing? After knowing she was sick? After seeing her run around like a headless chicken around town?" Runa said annoyed.

"Not anymore, no," James said coldly. "Before you broke her heart, then yes."

"She left the Silver Swans, I…" Runa hissed.

"She left because of you," James said and turned his gaze from the book to Runa.

Runa clenched her jaw.

"And she ran straight back into your loving arms, is that right?" Runa said. "You think you're so fucking good, don't you."

"I'm not the murderer here," James answered.

"No, you just torture women half your age so they won't spill your secrets," Runa said, her voice dripping with venom.

"I didn't…" James started but he could feel all the colour drain from his face.

"Yeah? So what do you call having someone delirious in pain, her side slashed open, begging for help and you take the fucking opportunity to press your thumb into my open wound, digging around inside with the intent of making me suffer, while threatening to let me die if I ever tell anyone what I know?" Runa yelled. She stood up from where she'd been sitting, her chair falling back. She had risen too fast and for a second, it looked like she was going to pass out. James reached for her, trying to help her so she wouldn't fall.

"Don't touch me!" Runa screamed and took another step back and stumbled over the knocked over chair and crashed to the floor.

James could see that she was in pain, she was clutching her wounded arm but she didn't make a single sound but he could see how she was holding her breath and her entire body was tense. He couldn't do anything, he knew he couldn't, not for her, not here.

Runa's words spun around in his head and he felt sick, he remembered doing it. He'd been desperate. He knew that Runa and Anya were close and she would have told her, it would have just been a matter of time and James couldn't let Anya know. Not this. It wasn't one of his best moments and looking back at it, he barely felt like himself.

At least not the man he'd tried to become over the last couple of years. The man that had stood and made Runa suffer and promise not to tell anyone was the man that had seen countless deaths, had his hands in countless guts and failed to help countless lives. A man he wasn't proud of ever having been.

"I am sorry, Runa," James said. It was true, he was sorry but he wouldn't take it back. He knew the only language Runa and people like her knew was violence, that's why he'd done it. But compared to him, both Runa and Anya, they were so young and he had not enjoyed making Runa's youth more miserable.

"I don't want your fucking pity," Runa said between pained breaths.

"I know," James said.

Silence.

"Anya deserves better than you," Runa spat out.

"She deserves better than you too," James said back.

Runa shot him a violent glance.

"The difference is that I know that," Runa hissed.

James stared at her for a few seconds, then without saying another word or trying to help her up from the floor, he turned back to reading his book.

***

James couldn't help but to glance at the door every other second. Ever since the Mark, Anya had tried to be home right around sundown but it had been dark for some time now which sent alarm bells ringing in his head. He tried to tell himself it was fine, Anya could take care of herself and she wouldn't be unnecessarily reckless, not right now.

Still, the last time he'd thought that Anya had come home with the Mark and almost died of fever, perhaps that was why he was more on edge than normally. Runa had long since gotten up from the floor but instead of sitting down on a chair again, she stood by the door, far away from James. Her dark skin was ashy and he could see the tiredness in her eyes.

Her legs were shaking ever so slightly from the strain of standing up but James knew it was pointless to tell her to sit down, not after what had just happened. Runa would rather collapse again or sit down on the floor as far from him as possible than be that close again.

James had reread the same four sentences five times now, he simply couldn't concentrate anymore so with a sigh he put down the book. James rubbed his bad leg, it was still not completely recovered from the night of the storm even though it had been over a week; he really had put too much stress on it and would pay for it for a while. He could feel Runa's eyes stare right at him but he couldn't find it in himself to care.

If she wanted to say something, he knew very well that she would just say it. The silence grew uncomfortable, or perhaps it had been uncomfortable this whole time, he just hadn't realised it because he'd been busy reading but now it was almost suffocating.

James rose from his seat, leaning heavily on his cane when the door slammed open. The silence broke into borderline panic as Anya ran into the house and closed the door quickly behind her.

Her dark hair that was usually put up into a neat ponytail was now scruffy and hair had fallen out onto her face. James quickly noticed she had blood on her face and her hands but she didn't seem wounded. The worst, the most worrisome part was that she looked manic, her eyes frantically looked around and she was moving so fast it was hard to keep his eyes on her.

She was pale but there was a healthy flush on her face and even though she wasn't smiling in the slightest, there was something…something elated about her look.

"Anya," Runa's voice almost came out as a whisper.

"What happened?" James asked, trying his best to stay calm. Something was very clearly wrong; bad things they could fix but he couldn't stand the thought of Anya getting hurt.

At Runa's voice, Anya quickly turned and looked at her with wide eyes.

"No…no…" Anya said. "Get out."

"What?" Runa said with a frown. "I came here to talk to you, I'm not leaving."

"Get out, right now!" Anya almost yelled and there was a flash of intensity in her eyes. James had never seen before and even he flinched at that.

Runa almost looked scared before she managed to pull herself together.

"What has happened?" Runa pushed.

James walked up to Anya and touched her arm to get her attention, but the moment he touched her, his hand immediately recoiled from the heat. Anya snapped her attention to James. "We have to leave. Right now," Anya said. "Pack only the necessary things and then we leave, right now," Anya said and started to make her way towards her room upstairs.

James grabbed Anya's arm, now ready for the intense heat so he pushed through it, even if it felt like touching hot water.

"Please," James said. "You're frightening me. What's happening?"

Anya stopped in her tracks and turned back to James and Runa. She was shaking slightly but finally took a deep breath.

"Runa, you need to leave," Anya said again. "Just leave, forget about me and stay alive."

Runa frowned and walked closer.

"I'm not leaving until you tell me what's happening," Runa said, finding some strength in her voice. "Why are you leaving the city?"

Anya shot James a worried gaze. He understood Anya didn't want to involve Runa in whatever was happening, he also understood that it was too late for him to back out so whatever happened he'd be right beside her.

"Please," Anya said, her voice almost pleading now. "I don't want you to get involved and I don't have the time to explain everything to you. Just please, trust me."

Runa's frown deepened.

"Trust you…" Runa repeated. "Like you've trusted me?"

Anya looked away at that comment.

"Do they know?" James asked, keeping it vague enough but still asking a serious question. It seemed the only logical explanation at this time for Anya to be this desperate.

Anya only nodded, her eyes a mix of fear and mania.

"Does who knows?" Runa asked, annoyed. "Stop talking like I'm not here!"

James started to walk over to his medicine cabinet. If he needed to move immediately, that meant only taking the most necessary things. He started to throw everything important into a bag, he could start packing while Anya dealt with Runa.

"I'm going to be in real big trouble if I don't leave right now," Anya finally said. "They will trace me back to James so he has to leave as well, they will never believe he didn't know. If you leave now, before they come, they have no reason to involve you, so please!"

James glanced over at them and Runa looked shocked. She looked more her age than James had ever seen her, just a young woman on her own in a ruthless town. Then her face hardened.

"I'll come with you," Runa said.

"What?" Anya said.

"I'll come with you," Runa repeated. "If you can't explain everything now, then I'll come with you and you can explain then."

"I know you don't want to leave this city, Runa," Anya said with a sad, knowing expression.

"I would, for you," Runa almost whispered.

James couldn't see Anya's expression but he could almost hear the soft gasp escape her lips.

"You'll be hunted," Anya said.

"Already a daily thing," Runa said jokingly.

Silence, the only noise was James packing.

"Okay," Anya finally said. "Get your stuff. You and James leave through the main gate, you should be fine if you leave before everyone knows. I'll take the secret exist and we meet out in the woods, okay?"

Runa made a noise of agreement and when Anya looked over at James, all he could do was nod, though his gaze caught Runa's. In that moment, all the hostility had momentarily been put away and there was only understanding. They both wanted to help and keep Anya alive.

Anya was about to run up to her room and Runa was about to leave to get her own stuff, when once again the front door was slammed open. The entire room was quickly flooded by guards, seizing them all, not caring how rough they were. James quickly raised his cane and cracked it across one of the guard's face, blood spurting out of their mouth. The crack, the blood, the violence he hadn't properly seen or been a part of in years made him slightly dizzy.

It almost scared him how easily he'd raised his cane to strike that guard, it was by reflex. When he'd frozen for just a second was when the other guard grabbed him. They took James' cane away and forced him down on the floor. His bad leg protested, he tried to resist but there wasn't much he could do as the guard had gotten the upper hand when he'd frozen.

Two others went for Runa, they didn't find much resistance in her. She tried to thrash and get out of their grip but there was no strength left in her body. If she hadn't been suffering from blood loss, James was sure she would have taken out at least one of them before being shoved to the floor. They grabbed her arms and bent them behind her back and roughly held her down, she yelped in pain when her wounded arm was wrenched hard behind her back.

James could see the moment they put pressure on her wounded arm when they had her on the ground because Runa went rigid and he could see she was doing everything to not scream in pain. He even thought he could see tears forming in the corner of her eyes.

The rest went for Anya, and when James finally managed to take in the scene, all the guards were wearing their usual uniforms except one woman who was wearing a scarf tightly wrapped around her head. She was large, tall and had a strict face that almost seemed carved out of stone; she didn't look like someone who would show mercy. James could tell she'd suffered a wound to her head from the wet patch on her scarf on the side of her head. The rest of her face showed signs of a fight as well.

The woman seemed to be staying back a little and she wasn't wearing a guard uniform. Was she some citizen that had noticed Anya's hand and then gone straight to the guards? The way the woman was holding herself and commanded the room, James highly doubted she was just a citizen. She was here with a purpose.

James heard Anya scream and looked over to her, she was fighting them, screaming, shouting, but James couldn't make out the words she was saying. He had never seen her acting like this, almost like a cornered rabid animal. She was moving impossible fast and ducked and side stepped all the guards trying to get a grip on her. Anya suddenly had one of her knives in her hand and slashed towards one of the guards. James had never seen her actually use it on someone, only used it to threaten.

She cut a deep slash in a guard's arm, the guard screamed out in pain and there was a single moment after when Anya just stood still. She looked over at Runa, who looked as shocked as James felt. Anya's mouth turned up into the tiniest smile and he could see that she'd gained renewed energy, from where he really had no idea. The smile sent a shiver down James' spine, she barely looked like Anya right now. Maybe it was the low light, the quick movements or the pain from his bad leg, but it was almost like she was glowing.

Then finally, after what felt both like seconds and an eternity, a voice spoke up.

"Stop it, Anya, or she dies." It was the woman with the scarf. Her face was stone and her voice had been steady and when he properly looked, he saw that she had a sword drawn and had it pointed at Runa's throat. All the guards took a step back from Anya. They all looked tired and slightly scared but also thankful to be able to get away from her.

"You wouldn't," Anya said.

The woman lifted her chin and lightly pressed the point of the sword into Runa's throat, she left out a small sound at the cold steel against her skin.

"I don't want to," the woman said. "I'm not a killer. But things can get ugly in a fight like this." The woman and Anya shared a knowing glance before Anya looked at Runa on the ground, one guard almost on top of her and with the sword pressed against the side of her throat. James wanted to speak, he wanted to help but the words died on his lips. This was far beyond him and he realised how little he knew about all of this compared to Anya.

Anya's face softened and she tilted her head to the left a little, almost like someone was talking to her and she was listening intently. James didn't like the look of that. Then her eyes shot back up to the woman.

"Now," Anya said.

Anya quickly spread her arms and bright flames shot from her and went in an arc around the room. The heat was unbearable and he hadn't even been hit with it. But everyone standing up had and he could hear the screams of the guards and crackling from the ruthless fire. James' eyes filled with tears from the heat and the smoke that was coming from the whole house being set on fire. He felt the hands that had been holding him release him and he managed to roll away slightly and grab his cane.

He tried to look at what was happening but it was utter chaos. He couldn't see Anya or Runa beyond the fire and smoke and the screaming guards. James could now see that the damages weren't as bad as he'd thought. Almost everything was on fire but it was contained and at this point, it looked like almost all the guards had been able to put out the fire that had consumed them with only some light burns and damaged clothes.

Then James heard a crack and what sounded like a body hitting the floor and all the flames went out in an instance. It was like the fire had never been there except for the scorch marks on his walls, floor and furniture. James got up from where he'd been laying and now when he could see properly again, he saw that

Runa was lying unconscious on the ground or at least he hoped she was unconscious.

He couldn't see if she was breathing from where he was, he'd have to get closer but it was difficult because of the chaos. He just hoped she was alive, if nothing else for Anya's sake.

His gaze then found Anya's limp body on the floor, blood trickling from a wound on the side of her head and the woman with the scarf standing above her with her sword ready. James felt his heart drop as he saw Anya's unconscious body, all he wanted was to run up to her and make sure she was okay. The woman with the scarf seemed the least affected by the damages of the fire when James looked closer.

"Take them all into custody," the woman spoke but now there were cracks in her steady voice and the frown on her face could almost be of worry.

Almost immediately, James felt hands on himself again and before he could do anything, he felt something blunt hit him over the face, knocking him unconscious.

Chapter 23

ANYA

Anya opened her eyes and stared into the face of Andrew, or rather Fire who was wearing his face. It seemed as disinterested as always, that hollow look in its eyes staring back at her. She was standing in the same darkness she'd always done in these dreams but it seemed brighter than before, like the two of them were generating light together.

"You said you could take them out," Anya said through gritted teeth.

"I could have. If you'd taken one of their lives. You simply didn't have enough power to do proper damage," it answered. "With enough power, you could have cleaved them all in half without breaking a sweat."

Anya groaned in annoyance.

"Why do I even have to kill someone or shed blood to get more powerful? I don't understand!" Anya almost yelled. "Can't you just do things!"

It sighed and turned it's gaze towards the little sliver of sky high above them.

"See it like this, Anya," it started. "You survived merging with me because you had enough fire, enough will, enough life force, call it whatever you want. Every time you use me, I take from that energy. Doing that over a long time will result in your death, it is what happened to everyone who didn't have enough to merge with me."

"When your life energy runs out, so do you. When you take someone else's life, I store that and instead of using you, I use the life you took. Which means you will become stronger the more lives you take." *Anya frowned.*

"You need fuel to keep going. So do I," *it finally said.*

"But you're magic, you're supp..." *Anya started.*

"I'm supposed to what?" *It interrupted and Anya thought she could almost hear annoyance in it's voice, which she'd never heard before.* "You know nothing of magic. I am pure fire, I am pure magic but there is nothing in this universe that can function without some sort of fuel. Magic comes with a price, whether it's you or someone else who pays it, I do not care."

"I don't want to kill," Anya said.

"But you want to use me," it said.

Anya averted her gaze.

"Be careful, Anya, or you will burn yourself out," it said. "And I will have to find another host to share my gifts with."

Anya was silent. She didn't know what to say, she didn't know if she had anything to say.

"Shedding blood only takes you so far, you've barely scratched the surface of what you could do. The real power you could possess with my help," it said. "But now you have to live with the consequences of not taking a life, having put not only yourself but your friends in immediate danger as well."

Anya's gaze shot back to it, worry clear in her eyes. What had she done?

"Things will be difficult now, I wonder if you will survive it," it said.

"I don't want to die," Anya almost whispered.

It frowned, a flash of anger came across its face before it went back to it's neutral look. "Don't be a child, Anya," it said. "You cannot have everything and pay nothing. That is not how this works."

"I know that," Anya hissed.

"Do you? Do you truly?" It asked and leaned closer. "You have been running your entire life. The moment something goes awry, you leave. You despise consequences and you despise the ones who deal with theirs."

Anya frowned. "That's not true," she said low.

"What is it your friend said?" It started. "Ah yes. Sometimes there is no 'figuring it out later'." Anya clenched her fist.

"Sounds familiar?" It said, its head cocked slightly to the side. "Do something for once, Anya, don't just let things happen to you. Even I was forced upon you by some stranger, you had no choice in it. Like a lot of things in your life. Do something to make them know who you are."

Those words hit harder than Anya would have thought but she realised it was right. Her entire life, things had been done to her, things had happened and she'd run away from them, side stepped them or ignored them. Never once had she actively done something that had risk to it. The first sign of danger or something she didn't like and she was gone.

Anya didn't want that to be her life. She wanted to be someone, anyone. She wanted to have control. She wanted to have power even if it was just a sliver of it.

"Whatever you choose, you will pay a price for it. So for once, pay for something you truly want," it said. "There is strength in you, there is power, you just have to let them out. Let go of the fear."

Anya closed her eyes and took a deep breath; it was almost like a stone had been lifted from her chest. She opened them and stared at it; newly lit determination clear in her eyes. Anya didn't want to kill but if she had just ended Inara's life, both James and Runa would be safe and so would she.

It wasn't that she regretted not killing Inara, she regretted the outcome and that was the problem. She had done nothing, she had let Inara make the move, make the choice that would change Anya's life.

"I want to be powerful," Anya said, her voice steadier than she would have thought. "I want to keep the people I care about safe."

"Are you willing to pay the price for that?" It asked.

Anya took another deep breath.

"I hope so," she simply said.

Chapter 24

INARA

Inara woke up in the small, closet-like room she'd been allowed to use to get some rest. Her head still felt like she'd been hit by a horde of galloping horses and she knew her face was filled with bruises but the worst damages had been addressed immediately after they had apprehended them all. It both surprised Inara and not that they took Anya and the other two to the Castle, she had never stepped foot in here.

It was way above her pay grade as a foot patrol guard. The entire way to the Castle, Inara couldn't help but to glance at Anya's unconscious body from time to time, she hoped it wasn't obvious. What Inara had seen her do, it was beyond anything she could have imagined. Even now, she wondered if she had dreamt it all, after all, no human could conjure fire at will from nothing. It was impossible.

But it wasn't just her that had seen it, if it had, she would have thought she'd been going crazy. Though she still felt like she was going a little crazy, it was just so much to take in. Inara had barely managed to duck beneath the arc of flames that had shot towards them, the rest of the guards had not been as lucky but most of them just had some damaged uniforms and some burns. The burns looked nasty but the doctors assured them all that it would not lead to any permanent damage, it would just hurt for a while.

Inara appreciated the room she'd been given to recover in but she hadn't managed to sleep a lot, her thoughts spinning in a thousand miles an hour without reprieve. The thought if she had done the right thing or not but after seeing what Anya was capable of, she leaned more than ever towards yes. She had to be contained and helped. Inara hoped that what was going to happen to her and that she wasn't just going to be thrown into The Grove.

Inara had never set foot in The Grove but she had heard the stories just like everyone else. The Grove was far below the Castle, carved out of the rock. The cells were small and it was always damp and cold down there. There were no windows and no way to know the passage of time.

It was always in a perpetual state of dim light, the hallways having torches for the guards to see the prisoners. They said that most people went mad down there and Inara could see why, it sent a shiver down her spine to even think about.

Inara had arrested people but only for the small holding cells in the guard house, where they kept the minor criminals. The ones who stole a piece of bread, caused a ruckus or got into a drunken fight. The Grove was reserved for the real monsters, or at least that was the thought behind it.

Even though Inara's head felt like it was made out of lead, she swung her feet out of her bed and got dressed. She had been given a new and clean guards' outfit to wear around the Castle; she guessed they couldn't have her looking ragged in the clothes she'd had in the fight. She had also been given a new scarf which she appreciated, it was a light grey not her usual black but she didn't mind the change.

A lot of things had changed. Inara knew the moment they had arrived at the Castle and word had spread between the important people that this would give her a good reputation, something she had hoped for. She had been congratulated on a job well done and she had spoken with more doctors and high guards than she had ever done before. Though she wasn't completely unaware of some of the glances she got from the guards that had been with her during the arrest, they had gotten burns and been wounded, and yet it seemed like Inara got all the praise.

For once, Inara couldn't be bothered to care. Their jealousy wasn't her problem. As Inara opened her door and peaked out into the corridor, she noticed that another guard had been stationed right outside her room. It wasn't anyone she recognised so she assumed it was a lower royal guard and when she looked closer and saw the little sigil of the king on her uniform, it confirmed it. The woman smiled to Inara.

"I hope you slept well," she said pleasantly.

"Well enough," Inara answered.

"Can I help you with something?" The woman asked.

Inara cleared her throat, there was only one thing on her mind right now.

"I would like to see the prisoners I brought in yesterday," Inara said.

The guard frowned slightly before returning to her pleasant smile.

"The man and the…the woman without the Mark are in the holding cells further down," the woman said. "The woman with the Mark has been moved for now and is not to be visited by any unauthorised personnel."

"I caught her," Inara said. "Shouldn't I be authorised?"

"Unfortunately not," the woman said. "But I can take you to the other two if you wish? They are to be interrogated properly soon, I'm sure they wouldn't mind if you held those."

Inara frowned slightly.

"They haven't started the interviews yet?" Inara asked. It must have been at least five or six hours since they'd been arrested, it seemed strange that they hadn't even begun the interrogation.

"There is a lot of paperwork," the woman said. "And we have been busy with the damaged guards. It's been a lot."

Inara nodded slowly at that. She could understand that after everything that had happened yesterday that things must be quite chaotic right now. Inara knew that the people in charge didn't want the people of the city to know about this Mark, so she heavily assumed they didn't want anyone outside the Castle to know what Anya could do. It would cause widespread panic at best.

At worst…Inara couldn't even imagine. They must have kept everyone involved in the Castle until they felt sure they could keep the secret or until further notice. Inara wouldn't be surprised if she would be staying at the Castle for a while, while this was all being figured out.

"Please take me to them," Inara said.

The woman nodded and started walking down the corridor. This was clearly closer to the servants' quarters, it wasn't anything fancy. The rooms were small and could basically only fit a bed. It was meant to house as many people as possible without really thinking about comfort. Inara didn't mind; she didn't need much and she would have felt more out of place if they had given her a grand bedroom.

When they exited the corridor, it was almost like stepping into another plane. Inara must have been really out of it yesterday because she had barely noticed how grandiose this place had been. It was almost absurd. Almost everything was plated in what looked like gold and the fabrics hanging as curtains or as decorations were all a royal purple, and wherever she looked, she could see the royal sigil. Inara finally noticed the lack of torches, yet all the rooms and corridors were filled with light. Bright light that seemed to emanate from small lanterns hanging from the walls. It didn't look like light from a fire, it was brighter and crisper. Inara had never seen anything like it.

They went down a pair of large stairs and kept going down, and for a short moment she wondered if the guard was taking her to The Grove, but surely not? The two they had apprehended with Anya hadn't been convicted yet or even been proved to be involved properly, they wouldn't throw them into The Grove? But when they came to the bottom floor, they stopped going down and kept moving from corridor to corridor.

It was an absolute maze. It felt like they were going in circles and Inara was sure they had passed the same vase four times when the guard finally opened a door into a place Inara felt more comfortable in. It was more sterile and clean, a place for the guards to work and Inara could see multiple rows of doors with a small window looking into it. Clearly holding cells.

"Thank you," Inara said.

The woman smiled and left the way they came from. Inara hoped she wouldn't have to find her way back to her room by herself because she would get lost and it felt like she could wander around in this place forever without ever getting back to her room.

At a desk sat a woman with deep skin and large prominent, almost black eyes. She had a couple of stark white scars that stuck out against her skin, one going down her cheek onto her throat.

The woman rubbed her eyes and she made eye contact with Inara.

"Ah, you must be the infamous Inara, correct?" She said.

Inara only nodded as a response.

"I'm Fatima," she said and reached out a hand.

Inara took it, they had a similarly strong hand shake which made them both smile vaguely. A handshake could tell a lot about a person after all.

"What can I do for you?" Fatima said and leaned back in her chair.

"I would like to see the two people I brought in yesterday," Inara said.

"Go ahead," Fatima said and used her head to point to the left side. "Some of your other guard friends have been in and out but I don't think they've actually done anything."

Inara frowned.

"What do you mean?" Inara asked.

Fatima shrugged.

"All of you who took them in have free access to the prisoners, some seem to have entered the room of the two of them only to exit a few minutes later. Not enough time to have done any real interrogation," Fatima said.

"What did they do?" Inara asked seriously.

"I don't know," Fatima said. "I'm only here to make sure the prisoners don't escape and that nothing gets out of hand. I'm not about to go and meddle with all the things going on right now. No offence but from the little I've heard, I'd rather spend a month in The Grove than deal with that."

Inara let out a small laugh.

"That's fair I suppose," Inara said.

Fatima smiled lightly.

"The man is in cell two and the woman is in cell three," Fatima said. "Take all the time you want. They will probably be here for a while."

Inara nodded and made her way towards cell two. Inara took a deep breath and took a quick peek into the small window on the door to assess the situation. The man, whose name Inara was pretty sure was James Braelish, was sitting on a chair with a table in front of him and his hands were chained to the table. It gave him some mobility but not enough to do anything really, mostly just so he could move his hands a little from time to time.

His eyes were closed but Inara could see that the wound on his head had not been cleaned, his hair was crusted with dried blood and he looked pale.

Inara frowned and instead of entering, she made her way to cell three and peaked into that window. She saw the dark skinned woman but her skin was ashy and dull and she had deep, dark circles under her eyes. Her arms were restrained in the same way as the man's and Inara could see the bandage on her arm, which she must have had from before the fight. It had bled through completely and it had dried on some patches but on others it looked fresh.

If James had looked bad, this woman looked like she could fall dead at any moment. Had they not given them medical attention? What good were suspects if they were dead? Slightly horrified, Inara returned to Fatima, who only gave her a raised eyebrow as a question.

"Have the suspects not received medical attention?" Inara asked seriously.

"I don't know," Fatima said. "I started my shift three hours ago. None of your guards have mentioned that the suspects would need medical attention."

Inara clenched her jaw as she felt anger swell up inside her.

"Have they received food and water?" Inara asked, trying to keep the anger from her voice.

"Not as long as I've been here," Fatima said. "I assume all of that got taken cared of before I got here. As I said, none of your guards…"

"Have mentioned anything, yes thank you," Inara said. "Could you please call for a doctor and for some water and food for the suspects?"

Fatima frowned slightly but finally just shrugged.

"Whatever you say, boss," She said.

"I'm not…" Inara started.

Fatima smiled gently. "You certainly outrank me after what you did yesterday."

Fatima rose from her seat and opened the door into the hallway and Inara could hear her shout something but she didn't care enough to actually listen. As long as she was following her orders, that was all that mattered.

Inara was a lot of things. She had betrayed someone she almost had considered a friend, not something she'd ever had very many of. She had been a very lonely child, perhaps by choice, perhaps by her upbringing, it was impossible to know at this point, now it was just who she was. Someone without friends. Anya had helped her and she meant something to someone who meant very much to Inara.

Inara did not want to think too closely to what Mara would say if or rather when she found out what had happened. Inara knew she wouldn't be able to lie to her, and she also knew that Mara wouldn't understand because they were fundamentally different. They valued different things.

Inara was a lot of things but corrupt was not one of them; cruel was not one of them either. She did what was necessary for justice to be made, for things to be set right, that was it.

Inara didn't like to see people suffer unnecessarily. But she knew people would suffer.

Chapter 25

INARA

Inara waited outside the cells until Fatima returned with a tray; on it stood two large glasses of water and some simple bread.

"It was the fastest thing I could get," Fatima said with a slightly apologetic look. "A healer is supposed to come down within the hour. They said they had a lot on their hands right now and couldn't prioritise suspects."

Inara frowned slightly. They were suspects, not convicted criminals which still made them innocent citizens until proven guilty and they should be treated as such, but she guessed they did indeed have other priorities.

"Thank you," Inara said and took one of the glasses and a piece of bread. "You can put the tray by your table, I'll be by to get the rest later."

"As you wish," Fatima said and went back to her chair and small table.

Inara took a deep breath. She had a feeling this wasn't going to go particularly well but she knew that both the man and the woman had better chances of not being severely punished if they were involved with her than with anyone else, at least as far as she knew. Inara knocked on cell two before she opened it. She saw the man startle awake, he must have fallen asleep and Inara couldn't blame him.

He looked at her and straightened himself in his chair. The only sound was the light rattling of the chains around his wrists when they dragged across the table. Inara sat down in front of him and slowly and with her eyes trained on him, she placed the glass of water and the piece of bread within his reach. He did not take it immediately, only stared at her.

"You are James Braelish, correct?" Inara said, breaking the silence.

A look of slight surprise flashed across his face.

"You know me?" He said and cleared his throat.

Inara nodded and tried to smile gently.

"I am from the east side myself and you are somewhat of a celebrity I would say," Inara said. "You have actual medical training and you help anyone, whether they can pay or not. That is unusual."

James closed his eyes, she could see how tired he was.

"How is your head?" Inara asked.

"Been better," he answered shortly. "But I doubt I have a concussion and the bleeding stopped a good while ago, so I'm going to be fine."

A short uncomfortable silence spread through the room.

"Please, eat, drink," Inara said and gestured to the glass and piece of bread. "I understand that the other guards haven't fed you?" A small scoff escaped his lips.

"No," he said. "So why are you?"

Inara frowned slightly.

"Because food and water are basic necessities that anyone deserves to have," Inara simply said. "A healer will be down soon as well to look at your wounds."

James just stared at her for a moment, it looked like he was studying her face before he spoke again.

"How is your head?" He asked and took a small sip from the glass of water.

Inara's hand went up to where Anya had hit her by pure reflex, it still throbbed with pain.

"Been better," Inara said gently.

When James started to drink, he didn't stop and he finished the entire glass in seconds, almost seeming to forget to breathe. Finally, he put down the empty glass.

"I can get you some more water if you'd like?" Inara asked.

James shook his head.

"It's fine, but thank you," he said and started to slowly pull off pieces of the bread and shoving them into his mouth. "But I don't think you're here to just give me water and food. You were there, at the arrest."

"I was," Inara said.

"How is Anya? Runa?" James asked low.

Inara frowned slightly.

"I don't know where Anya is being kept right now," Inara said honestly. "And I assume the woman we arrested is Runa?"

"You don't know where she is?" James asked. "How can you not know? You arrested her."

"It is above my paygrade apparently," Inara said, trying to not sound annoyed. "And Runa, as you call her, is alive and is in the cell next to this one but…"

Inara took a careful look at James, to see his reaction.

"She isn't doing particularly well from what I could see," Inara said. "She is in worse shape than you."

James' face was unmoving and unreadable and Inara didn't know if that was from lack of care for this woman or from being exhausted.

"I promise the healer will see her as soon as possible," Inara finished.

James said nothing to that.

"Now," Inara said, time to get to the important things. "Did you know?"

"Know what?" James asked, sounding exasperated.

"About Anya. She lived with you, correct?" Inara said.

"She lived in a room in my house, yes," James said.

"So you know her well? Would know her comings and goings and what she's doing?" Inara asked.

James laughed low.

"Not really," he said. "She came and went as she wished. She often didn't even use the front door, simply climbed into her room from the window on the second floor."

"So you weren't close?" Inara asked. "She didn't confide in you?"

There was a short moment of silence.

"No," James said.

Inara didn't believe him, his voice might be steady and true but his eyes betrayed him with worry.

"So you know nothing of a mark on one of her hands or so?" Inara continued.

James shook his head. "She almost always wore gloves when I saw her."

That tracked with what Inara had seen during her time with Anya but she still did not believe that James did not know anything about this.

"Alright," Inara said. "What do you remember from the arrest?"

"Chaos," James answered. "Guards bursting in, assaulting us…"

"They were a little rougher than I expected," Inara confirmed.

"Says the woman who held a sword to an already wounded and helpless woman on the floor," James said calmly.

Silence.

"I would not have harmed her," Inara said. "She was close by and I took a chance that they knew each other and I seemed to have been correct. I just didn't want there to be any more bloodshed." The question though was if Inara would have hurt the woman if Anya hadn't stood down or spewed fire at them. Was it righteous to hurt someone potentially innocent to apprehend someone potentially very dangerous? Did they outweigh each other? Inara wasn't so sure anymore.

"And then, what did you see?" Inara asked.

James shrugged. "Fire. Someone must have knocked a candle over something flammable that caught real fast. From there, I saw nothing until the fire was put out and I was knocked unconscious."

"You did not see where the fire came from?" Inara asked slowly.

He shook his head. "I didn't exactly have a good view from being shoved into the floor, I saw very little of anything."

Inara did not believe him. He had seen more than he admitted but how much she couldn't be sure of, but he was lying to save himself, something Inara couldn't entirely fault him for. It wasn't his fault that he housed Anya or helped people, he shouldn't be punished for that. Inara also knew he used a cane and she found it unlikely that he would have helped Anya steal from the Castle, it didn't make sense.

At worst, he had seen the Mark and then said nothing because he didn't know what it was, perhaps he too thought it was just another tattoo.

"Thank you, James," Inara said. "I will let you rest and if you need more water or food, please just give me a shout alright?"

"That's it?" James asked, slightly confused.

"I think I have everything I need from you," Inara said. "Unless you have something you want to add? Any help you can give would be of great use."

"Anya is innocent. I don't know what you think she's done but she isn't that kind of person," James said.

The fight Inara had with Anya flashed before her eyes, the brutality in the way she moved and the force in her hits. But then in the end, Anya had not killed her even with ample opportunity and a fairly good reason, at least from her perspective. Anya might be a thief but she wasn't a murderer, that much was clear.

"I will let my superiors know what you've told me," Inara simply said.

Inara gave him a small nod before she exited the room. The moment the door closed behind her, she released a deep breath and leaned against the steel door. Her head was pounding more than it had done since the fight.

Inara had to keep going, this was no time to slow down and relax. There was still so much that Inara didn't know about all of this and at this point, she felt like she was in far too deep to back out. The only way left was forward, there was no going back anymore.

Inara got the other glass from Fatima's desk and the last piece of bread before she went to cell three. Before she opened, she took a deep breath. With James, she had heard rumours and had known somewhat what to expect from him but this woman, Inara had no idea. Inara knocked before she opened the door. The woman was sitting in the same position that Inara had seen her in when she'd peaked in earlier and her eyes were fixed on a point on the wall to the left.

She barely even registered Inara entering. Inara slowly placed the glass of water and the piece of bread within her reach but still, she did not move.

"My name is Inara," she said. "I would…"

"I don't care," the woman said, interrupting her with a hoarse voice.

Inara cleared her throat.

"You are Runa, correct?" Inara said. "A last name?"

"Yes. No," Runa said shortly.

"Please, drink, eat," Inara said. "I found out the other guards hadn't given you any so I…"

"I'm not fucking touching anything you're giving me," Runa said with a surprising amount of hostility compared to the state she seemed to be in.

Inara frowned.

"It is your choice of course, but you don't look too well," Inara said. "A healer will be down soon…"

"Does this usually work?" Runa snapped and finally turned her head and looked at Inara.

"What do you mean?" Inara asked.

Runa scoffed.

"The whole, first you starve me, don't give me any water or anything and have other guards come in just to be cruel so that you can swoop in like a saint and help, so I'll tell you everything I know," Runa said with a scowl. "It's pathetic."

Inara frowned and felt offended by her comments. Inara would never play such cruel tactics, she simply tried to give them some amount of comfort during their time here.

"That is not what this is," Inara said sincerely. "And I apologise if the other guards have treated you badly."

"Why would I even want your apology?" Runa said. "One of the last things I remember is the cold steel of your blade pressing into my neck."

Inara almost apologised again but realised that would probably only upset her even more.

"I would not have hurt you," Inara said.

Runa let out a laugh of contempt.

"Oh yeah? Thanks for letting me know. I totally believe you," Runa said.

Inara looked at Runa's wounded arm, it didn't look good. Inara wasn't a doctor or healer by any means but it seemed like it could be in the danger zone of becoming infected. Runa must have seen her staring because she moved uncomfortably in her chair but she was chained to the table, so she couldn't get anywhere.

"Tell me about Anya," Inara said, changing the topic.

Inara could see Runa's eyes widen for just a second before her face returned to the scowl she'd worn almost the entire time. Runa was silent for a moment and Inara almost thought she wouldn't say anything at all.

"We were friends. A long time ago," Runa finally said. "She was part of the Silver Swans, then she left. End of story."

"The Silver Swans," Inara muttered more to herself than to her. Inara had a vague grasp of the dussin or so gangs residing on the east side, but there always seemed to be new ones and old ones were suddenly gone. The gangs were not something Inara wanted to get involved with, not until she had some power to change things on a larger scale.

If she went in as a patrol guard, there was a chance they'd either laugh at her or kill her and dump her body so no one knew a crime had been committed. The Silver Swans was not a gang she was familiar with.

"Is that why you were at James' house?" Inara asked. "To speak with Anya?"

Runa cleared her throat. "No, I'd just gotten hurt in a fight." Runa gestured with her head towards the wound on her arm. "I needed someone to fix me up, so I went to James. I haven't properly spoken to Anya since she left the Silver Swans."

"But surely you must see her if you go to James often?" Inara said.

"I don't go there often," Runa hissed. "I don't tend to get hurt enough, I'm not an amateur."

"So what you're saying is that you were simply there at the wrong time?" Inara asked. Runa nodded. Inara did not believe her either. Runa was a better liar than James by a mile, but her eyes betrayed her just as much. Every time she spoke Anya's name, something would light up in her eyes. Anya meant more to her than she let on.

"Alright. So you wouldn't know if Anya has seemed different in recent times or if she has done anything she shouldn't have done?" Inara asked with a knowing look.

"No. Sorry," Runa said coldly. "She works alone, so you should ask her."

"I don't have authorisation to see her," Inara answered truthfully.

Runa frowned slightly.

"She isn't here?" Runa asked, confused.

"I don't know where she is," Inara said.

"But she's alive?" Runa asked, obviously trying to keep her voice calm.

"I would assume so," Inara said, she would have found it extremely confusing if they had disposed of her; in that case what had all of this been for?

Runa didn't say anything in response.

"What do you remember during the arrest?" Inara asked.

"Lots of guards, you threatening to kill me. That's about it," Runa said.

Inara narrowed her eyes.

"What about the fire?" Inara said.

"What fire?" Runa asked. "One of your guards knocked me unconscious right after your sword left my throat."

It wasn't impossible. Inara remembered that Runa had been unconscious when the fire had died down while James had been taken down after. Things had happened so fast from Inara pointing her sword at Runa to the fire erupting, she really couldn't be sure if Runa had been conscious or not. It was really convenient that neither of them had seen the fire coming from Anya, it was deniability.

Inara wasn't sure she believed either of them but somehow she felt a slight relief that this was the story they went with. If they had seen something incriminating, Inara was no longer sure if they would leave this Castle, she was still unsure if she could herself. It was an uncomfortable thought. They wanted no one to know about this that was obvious but how far would they go to keep it a secret?

"Alright. Thank you, Runa," Inara said.

Runa narrowed her eyes in suspicion.

"That's it? No threats? Nothing?" Runa said.

"If you have nothing else to add?" Inara asked. "I just want justice to be served, Runa." Rage filled Runa's soft face and Inara was sure that if she hadn't been chained, she would have jumped at her.

"Justice?" Runa said, her breathing coming in heavy. "Whose justice? Yours?"

Inara frowned in confusion.

"Justice is impartial," Inara answered.

"So your justice must be served," Runa said. "That's what you mean. Your idea of justice."

"That's not..." Inara started.

"I hope one day you'll feel my idea of justice," Runa hissed. "And we'll see if it's the same." Inara said nothing and only made her way towards the door, right before she opened it, she turned back to Runa.

"Please, eat and drink. It's good to no one if you drop dead in this cell," Inara said.

Runa's face turned to stone. "Don't be so sure about that," Runa said coldly.

Inara felt her face drop at the comment and she quickly left the room.

This wasn't how it was supposed to be, Inara thought desperately. Things had always been easy; stealing was wrong, but the punishment wouldn't be too severe. Killing someone was wrong and would be punished severely. But this was all blurred. Guards who were supposed to help had left both Runa and James without food, water or medical care, that in itself was a crime to Inara.

Runa and James were simply in custody because they might have seen something someone didn't want them to see and if they knew more about it. They hadn't done anything. Inara wasn't even sure if Anya was guilty. Yes, Inara had seen her conjure fire from nothing and that was dangerous in itself but after their talk and fight, the desperation and conviction that Anya had spoken with when she said she hadn't stolen anything.

Inara believed her.

The horrifying thought entered Inara's mind. Had she made the wrong choice?

Chapter 26

A N Y A

Anya opened her eyes, being immediately blinded by bright light and everything went past her in a blur. She tried to sit up but found herself quickly being forced down onto whatever surface she was laying on. Suddenly, she was back at the Red Rose, being forced back into a bed by arms older and stronger than her and held down no matter what she said, how much she said it hurt.

Panic flooded Anya as straps were secured to her wrist and ankles. She just saw hands and what looked like distorted faces when she tried to look around. Anya wanted to plead, to scream to please let her go. She'd go with them, she'd do whatever as long as they released her.

She thought she might have started crying because her cheeks were suddenly wet and she could hear her breath hitch every few seconds. The only sounds she could hear were her own panicked breaths and what sounded like wheels rolling on a flat surface.

"Please don't move," a distorted voice said almost in slow motion. "We're here to help you."

"P-Please…" Anya managed to say, barely getting any sound out.

Anya tried to fight the straps holding her down. She didn't know where she was or who these people were. They were just anonymous faces taking her somewhere she had a feeling she didn't want to go.

"Relax," another slowed voice spoke.

That almost made Anya panic more. Her breathing was getting out of control. She was here, wherever here was, but at the same time she was back at the Red Rose being fifteen again, feeling like the world was swallowing her whole. Feeling helpless and out of control. Everything was spinning and for a moment she thought this was it, she was dying. Her heart was beating so fast it felt like it was going to burn itself out and no matter what she did she couldn't get enough oxygen into her lungs.

Then there it was, the spark of the flame inside her. Anya clenched her fists and she closed her eyes tightly. Anya was in control, she had power, she was not helpless. Not anymore. Just as she felt the fleeting grip of the flame, something sharp poked her neck and her whole body went limp before she drifted back into darkness.

***

"Open your eyes."

Anya woke up with a gasp, feeling nausea almost overtaking her but she managed to keep it down. The first thing she noticed was that she was no longer strapped down, she was able to move freely and it sent calm through her body. She was in control.

Then she noticed the rest. As Anya looked around she saw that she was in a small transparent box, in it were a simple bed bolted to the floor and a toilet. The inside of the box was lit up but she couldn't see any torches or similar. All the light seemed to come from a small orb in the ceiling. Outside the box was complete darkness, she could see nothing. How large the space outside the box was impossible to know, it could be as small as James' living room or as big as infinity.

It strangely reminded her of her dreams when she was standing in the chasm far below the sky, the only thing giving light was herself and It. Anya rose from where she'd been laying, her body felt stiff and unused. For the first few moments, every step was painful. Finally, Anya managed to stumble up to the transparent wall and put both her hands on it.

It felt like some form of glass, or at least that was the only thing coming to her mind. It was cold beneath her skin and she could see the mark clear on her left hand, there was no glow to it like it had sometimes, it was dull, like it had run out of energy. "Hello?" Anya spoke low and she shuddered when she heard herself, she sounded like a scared child. "Hello?" She tried again with a little more force behind it.

There was no answer.

"Please?" Anya said, her voice was back to sounding vulnerable. "Anyone?"

Still there was no answer, there was no sound at all except her breathing and the sound of her heart drumming in her ears. She wasn't even sure if her voice reached outside the box. Maybe no one could hear her at all, no matter how much she would scream and shout.

"*I'm not sure you want one of them to come,*" it spoke softly. "*After all, they put you in here.*"

"C-Can you get me out?" Anya asked, her voice shaking.

"*If I did, you would die,*" it simply said. "*You don't have the excess energy to accomplish something like that right now. I would burn right through you.*"

Anya tried hard to stay silent but a soft sob managed to slip past her lips, she knew she was being silly. The Mark, Fire was obviously inside her head and could tell what state of mind she was in but she felt as if she managed to keep it inside, if she managed to not show any weakness on the outside, she would be fine. She was wrong.

After letting out the first sob, Anya couldn't help it; it all came out of her like water out of a broken dam. Tears flowed down her face and she barely recognised the noises she was making as she cried harder than she had done since her mother had passed.

The thought of James laying on the floor inside his house, the thought of Runa yelping in pain when they wrenched her wounded arm, those images spiralled through her. Where were they? Were they safe? Were they dead? Anya managed to drag herself over to the toilet before she threw up at that thought. Her hair stuck to the sweat on her forehead and she rolled onto her back on the floor.

Anya closed her eyes, she was so tired, so exhausted. Memories flashed before her eyes, of another time when she'd been younger. A bright sunny day laying in the grass with the person she loved, at first barely touching but then felt their hands clasped together, like they were moulded to be like that forever. The sound of laughter, the smell of someone cooking her food after a long day, making sure she wasn't wounded.

Anya wished she could live in these memories and forget the present reality she lived in. Her past had been filled with horrendous things but the things she would do to be back there right now, she didn't care what she'd have to pay.

Anya finally opened her eyes, tears streaming down her face. She knew she would drown in those memories if she wasn't careful and if she wanted to continue to live, she couldn't stay in the past. Only let it strengthen her with the promise that things could be good once again, if only she kept moving forward.

Chapter 27

INARA

With a heavy head, Inara walked back to the front desk. Fatima looked up from a stack of papers she had been looking through, she seemed busier than before.

"How did it go?" Fatima asked.

Inara rubbed her eyes.

"Fine," Inara said. "I got what I wanted to know."

"That's great!" Fatima said. "You should report what you found out to Malik Bron."

"The War Councillor to the King?" Inara asked slightly shocked. "I know he's in charge of the guard force but he must be busy and I don't think…"

"He's very invested in this," Fatima said seriously. "He's going to want to know what you found out. I'm actually a little surprised he hasn't talked to you yet. All the other guards coming in here couldn't stop talking about meeting him."

Inara frowned slightly. Involving the War Councillor to the King in this made things a lot more complicated and a thousand times scarier. Something was really happening and for some reason, it all revolved around Anya. Inara had known the first moment she had set her eyes on that Mark that something was wrong with it, it just wasn't natural.

No one else seemed to really mention it but surely she couldn't be the only one feeling the strange pull coming from it? Like it was calling to her and it was terrifying.

"Thank you," Inara said. "I suppose I'll go find him."

Fatima gave her a soft smile. Inara started to make her way towards the exit door, she did not look forward to trying to find her way back out of here.

"Oh right, wait, one more thing!" Fatima yelled after her.

Inara turned around with a questioning look.

"Some guards took in another person of interest in this if you want to talk to them as well?" Fatima asked.

"Another person?" Inara asked with a frown. As far as Inara had been aware of the only people who had been involved in the arrest and had seen anything were currently somewhere in the Castle, who could they have brought in?

"Yes, apparently they traced some of the books in the house to this person. At least the books that weren't consumed by the fire," Fatima answered. "Though I'm not sure if you'll get much out of her. She didn't seem to understand anything any of us said. We're not sure if it's because she doesn't know our language or what it is but you can have a go anyway if you wish." Inara's face dropped. No, it couldn't be. There was no way that she could be involved in this.

Without saying another word, Inara turned back towards the cells.

"Cell five!" Fatima shouted after her.

Inara stopped in front of cell five, not daring to look into the small window leading into the room. She didn't want to see. If she didn't see it wasn't real, it was still just a hypothetical.

Finally, Inara glanced inside and she felt all the colour drain from her face. In the small cell sat Mara, with her bouncy red hair and pale freckled face but she wasn't smiling like usual, there was obvious confusion and fear in her eyes. Inara stormed back to the front desk, trying to keep calm.

"I need a pen and paper," Inara said.

"What?" Fatima said confused.

"Pen. Paper. Now," Inara said in a commanding voice.

Fatima didn't hesitate, she immediately picked up a few stacks of paper and a pen and handed them to Inara. Inara could see that Fatima wanted to ask something but she decided to keep her mouth shut when she saw the look on Inara's face. Smart woman. This time without hesitating, because Inara was afraid that if she paused for even a moment she would not go through with it. Inara opened the door to cell five.

The confusion and fear in Mara's eyes didn't disappear but there was a small sigh of relief. Mara instantly started to sign, trying to communicate with Inara. With sad eyes, Inara simply shook her head and sat down and placed down the pieces of paper and the pen.

"Write," Inara said and made the motion as if she was writing.

Mara lowered her hands almost in defeat before she picked up the pen and started writing.

"What's happening?" Mara wrote.

Mara passed over the pen and Inara just held it for a moment, feeling her hands shake ever so slightly, just thinking what she was going to tell her.

"Some of your books have been found on a potential crime scene," Inara finally wrote; it was honest but vague enough.

Mara read what she'd written and then looked up in confusion.

"What crime scene?" Mara wrote, her brow furrowed.

Inara took a deep breath.

"Did you lend some books to James or Anya? Or did they buy some books from you recently?" Inara wrote.

Mara just stared at her for a moment. Inara could tell she was reading her facial expressions and contemplating what to write next.

"Yes," Mara simply wrote.

Inara closed her eyes. Shit. That did complicate things but it wasn't too bad, she wasn't in the same position as James or Runa. Mara could have given those books without having any idea what they were going to be used for.

"Did they say what they were going to use them for?" Inara wrote.

"Are James and Anya in trouble?" Mara wrote, ignoring her question.

Inara took a deep breath.

"What were the books for?" Inara tried again.

Mara read and then slowly looked around the room, almost like she was afraid someone was watching them which was impossible. There was no one else in here and there was no possibility that Fatima or anyone else outside the cell could know what they were talking about.

"Anya requested them. Asked if I had books about markings regarding fire," Mara wrote slowly.

"Did you?" Inara wrote immediately.

"I have a lot of books. I gave them what I thought could help," Mara wrote.

"But you don't know why they wanted those books?" Inara asked.

Mara shook her head. Inara turned around in her chair and looked at the door and the small window giving insight into the room before she turned back.

"Tell no one that Anya requested books about markings regarding fire," Inara wrote quickly. Mara read it and frowned deeply and it looked like she was going to question it until she met Inara's pleading eyes. Mara nodded slowly in response.

"I'm going to get you out, I promise. Just say you know nothing if anyone else asks, okay?"

Inara said.

"You mean write," Mara wrote back.

Inara sighed and she very clumsily and slowly signed "I'm sorry." It was bad but by Mara's face at least it was comprehensible. A sad small smile came across Mara's face for just a split second.

"Can you get Anya and James out as well?" Mara asked.

Inara didn't write back for a few seconds, just staring at the piece of paper.

"I'm going to try," Inara finally wrote. "It's complicated and you should not get involved."

Mara nodded in understanding.

"I'll get you out, I swear," Inara wrote and tried to smile.

"You're a good person. I'm sorry that I am hard on you sometimes," Mara wrote back.

Inara felt nauseous at reading that. Mara would not be writing that if she knew that it was Inara's fault that both Anya and James were in trouble right now. That this was all because of her. Inara gave her a quick nod and tried to smile but it turned more into a grimace. Inara quickly got up but left the pen and paper with Mara and closed the door to the cell behind her.

***

Inara did not waste time after she left cell five. She immediately asked Fatima where she could find Malik, the War Councillor, and Fatima had said with some hesitation that she didn't know but if Inara asked one of the royal guards, they should be able to lead her to him. Inara had said thank you but it had barely been audible as she left the holding cell area. The moment she stepped back into the 'official' Castle, it was almost like she'd forgotten how gaudy it looked.

The gold covering nearly everything and the drapes of purple with the royal emblem, almost like they were afraid that someone would forget whose Castle they were in. Inara had little memory of how to get back from where she'd come but she managed to get through the multiple corridors and out into a larger area, though one she didn't recognise. A guard patrolling the area caught her eye and she walked towards them with purpose.

She could see a flash of fear in the guards eyes as Inara closed in. Inara knew how intimidating she could look and right now it was only to her advantage.

"I need to see Malik Bron," Inara said.

The guard looked surprised and took a few seconds to answer.

"Do you have business with the War Councillor?" The guard asked low.

"I'm from yesterday's arrest," Inara simply said.

"Oh," the guard said. "Please follow me, he is usually in his War Room."

Inara only nodded and the guard started to walk with quick steps but Inara's legs were far longer and she almost had to slow down not to overtake the guard. They said nothing on the entire walk and it suited Inara well. She was bad at casual chatter in the best of cases and right now that was the last thing she needed and it was like the guard could tell. It took another eternity to get to the War Room, this Castle was simply too big.

Inara couldn't fathom what all the rooms could be used for. Why did one family need all of this? The guard looked at Inara before she carefully knocked on the door to the War Room.

"Who is it?" A raspy voice yelled through the door.

"Ehm…Someone from yesterday's arrest, Sir," the guard said.

Silence.

"Let them in," the voice answered calmly.

The guard simply gave Inara a nod before they almost ran away. Inara wasn't sure if it was out of fear of her or of Malik but she had a hunch. Inara opened the door and stepped inside and carefully closed the door behind her. She stopped and placed her hands behind her back and straightened her back. She wasn't entirely sure how to behave with these high ranking commanders.

Malik was standing at a large table with a map of the country on it, leaning on it casually but his head was cocked to the side and stared at her. Malik was a tall man with golden brown skin, his hair was short trimmed and his large beard was well kept. He looked like a man of status and money. Malik smiled and laughed when he laid his eyes on Inara and gestured for her to approach.

"No need for formalities I hope?" Malik said cheerfully. "I know that you are Inara Justifa, patrol guard on the east side. Correct?"

Inara slowly nodded.

"And I would hope you know who I am," he said almost like a joke.

"Of course, you are Malik Bron, War Councillor to the King," Inara answered.

Malik chuckled a little at that.

"What good is a War Councillor when this country hasn't been at war for over fifty years?" He said with a smile. "Nowadays, I simply make sure the guards all over the city do what they are supposed to and that things are in order."

"A big honour and a big task," Inara said.

"No need for flattery," he said. "After all, it should be me who should congratulate you, Miss Justifa."

"Inara," she said quickly.

Malik raised an eyebrow and then nodded.

"You brought in the girl with the Mark, correct?" Malik asked.

"Well, it was me and ten other guards but yes," Inara said.

"Ah yes, the other guards. I have spoken with them to get their story of the event. Even though there was obvious resentment and jealousy, they all spoke well of you. They all said it was you who discovered the girl," Malik said.

Inara simply nodded.

"How did you discover her?" Malik asked and his small eyes focused seriously on Inara.

Inara was silent for a moment.

"Pure luck I'm sad to say," Inara said and tried to smile.

"Come now, it can't have been pure luck," Malik said.

Inara frowned slightly; how had she known really? She hadn't but she'd suspected it ever since she'd shook Anya's hand. Was it because she had been wearing gloves the entire time and she had been asking around about the theft? Or was it because deep down, Inara had known that there had been something on her left hand, something that shouldn't be there. Something that wouldn't stop calling.

"Intuition then," Inara said. "I had no proof but I managed to remove her glove and I saw the Mark and knew I had the right person."

Malik studied Inara's face closely.

"You got hurt," he said.

"Could have been worse. She had the opportunity to kill me but she didn't," Inara said honestly.

"Strange," Malik muttered. "Well, in any case, this victory belongs to you and we are all in your debt. You saw what the girl could do. It was imperative that we got her back in custody before it got out and things got messy. I think you could imagine the chaos that could erupt from something like this coming out."

"I could," Inara agreed.

Malik smiled pleased with her response.

"From now on, you are going to work with me. I have spoken with the King and he agreed to place you in my own guard unit that works outside the rest of the guards in this city," Malik said.

"I'm sorry?" Inara said confused.

"You have gotten one big promotion, Inara," he said with a smile. "And because of what you know, you could be of immense help in this matter."

"What of the other ten guards?" Inara asked.

"Ah yes," Malik said. "They have all been immediately sent away to neighbouring cities, all of them split up to work to hold the peace there. They left no more than 30 minutes ago, I hope you didn't want to say goodbye to anyone?"

Inara shook her head and then frowned.

"Why?" She asked. "Why send them away?"

"To keep this from spreading to a minimum. This city is already on the brink of it getting out, we don't need patrol officers getting drunk and letting it slip," Malik said.

"But isn't this just risking that it spreads in the other cities, instead of just here?" Inara asked.

Malik put his hand on Inara's shoulder, it was a firm but not painful or threatening grip.

"Don't worry, we have thought this through and this is the best option for everyone," he said. "You don't have to think about them anymore. Your new job will be time consuming as it is."

Inara only nodded but something deep inside her felt wrong, but then again, she'd basically had a bad feeling ever since the arrest. Perhaps she was just being paranoid.

"Now we have some people in custody to speak with," Malik said and gestured for the door.

"I've already interviewed them," Inara said.

Malik stopped in his tracks and looked back at her.

"You've been busy. I would have thought you'd be resting for the first part of today," Malik said.

"I'm sorry if I overstepped, I just had to know…" Inara started.

"No, of course, you made the arrest, it is only right that you got to interview them," Malik said with a small smile. "What did you learn?"

Inara took a deep breath. Here it was, this moment would decide a lot of things. A lot of things Inara didn't really want to have in her hands.

"None of them saw how the fire started, nor did they know about the girl's Mark," Inara said.

Malik narrowed his eyes.

"And you believe them?" He asked.

No. "Yes," Inara said before she could think about it.

"Seems a little convenient, don't you think?" Malik said and stared at Inara.

"It was chaotic, Sir, and they had been brought to the ground, their faces basically on the floor. I believe them," Inara said, feeling her voice being unnervingly steady. "And the girl seems to have been somewhat isolated. It seemed she worked alone and didn't speak with many."

Malik stroked his beard and looked deep in thought.

"And the bookkeeper?" Malik asked.

"Just a bookkeeper," Inara answered. "Didn't know what the books were going to be used for. She apparently sells a lot of weird books to eccentric people."

Malik sat down in one of the many chairs in the room. It looked unbelievably comfortable but Inara remained standing, not even sure if she was allowed to sit down.

"So what do you suggest we do with them?" Malik asked, his eyes piercing into Inara. "We cannot afford the information about the Mark and what the girl can do to get out as it is right now."

Inara took a deep breath.

"I don't believe they are of any danger but I would suggest that we put at least two guards on the woman and the man for a shorter period, to see if they do anything suspicious. Just to be on the safe side," Inara said, just letting the words fall out of her mouth. She needed to make him believe and trust her in this.

"So you suggest we let them go and then shadow them?" Malik said.

Inara nodded.

"The man, James, is very well liked and a pillar on the east side. I think it would be more suspicious if he just disappeared and the chances of neighbours seeing us carrying his body from his home is high so they would know where to put the blame. He's the only doctor on the east side, he would be missed," Inara said.

"You make a fair point," Malik said with a nod. "We want to keep the suspicion down as much as possible. Well, if you are sure they didn't see or know anything?"

"I am," Inara said, her mouth felt impossibly dry.

There were a few moments of silence where Malik just stared at her. Then he clapped his hands together and with a smile rose from the chair.

"Then that is what we shall do," Malik said. "We'll place guards to shadow them and if they notice anything, we'll just take them right back in."

Inara nodded.

"Get some rest now. It's been a long day for you, Inara," Malik said. "Tomorrow will be even longer."

Malik dismissed her and pointed at the door, and Inara tried to smile in appreciation over everything he'd done but she wasn't sure it came out sincerely.

Now there truly was no turning back.

Chapter 28

RUNA

The moment the door to Runa's cell had been opened and her chains released, her first instinct had been to try and take down the guard to get out of here but she saw four more guards standing outside. They had changed the bandages on her wounded arm. It would seem because of all the struggles and moving, the scar was going to become quite prominent. It was a nasty wound, especially from having come from such a neat cut, but it seemed to be healing.

Runa still didn't feel completely like herself yet, but the bread and water which she had devoured about ten minutes after the woman with the scarf had left, had helped her feel a little better. Runa guessed it would be a couple of days before she would be back to herself. The blood loss and then everything that had happened after had really messed her up physically.

To Runa's surprise, she was guided out of the Castle; the large door closing behind her and that was it, she was free. She stood outside the doors for a brief moment, not entirely sure what had just happened. Had Inara really believed what she'd said about not seeing anything? Runa found that unlikely but she found it even more unlikely they would have let her out if they didn't believe her. Because Runa had seen it all.

She'd seen how the fire had emerged from Anya, like she had summoned it from nothing and then sent it in an arc towards the guards. Almost like slashing a sword. It was hard to believe but Runa trusted her senses and they would not have done all of this for something that wasn't extremely important and dangerous. Runa's eyes scanned the Castle, from the large front doors up to the tallest tower; it really was massive. And somewhere in there was Anya. Runa closed her eyes hard and willed her feet to move away.

I'll come with you. Her own words echoed in her mind, almost like it was mocking her. What had she been thinking? She hadn't, that was the answer. Runa the stupid idiot who let her heart lead her over cliff edges. The dream of getting out of here with Anya and building something bright, hopeful and new together far away from this city that had treated them so horrendous.

But that was all it had ever been, a stupid dream. Runa could feel her eyes starting to burn and she rubbed them hard. She refused to cry as she walked slowly back into the centre of the city, the Castle looming over her.

Dreams had always been what had kept her going, the dream of something more than this. Perhaps it no longer kept her going, it kept her back. Perhaps she needed new dreams, dreams that were actually achievable. Dreams of not being blissfully happy with someone she loved but to be content and safe instead.

Wasn't that better? To strive towards something actually achievable and not something that would only get her hurt and killed? To not actually dream at all but to live with the cards she'd been dealt. It wasn't a pleasant thought but neither was her reality.

Her feet led her to the Keg. All she wanted was to collapse in her bed and not leave her room for days, not until she was completely recovered. She swung open the door, it was as rowdy as ever and a few members of the Silver Swans were situated on their usual spots. Runa had planned on just going straight up to her room but then she saw that the bar was currently empty and she could really go for something strong right now after what had happened.

Just one drink and then straight to her room. Runa sat down on one of the barstools by the bardesk and leaned heavily on her elbows.

"I ain't seen you in this chair for a while," a gruff, deep voice spoke.

Runa smiled slightly and looked up at Egil. Egil smiled as they spoke.

"Egil," Runa said with a sigh.

"You're looking rough, everything alright?" Egil asked with a raised eyebrow.

"A Drowned Lady please," Runa said instead of answering.

Egil whistled at her request.

"Everything's not alright, got it," Egil said and started to pour up the drink she'd asked for.

"What happened to your arm?"

Runa looked down at her bandaged arm and shrugged.

"Got in a scuffle," she simply said.

Egil put the drink in front of Runa and she immediately started to take large gulps of it and when she put it down, it was almost two thirds gone. When she looked back at Egil's face, she saw their furrowed brow and slight worry.

"Anything fun happened since I was last here?" Runa asked and continued to sip her drink. Runa had barely been gone a day, strange how that time in the Castle had felt like an eternity but coming back here, no one had even noticed she'd been gone. It had just been another night of her not coming back to the Keg for whatever reason.

After all, she was on a personal mission that had a tight time limit. She'd have to talk to Mr Parker about how the situation had changed. "Not really. The Rusty Coffins are still encroaching on our territory," Egil said and started to clean glasses. "Then there is the usual you know. Married men complaining about their wives, bachelors complaining about not having a wife. The usual."

Runa chuckled low at that. She finished her drink in one swoop, feeling the heat of the alcohol soothe her inside, calm her down and dull the pain. Just what she had needed.

"I'm going to go have a nap," Runa said. "If anyone asks, I'm out."

Egil nodded. Runa liked Egil. They were a good person but they also worked under Mr Parker which made them impossible to completely trust. There was obviously no one she could really trust except herself and she could barely do that apparently. Runa gave them a small salute before she made her way over to the stairs leading up.

Runa managed to take one step before someone was blocking her way. She didn't have to look up to know who it was and with a deep sigh, she stepped down and moved aside slightly so Mr Parker could get past.

"You look absolutely dreadful," Mr Parker said.

"Thanks," Runa said. "Now if you'll excuse me, I'm going to take my dreadful body up to my room."

Runa made to move but was stopped by a firm hand placed on her chest, right below the throat. She closed her eyes, she really didn't want to do this right now. Runa had a reputation of being calm and collected but right now, she felt as if she was a powder keg, ready to explode by the tiniest spark.

"How is your mission going?" Mr Parker asked.

So that was how he wanted to do this this time. Last time he wanted no witnesses, this time he wanted everyone to witness. Runa cleared her throat.

"I was going to talk to you about that after getting some sleep," Runa said as politely as possible. "I am a bit tired."

"Well, the days I gave you are quickly running out, so I would like to hear your progress," Mr Parker said.

Runa had noticed the environmental shift in the bar. Everyone had gone silent and she could feel everyone's eyes burning in her back. There were a couple of ways this could end, very few of them in Runa's favour if she didn't play her cards right.

"She's been arrested," Runa said and looked up at Mr Parker.

Runa saw the flash of anger in his eyes, the slip of his polite costume, showing the man behind. "Arrested?" He asked, pushed Runa back with his hand gently but threateningly as he himself stepped closer to her.

"That's what I said," Runa said. "She's being kept in the Castle."

It was like the silence got heavier as she spoke those words. Everyone knew it was impossible to get in or out of there without being seen.

"Probably The Grove," Runa continued but she didn't entirely believe that. There was no way they were going to put Anya in some cell after what she'd been able to do. No, they were going to find some way to exploit that but none of these people needed to know that.

Mr Parker smiled but Runa saw what it really was, the warning that violence was just a second away if she said the wrong word.

"How…convenient for you," he said, every word was carefully chosen.

"If you are somehow suggesting that I had anything to do with her arrest, then spit it out," Runa said.

"Did you?" He asked through gritted teeth.

"No," Runa said. "That would be disobeying your orders and no one would ever dare to cross you."

Runa couldn't help but lace the last words with poison and sarcasm even though she knew she would pay for them. Mr Parker took another step closer to her but she didn't budge. She could smell the cigar smell mixed with alcohol on his breath. He observed her closely but quickly glanced around the room, scouting all the spectators. After what felt like too long of a silence, he spoke again.

"Well then, if she was arrested, there is only one thing to do," Mr Parker said.

Runa almost wanted to sigh of relief, he would drop this and find some other way for her to prove herself or perhaps Anya being imprisoned was enough for him? After all, she could not impact Runa's judgment from a cell. Mr Parker stared right into Runa's eyes and she immediately knew she'd been wrong and she felt her heart drop.

"Break her out, bring her here and then we can all witness your loyalty first hand," Mr Parker said.

Runa didn't manage to contain the scoff of disbelief that came out of her mouth, Mr Parker's face hardened.

"It's impossible to break into the Castle, not to mention The Grove and then break someone out of there as well? That is insanity," Runa said.

"Are you refusing to follow my order?" Mr Parker said.

"I can't fly either, what's next, you're going to ask me to fly to the next city over and deliver a message?" Runa said.

A quick burst of laughter filled the room but it dissipated immediately as Mr Parker looked around the room.

"I would follow your order, if it was a possibility," Runa continued.

Before Runa could react, she was slower because of the blood loss, Mr Parker had put his right hand around Runa's throat and pushed her into a wall. There was barely any pressure being applied to her throat but the threat of it was there. Runa didn't bat an eye, she just stared at him.

"I gave you a roof over your head, I've given you jobs to do, to earn real money. I am what kept you alive," Mr Parker hissed, then he shouted into the entire room. "I am what's keeping all of you alive! Without me, there would be no Silver Swans. There would be no protection for any of you and you would all be on the streets again! You'd be nothing again! I made you something."

Runa glanced around the room. She could see that everyone was on edge and they all looked like they were unsure of what to do. Runa turned back to Mr Parker.

"So kick me out then," Runa said. "Kick me out for refusing to do the impossible."

Then she turned to the rest of the room.

"I wonder which of you will be thrown out next after you can't comply with his insane demands," Runa said loudly.

"You insolent little…" Mr Parker said and applied pressure to her throat.

Runa's hands immediately went up to try and get his grip of her, she wheezed, desperately trying to get some air in her lungs. Mr Parker's face had turned red in anger and his eyes were dark and soulless, the costume now fully discarded. If Runa had been well rested, didn't suffer from blood loss, had barely slept or been fed or had any water in the last couple of hours, she could have gotten out of his grip easily but now all she did was thrash against him. Black dots were starting to form in her vision and it grew blurry.

"Boss."

Someone had spoken, she wasn't sure who as her blood was thrumming in her ears almost making her deaf. Suddenly, the pressure was gone and Runa collapsed to the floor, frantically trying to get air into her lungs. What she saw when she looked up was that five of the Silver Swans, with Trent in the lead, stood behind Mr Parker, their hands on their weapons.

The look on Mr Parker's face was something Runa would never forget and cherish forever. It was a true look of surprise and disbelief that someone stood up against him.

"So that's how it is," Mr Parker said.

"We don't kill our own," Trent said and gave Runa a quick glance. "That's our code."

Mr Parker straightened his back and for a moment, Runa thought he was going to fight all five of them, something he surely would lose. Mr Parker wasn't a fighter, he hadn't lived a rough life. He was a rich asshole who wanted people to depend on him and fear him. He wanted to hold people's lives in his hand and dangle threats over them to make them dance to his tune.

"I suggest you go to your room, Boss," Trent said. "Calm down and you'll see this in a new light."

Mr Parker looked down on Runa on the ground, hatred clear in his eyes. Then the costume slipped back on, like it had never been taken off.

"Of course," he said and took a deep breath. "You're right, I lost my temper there."

He gave the five Silver Swans a warning glance but with a smile on his lips.

"Silver Swans stick together. Loyalty is everything," Mr Parker said, trying to sound proud and cheerful but failing miserably. "I'll be in my room if I'm needed."

Mr Parker shot Runa another quick glance before he turned back to the stairs, she had never heard his footsteps sound so loud before. The Silver Swans let go of their weapons and it was like the entire bar let out a collective breath, the mood shifted immediately. Trent reached out a hand for Runa to grab, she took it and he pulled her up with ease.

"Thank you," Runa said with uncertainty as she rubbed her throat. Last time she'd talked with Trent, she had held a knife to his throat because he'd joked about her feelings for Anya and still he had come to her defence.

Trent nodded.

"Ain't nothing. You're one of us. We might brawl and threaten but we don't kill one of our own. Not even the boss is above that," Trent said.

Runa didn't know why but those words almost made her cry, she really hadn't thought anyone would have come to help her. She had made an attempt with her words but they were a last ditch effort more than anything else. Anything to stay alive.

Hearing 'you're one of us' had never felt as sweet.

Chapter 29

ANYA

The darkness surrounding the clear box Anya was situated in suddenly turned into a bright light and she could hear what sounded like heels on a hard surface coming closer. Anya rubbed her eyes, trying to see anything in the sudden brightness. She could finally see the rest of the room. It wasn't large but completely empty. It seemed completely made to store this box and nothing else.

In front of her stood a fat woman with large deep brown eyes and her skin had a golden hue to it, her long curly hair framed her face perfectly. She was dressed in nondescript but well-made looking clothes, and it only took Anya a second to connect where she'd seen clothes like that before. Andrew had worn similar clothes when she'd found him out in the woods. The woman smiled gently and she was holding a clipboard and a pen in her hands.

"Anya?" The woman asked calmly.

Anya swallowed hard but slowly moved closer to the wall of the box. She wanted to get closer, to get a better look.

"Who's asking?" Anya finally said.

"My name is Esther," she said. "I am head scientist for the King."

Anya just stared at her. What was she supposed to say to that? She could try and beg and plead with her to let her out but knew it would fall on deaf ears, which left her with very little to say. From what Esther had just said, Anya knew she was in the Castle somewhere and from the look of this box, they didn't want her to go anywhere.

"Can I ask you some questions, Anya?" Esther asked.

Anya closed her eyes and slowly sat down on the floor of the box.

"I don't have anything else to do, so go ahead," Anya said low.

"I am sorry about all of this," Esther said and tried to smile.

Anya said nothing and didn't even lift her head to look up at her. Esther cleared her throat.

"Where is Andrew?" Esther asked.

Anya frowned.

"Dead," Anya simply said.

Esther sighed.

"I assumed as much," she said, a tinge of sadness in her voice. "As you have the Mark. Did you kill him for it?"

"What?" Anya said and she couldn't help but let out an incredulous laugh. "You think I wanted this?"

"Why did you take it then?" Esther asked.

"I didn't take it. He forced it on me," Anya hissed.

Esther frowned deeply. It was almost like she couldn't really comprehend what Anya had just said.

"How did you get him out of here? How did you get in here?" Esther asked.

"What are you talking about?" Anya asked. "I've never been inside the Castle before. I'd never met him until…" Anya took a deep breath.

"Until?" Esther asked.

"Until the night of the storm weeks ago. I found him in the woods and he forced the Mark on me," Anya said.

Anya left out some parts because she wasn't a complete idiot and she didn't trust any of these people, but she also didn't find any use in lying about the actual events.

Esther's frown only deepened.

"So you claim to know nothing about this?" Esther asked.

Anya glanced at her left hand and the Mark on it and she clenched her jaw. She raised her hand so Esther could clearly see the Mark.

"I didn't ask for this. I didn't want this," Anya said. "I was simply at the wrong place at the wrong time. Now please, tell me what's going on here."

Esther sighed and quickly scribbled something down on her clipboard before she turned back to Anya, her eyes clearly drawn to the mark.

"During the night of the storm, Andrew disappeared and so did the Mark," Esther started. "We hadn't had any success with the previous…"

Esther looked at Anya carefully before she continued.

"The previous test subjects. They had all died within twenty-four hours of receiving the Mark," Esther said. "The last one was burning up from the inside slowly, something that seemed to be happening to all of them. It was Andrew's shift and he went to check on the subject. He never returned and when the next person entered the room, all they found was a slightly scorched bed and a pile of ashes on it."

Pause.

"We thought…We didn't really know what to think but Andrew had been right beside me the entire time during this project. We thought the last subject with the Mark must have done something to him, or someone had incredibly broken in or…" Esther said.

"He'd taken it and left," Anya almost whispered.

"He wouldn't," Esther said, her voice suddenly filled with harshness. "He was as dedicated to this project as me. He wouldn't take it and leave not when he knew…"

Esther cleared her throat.

"So far the Mark has had a 100% death rate," Esther said. "Apparently until you."

"Lucky me," Anya muttered.

Esther took a few steps closer to the box, so close that if the wall hadn't been there, they would have been able to touch. She observed Anya closely.

"Why did you survive?" Esther asked. "What makes you so special?"

Anya met her eyes and she could feel a spark of anger ignite inside of her and it must have shown on her face because Esther immediately took a step backwards. Anya could see it on her face as much as she could hear it in her voice. Esther saw nothing more than a child of the gutter in Anya. Anya would never have been seen as special without the Mark and that lit something deep inside of her.

She was more than this Mark. She was a living human being but because she was from the east side, she was nothing. To them, she was nothing more than a vessel to this thing.

"If you cooperate with us, this will be easy and painless," Esther said.

"And if I don't?" Anya asked.

Esther was silent for a moment.

"We have our orders from the King to get the answers no matter the cost," Esther said. "So please, cooperate."

Anya rubbed her eyes. She didn't feel like cooperating with them out of pure spite but she couldn't find it in herself to really see a reason why she shouldn't?

They had her already, perhaps if she cooperated with them, they could help her? They had studied this Mark, they seemed to know a little about it anyway, perhaps they knew of a way to remove it?

Perhaps they could free her from this. Anya couldn't lie, she enjoyed the power she felt with the Mark but the price she was paying was too high. She had no want to be special or someone with extraordinary power. Anya just wanted to have some power and control over her own life.

"If you want the Mark back, you can take it," Anya said. "I'm sure you'll find someone else to survive it. I don't want it."

Esther averted her eyes for a moment.

"I would like to know everything you know about the Mark," Esther said instead of answering her question. "We've never had a living and conscious subject before to tell us what it's like. What it and you can actually do."

"If I do? If I help you to the best of my ability with answering your questions, will you take the Mark off me?" Anya asked. "Please."

"I'm sorry," Esther said and there was genuine regret in her face. It reminded Anya of Andrew's face right before he'd forced the Mark on her. "There is no removing the Mark without killing you."

Anya felt like she'd been punched in the stomach.

"What?" Anya whispered.

"As far as we know from our research, removing the Mark kills the host immediately," Esther said. "The only way it is transferred between hosts is when the previous body is dying. We think it is a defence mechanism, a survival instinct. It only wants to move on once the host has nothing left to offer."

Anya felt like she was going to be sick and she stared back at the Mark. It hadn't told her that, perhaps for some specific reason or perhaps because it didn't see any point in it. Knowing this changed nothing, not really. It just cemented the fact that she was stuck with this until she died.

It cemented the fact that she and the Mark was now one and the same, no separation possible. "If we find a way to safely remove it, we could do that to you," Esther said and tried to smile but the sadness in her eyes was overwhelming. "But don't get your hopes up."

Anya didn't have a habit of getting her hopes up anymore, they'd been smashed too many times for that.

Chapter 30

JAMES

The moment they had released James from the cell, given him his cane back and showed him out from the Castle, he hadn't looked back. He didn't want to give them a chance to change their mind even if it would be easy to find him again if they truly wanted to. His head was still hurting slightly and his bad leg felt stiff and heavy. He leaned heavily on his cane as he made his way back towards his home.

He knew that if he looked back at the Castle he might not make it the entire way home, his head was only thinking about one thing. Anya. She was in there somewhere and he had to help her, he had to get her out. James stopped mid stride, his bad leg refusing to move for a moment and he tried to breathe through the pain. He glanced at the grip of his cane and almost let out a scoff.

How was he going to do anything when he couldn't even walk the entire way home from the Castle without stopping? He was no longer a soldier, no longer as strong as he'd been in his youth. Now he was just a wounded, broken old man. He wished he'd had this mindset when he'd been younger, the things he could have done with the knowledge he had today.

But he had been a reckless, selfish boy who couldn't see anything but his own misery which had cost him everything. James forced himself to continue walking, simply one foot in front of the other until he reached his home. One foot in front of the other over and over, no matter how much it hurt. James leaned against his door before he unlocked it and out of pure habit, he glanced behind him and out of the corner of his eyes, he saw two guards coming around the corner he'd come from. They met his gaze and the way they stopped in their tracks was all confirmation he needed, he was being shadowed. It wasn't surprising considering what had happened.

Frankly, he was quite surprised Inara had believed him and that he'd been let go but of course, they had set guards on him to make sure he didn't step out of line. The fact that he wanted to help Anya didn't really matter as he didn't have the first clue on how he would go about doing that, so he had nothing to fear from those guards. As long as they weren't here to kill him and make it look like it was done by some criminal from the east side, he really hoped they wouldn't stoop so low.

The guards of this city didn't do a whole lot to help the less fortunate but surely they wouldn't do something as horrific as killing a civilian? But perhaps this secret was worth the bloodshed.

James smiled gently towards the guards and then went into his house and carefully locked the door behind him. Now they knew he had seen them and knew they were there, perhaps that would make them more careful or simply make them move faster, he wasn't sure. As he entered his house, the marks of the fight were obvious. There were scorch marks on the walls, floor and some of his furniture.

Almost all of the chairs were turned over and all the books that had been on the table were gone. He swallowed hard, had they taken the books? How many of them had survived the fire? He wondered if they had made any connections with the books but as he was free, he guessed he'd been lucky. James didn't have any energy to try and fix the mess. He simply poured himself a glass of water, took some dried beef before he went to bed.

It had been a long night without any sleep and barely any water or food. If he had any plans on helping Anya, he first needed to take care of himself. He might not be as physically mighty as he'd once been but he was a lot more knowledgeable and wiser than in his youth and that could be of almost more use. At least he hoped so. James fell asleep almost the moment his head touched the pillow, his tense and aching body finally getting some rest.

James opened his eyes as he heard the familiar soft noise of feet jumping down from the window in the room upstairs. His heart jumped in his chest. The only person who used that window to enter was Anya. He quickly grabbed his cane and moved towards the stairs. He knew it couldn't be her but what if it was?

What if she had made it out just like he had by some miracle and she'd come home? He heard the footsteps move towards the stairs and when he looked up, the small tinge of hope in his eyes died when he saw Runa stand at the top of the stairs.

Runa looked bad; as ashy as before and he could see how unsteady she was on her otherwise steady feet but there was something alive in her eyes that hadn't been there last time he'd seen her.

"You're out," Runa said with a plain face.

"You look awful," James said, trying to hide his disappointment as he moved away from the stairs and pulled up one of the chairs from the floor to sit on.

Runa walked down the stairs with slow steps. James noticed that at least her bandage on her wound had been changed which was good.

"What are you doing here?" James asked tiredly.

Runa looked around the room, obviously noticing the marks from the fight just as James had.

Runa hesitated before she spoke.

"I didn't want to sleep at my usual place," Runa said and rubbed her neck. It almost looked as if there was a bruise forming there if James looked carefully.

"So you came here?" James asked with a raised eyebrow.

Runa averted her glance. "I don't have anywhere else to go," she muttered low, a hint of shame in her voice.

"What about Mara's place?" James asked.

"If you think I'm getting her involved in this, you're crazy," Runa said. "You're already involved and…"

Runa took a deep breath.

"Forget it," Runa finally said with a sigh. "I came here because I needed a place to sleep and I could check if you got out as well or not."

"You worried about me?" James asked with a slight surprise.

Runa laughed low. "Don't flatter yourself, old man. I wanted to check if you got out so if my wound got infected, I had somewhere to go. You're useful," Runa answered.

James shouldn't have been surprised by her reply but she almost always seemed to be able to surprise him no matter what. In both good and bad ways, though it seemed to be mostly in bad ways. The image of the two guards outside his house came to James' mind and he frowned in worry.

"Did anyone see you?" James asked.

"If you mean the Blue Birds stationed to watch us?" Runa said. "What do you take me for, an amateur? Of course they didn't see me."

"You're not exactly in top form," James said.

"Me in my worst state is still leagues better than two foot patrol guards who don't want to do their job," Runa said.

Runa ran a hand through her thick hair.

"I got my place covered, I told a friend that if one of the Blue Birds comes inside to check for me, that I'm simply sleeping in my room. They'll need a warrant to actually check it and they're not going to do that. They don't get paid enough to go through the trouble of getting a warrant, especially not for a gang place. All I needed to do was slip out the back way and then take the roof way here and climb in Anya's window. Your Blue Birds only check the front doors. They're not good at this."

James was actually a little impressed by Runa and for once it wasn't in a horrifying way.

"So can I sleep here tonight?" Runa asked low. "I'll be gone before dawn."

James sighed slightly.

"Of course," James answered. "You're welcome to come and go as you please."

Runa frowned deeply.

"Why?" Runa asked.

James rubbed his eyes.

"Because I'm going to need your help," James said. "So if I can provide some sanctuary in exchange, that's a good deal."

"Help with what?" Runa said suspiciously.

"To get Anya out of the Castle," James said.

Runa let out a laugh in disbelief.

"You can't be serious," she said. "You too? What's with everyone suddenly thinking it's possible to break into the Castle?"

"You too?" James asked confused. "What are you talking about?"

"Forget it," Runa said. "It's not happening."

"I thought you cared about Anya," James said.

Runa took a quick step forward, her eyes suddenly ablaze with anger.

"Don't," Runa said low, a real threat in her voice. "Just don't."

James stared at her.

"I don't owe her anything," Runa continued, her voice wavering ever so slightly. "And I have nothing to do with any of this. Whatever she got herself involved with is on her. I'm not going to get locked up in The Grove forever for that."

"She didn't do anything," James said, now feeling anger rise inside of him, matching the sudden anger that had erupted from Runa. "And the last thing I remember is that you said you'd follow her out of this city, so she could explain it all. Was that just a lie?"

"Things changed," Runa hissed. "I would have…I would have followed her but Gods, you saw what she did!"

A heavy silence fell over the room. The only thing that could be heard was their slightly heavy breathing from their shouting match.

"I did," James said. "Which is why I know she needs help."

"She conjured fire from nothing!" Runa said. "What she did isn't normal! And we got arrested for simply being in the same room as her! We could have been thrown into The Grove to rot because of her!"

James said nothing; he could hear the true message behind her words. *She conjured fire and she never told me about any of it.* Runa was hurt and even if James could understand that, he didn't have the time or patience to deal with that right now. She wasn't a child anymore and he wasn't her parent or protector. He had enough to worry about with Anya, he couldn't add Runa's hurt feelings to the list.

"Listen to me. It is impossible to break into the Castle, so don't even entertain the idea," Runa said. "We just have to…to keep going with our lives."

James stared at Runa in disbelief, his mouth hanging slightly open in surprise.

"Now I truly see why Anya left you," James finally said.

"What?" Runa said low and there was a hint of fear in her voice.

"You do nothing that doesn't profit yourself. You have no heart," James said.

Runa took a step back, her face was neutral. The only crack in her facade was her lip trembling once before she clenched her jaw and straightened her back but it was too late, James had seen right through her.

"At least I'll survive," Runa said coldly.

"But you'll never live," James said, his words laced with venom.

James thought he might have seen the first signs of tears in Runa's eyes but she quickly turned around and without saying another word, she went back up the stairs to Anya's room and slammed the door shut behind her.

Chapter 31

INARA

That night, Inara slept better than she had in years. The knowledge that James, Runa and Mara had been released helped to settle her somewhat guilty conscience but she couldn't stop thinking about Anya. She needed to see her, to see how she was treated and what they were going to do with her, only then would she know any amount of peace. It was a strange war going on in her head because Anya had the Mark.

The thing they'd been looking for which meant she was involved in the theft in some way and she had conjured fire from nothing and almost burnt them alive. Those were facts, yet it was impossible for Inara to get their last conversation out of her head. Anya could have easily killed her and none of this would have happened yet she hadn't. Inara guessed she felt some sort of shame in that.

Anya had spared her but Inara had not done her the same courtesy, because it was true as Anya had said, Inara could have just let her go. Inara could have let her go, get out of this city but it simply wasn't in her nature. She wasn't one to pass problems onto someone else, not if she could do something about it. Yet there was a part of Inara that believed Anya was innocent and had been dragged into something a lot bigger than herself, like all of them at this point.

That Mark, all of this because of a Mark on a left hand that apparently could grant a person the ability to conjure fire, because Inara had a hard time believing Anya had been able to do that before. Inara knew there was something with the Mark. It had been obvious since the first time she'd shaken Anya's hand, it was the source of all this commotion. It was dangerous.

Inara opened her eyes and stared into the ceiling of the small, closet-like room she'd been staying in. She took a deep breath before she rose, got dressed and exited her room. There was still a lot to do. As Inara opened her door, she was met with Fatima's smiling face.

"Good morning," Fatima said cheerfully.

Inara was silent for a moment, slightly shocked at seeing her outside her door and the exact moment she had exited.

"Good morning, Fatima," Inara replied. "What are you doing here?"

Fatima's face lit up when Inara said her name, had she thought she'd forgotten her already? Or was Fatima simply relieved she didn't have to introduce herself again? Inara wasn't sure. "I'm here to wake you up and get some breakfast with you, then take you to the War Counsellor," Fatima said.

"I thought you worked down by The Grove. Or at least the holding cells," Inara said slowly.

"I work all over the Castle," Fatima answered. "Wherever I'm needed is where I am. The War Counsellor knew you'd met me when you talked to the suspects yesterday so he thought a familiar face to walk you around would be nice."

"You work for him?" Inara asked.

"All guards do in some capacity," Fatima said and started to walk. Inara followed.

"I thought you didn't want to get involved in all of this," Inara said.

Fatima's smile faltered slightly and she lowered her head, then she looked back up, her smile restored.

"Wherever I'm needed is where I am," Fatima repeated. "We are all servants for the Crown."

"I'm sorry if I got you invol…" Inara started.

"Don't be ridiculous," Fatima said with a laugh. "We're all involved to some degree. Sure I wanted to try and stay on the outskirts of it but we don't always get what we want now do we?"

Inara didn't answer her.

"Now I hope you're hungry. One of the perks of working in the Castle is the food," Fatima said with a wink. "A word of advice, sneak some of the bread with the seeds on top in your uniform for later, it's a fantastic snack for a slow day."

Inara found herself smiling gently back at Fatima. It then disappeared as quickly as it had appeared. Fatima had been commanded by the War Counsellor to accompany Inara, she wasn't here because she wanted to be her friend or because she liked her. Nonetheless, Fatima was a breath of fresh air in this otherwise quite serious situation Inara had found herself in.

***

The breakfast passed in a flash. Inara couldn't help but be a little overwhelmed at the whole situation. She was mostly used to eating and being alone but here, there were hundreds of people. The breakfast room for the Castle guards was filled with talking, laughing people, eating to their hearts' content and Fatima hadn't been lying, the food was like nothing Inara had ever had.

A literal buffet to choose from, anything your heart desired could apparently be requested and be done by actual chefs in place. Inara had noticed Fatima talking to her and laughing and she just tried to nod along and smile whenever it seemed appropriate, but it was like her thoughts were elsewhere. Before she even knew it, she and Fatima stood outside the War Room.

"Inara?" Fatima said gently.

Finally, Inara snapped out of whatever haze she'd been in and looked at Fatima questioningly. "If you ever need anything, don't be afraid to ask," Fatima said with a small smile. "You're good, try and keep it that way, okay?"

"What do you mean?" Inara said with a frown.

Fatima's eyes flashed further down the hallway before returning to Inara.

"Nothing," she said. "Just that I'm here if you need a friend. It's good to have friends." With that, Fatima gave a little nod and then quickly walked down the hallway she'd been glancing down earlier. Inara couldn't help but follow her with her gaze at least for a moment, she wondered what was down there?

Inara knocked on the War Room door and it quickly opened, almost like the person on the other side had been listening and waiting patiently on the opposite side. Malik smiled pleasantly at her and made a gesture for her to enter. The room looked practically identical to how it had done the day before and Inara stopped at the same spot she'd stood yesterday. "How have you slept?" Malik asked. "You look better than yesterday."

Inara nodded. "The breakfast helped as well," she said.

Malik looked pleased by that answer.

"I hope Ms Thorne was good company," Malik said.

Ms Thorne. He had to be referring to Fatima. Inara only nodded as an answer.

"You're not much of a talker, are you?" Malik said with a small laugh.

"To be honest, this is all a little overwhelming and I tend to talk less and observe more in those situations," Inara said.

"I like the honesty! And that is a good trait!" Malik said. "I, on the other hand, talk far too much I've been told."

He laughed again.

"Is there anything I can help with to make this a little less overwhelming?" Malik asked.

Inara was silent for a moment.

"If I knew what I was supposed to do here, that would help," Inara said slowly.

Malik clapped his hands together.

"Of course!" Malik said. "That's very rude of me."

"I meant no…" Inara started but Malik just waved it off.

"I'll quickly show you around today and get you accustomed to the situation. It's not often we have someone climb from foot patrol guard to being in the War Counsellor's own guard force. Things will be quite different here," Malik said with a hint of seriousness. "Are you ready for that?"

"Yes," Inara answered quickly.

"Good," Malik said. "As you have witnessed what the girl with the Mark can do and brought her in, you will work closely with that project. Most people in the Castle know a little about it but do not be mistaken, it is extremely confidential and leaks or gossip of this will not be tolerated."

Inara could almost feel her heart jump in her chest. She'd be working closely with Anya which meant she could check on her, make sure she was fine and being treated okay. Inara could make sure she hadn't made a mistake.

"You will also be presented to the Royal family later today," Malik continued slowly.

That sentence sent a chill down Inara's spine.

"Why?" Inara asked low.

Malik smiled but the warmth wasn't there as it had been before.

"The King is the one who is in charge of this project, it's his golden idea and a lot of his focus is on it. So he wants to meet the person who brought the mMrk back to its rightful place," Malik said. "Don't be worried, it's an honour."

"It is an honour," Inara said. "I'm just not sure I deserve it."

The fact was that Inara didn't want to meet the Royal family, not right now. Even though she had always dreamt of an audience with the King to speak about her thoughts for reforms of the east side, this was not how she'd imagined it happening. She wasn't here to speak about the east side, she was here because she'd captured Anya. She had heard little about them but what she'd heard wasn't the most flattering talk. Most people talked about them as lazy rulers, more worried about throwing extravagant balls and parties and keeping the Castle in pristine condition, and Inara hadn't exactly seen a lot to go against those rumours. The fact that the King was so focused on this Mark instead of trying to make this city a better place to live was infuriating to Inara.

That Mark was wrong. It wasn't anything of this natural world and yet he placed it above the living and breathing people struggling in the city he was supposed to keep safe. The more Inara learnt of the King, the more she realized that she had been naïve in thinking that he would listen to her about her ideas.

"Don't be shy, of course you deserve it," Malik said. "And it might be good for you to meet them now as you'll have to attend the princess' 20th birthday party in three days."

"What?" Inara said confused.

Malik placed a gentle hand on her shoulder.

"This is a lot. Let's start with one thing and we'll get to the rest as we go along, okay?" Malik said.

Inara slowly nodded but now more than ever she felt like she was in over her head. This had all gone too fast. She didn't feel like she belonged here and she felt like a traitor with the doubts she had in her mind. Inara forced herself to take a deep breath. One thing at a time was how she was going to do this just as he'd said.

Chapter 32

RUNA

The moment Runa had entered Anya's room, she'd basically thrown herself into the bed but as her eyes scanned the room, they stopped on something peculiar on the wall. Runa placed her feet on the cold floor and with slow steps walked over to a piece of the wall, a piece that had what looked like a handprint seared into it. With a featherlight touch, Runa ran her fingers over the scorch mark in the form of a hand. Something uneasy filled her the moment she touched it and she quickly withdrew her hand.

It almost felt warm to the touch.

Runa fell asleep and when she woke, she kept her promise and was out the window of James' house before the sun rose in the distance. She wasn't in a good mood after their talk yesterday and didn't want to see his face. Though, after finally having a good night's sleep, Runa felt some of her strength return to her. She hated feeling weak, sluggish and not up to her usual standard.

Being sloppy and weak got you killed, which had been almost proven by her little altercation with Mr Parker. When Runa had walked up to her room at the Keg, she'd met Tamara who'd calmly told her that two Blue Birds were outside watching the place. It was obvious they were here for her, of course they wouldn't just let her go unwatched after what had happened. At that moment, Runa had decided that she wasn't going to sleep at the Keg that night, not after everything.

Sure her door had a lock, as did every door but Mr Parker had the master key and could enter whenever he wished. Runa knew she was paranoid but that trait had saved her life more than once. Besides she wanted to see if they'd released James as well. Not because she was worried but because he could be useful, when he wasn't being an asshole.

Runa knew she had to be back at the Keg before the Blue Birds outside noticed and she wanted to check in with everything again. Hopefully Mr Parker had calmed down and some agreement could be reached, even though she had her doubts. Runa took the roof way over to the Keg and as she felt the wind blow in her hair. She could almost hear Anya's steps beside her as they made their way through the city.

It had been Anya who had taught Runa how to properly make her way across the roofs, which gaps were too far to jump and which ways were the fastest. It had been another time, it almost felt like another lifetime at this point.

Runa climbed inside her window of the Keg, which she'd left just the tiniest bit open for easy access later. Luckily, her room was on towards the backside of the bar, so the Blue Birds had no chance of seeing her coming or going. Her room looked untouched but then again, there wasn't much to touch. As she grabbed the handle of the door, she quickly realised it wasn't locked.

She was sure she had locked it before she left the night before, it was by pure instinct at this point. Runa felt a chill go down her spine as she opened her door. The corridor was empty and it was unusually quiet. It was often quieter up on the second floor but you could always hear some of the talk and songs from downstairs but now, there was nothing. It was like everyone had just disappeared. Runa hunched slightly and walked with slow, deliberate and almost silent steps as she made her way down the stairs.

The first thing she noticed was that there were indeed no customers in the bar and she knew that the Keg was never properly closed. The second thing she noticed were the five bodies hanging from the roof. Runa stopped in her tracks, almost frozen in place because she couldn't entirely make sense of what she was seeing.

It was Trent and the other four people who had come to her help against Mr Parker yesterday, just hanging from hooks in the ceiling. Their throats were slashed open and blood covered their clothes, they'd been killed and then hung up after in some morbid show. Runa couldn't tear her eyes from Trent's lifeless and cloudy eyes, staring into nothing. They were empty and Runa felt like she was about to fall into the darkness when she heard a movement to her side that snapped her out of it.

Runa saw Mr Parker sat in a chair, his legs crossed and a glass of whiskey in his hands. All around him were members of the Silver Swans. Runa thought she might throw up and she urged her legs to move, to force her mouth to speak but she was frozen.

"Runa!" Mr Parker said, glee in his voice. "Everyone, welcome her back please."

There was a murmur going through the group but that was it. Mr Parker rose from his seat and walked up to the five hanging bodies. With a nonchalant hand, he pushed on Trent's body and it slowly swung forwards and backwards as he took another sip of his drink.

"You weren't here last night. You always were a smart one," Mr Parker said. "But you've reached the end of the line now."

"What have you done?" Runa finally managed to speak.

"Me?" Mr Parker said. "I've simply culled the unloyal from the herd. Loyalty is the most important thing after all."

Runa's eyes shot back to the five bodies before going back to him.

"The rule…we don't k…" Runa started.

"We don't kill our own?" Mr Parker said. "They stopped being our own the moment they betrayed me."

"They stood up against you!" Runa almost screamed. "Against your insanity!"

Mr Parker's gaze darkened and Runa saw his grip of the glass tighten slightly. "These people," Mr Parker said and raised his arms to show the people behind him. "Are loyal to me. They appreciate what I give them. Unlike you."

Mr Parker sighed but it was just for show, there was no emotion in it.

"You really had such potential. Pretty, ruthless and loyal," Mr Parker said. "That loyalty just never belonged to me. So here we are."

"You're going to kill me?" Runa asked. Her eyes shifting from all the Silver Swans members and mentally going through every place on her body she had a knife.

Mr Parker downed the last part of his drink and threw it straight into a wall, it broke in a million little pieces.

"You know too much," Mr Parker said. "All our operations, all our secret hideouts. You could sell that to any competing gang in the city for a pretty penny."

Mr Parker laughed slightly.

"But honestly, yes I mostly just want to kill you because you've done nothing but go against me. I don't need people who think for themselves, I just need obedient soldiers. And there are a thousand more of you out there in the city, an overabundance of people desperate to prove themselves and make some money. People desperate to survive, desperate enough to do anything I tell them."

A short pause.

"So yes, I am going to kill you," Mr Parker said and then turned to the people behind him.

"Apprehend her, do whatever you want, just keep her alive. I want her to myself before she dies."

Runa quickly unsheathed two of her knives before any of the Silver Swans had moved. She could see remorse and doubt in some of them, like Irena and Tamara who barely moved from their spots in the back. Others looked like it was their birthday and they'd just received the best gift ever imaginable.

Three of them rushed towards her but Runa easily sidestepped all three of them, while cutting open the side of one of them. There were at least fifteen of them and only one of her, and even if five people refused to attack her outright, she was still outnumbered. This wasn't a fight she could win, this was a fight she had to run from if she wanted to live.

The door to the outside was immediately blocked by two people and a few of them had moved so they were in her path for the stairs, she had to choose one of the ways. If she went for the doors perhaps the Blue Birds were still outside and if she was really lucky, that might just buy her enough time to save her life, even if they arrested her. The Grove or whatever place they would put her in would be preferable to death; prisons you could get out of but death was permanent.

Runa ducked beneath a sword being swung at her and she stepped slightly to the right, trying to go for the front door and hoping she could get past the two men standing there. Then it was like the world stopped moving for a moment. Runa was off her feet as a blast filled the room and pieces of wood went flying. Runa landed on the ground, her ears ringing and the air was filled with smoke and it took her a few seconds to understand what she was hearing. It was screaming.

Coughing, Runa slowly got up and looked around, the Keg had taken a big blow and the entire front door was gone. She could see members of the Silver Swans on the floor, a lot of them bleeding from their faces from cuts from the wood pieces. Then amidst the smoke, she saw other people running into the Keg and ruthlessly attacking anyone they noticed. Runa rolled behind one of the tables that had been turned in the blast to hide.

It was hard to see what was happening, it was impossible to know who was a Silver Swan and who was an intruder in the smoke and chaos. The things she did see was blood being splattered on the ground and people falling to the floor and then not moving. Screams of pain and anger were all that could be heard and part of Runa was surprised no Blue Birds had come, especially if the two outside were still stationed there.

Though the chance of them being either dead or bribed to go somewhere else was high and the chance of anyone coming to their rescue was incredibly low. The funny thing was that whatever gang had attacked had probably saved her and Runa had a good guess it was the Rusty Coffins. They had been trying to get into their territory for weeks now.

The door out was now clear as everyone had entered and the fight was towards the back of the bar, but out of the corner of her eyes, she saw movement. It was Mr Parker; the first person she'd really seen this entire time and he was fleeing up the stairs.

Without thinking, Runa was on her feet and moving towards the stairs, with only a singular purpose in her mind. No one paid her any real attention as she weaved through the people fighting, they were too busy trying to stay alive and she was far quicker than Mr Parker. It was obvious that he was out of breath and he had somehow managed to get up the stairs without being followed, except by Runa.

He must have thought himself somewhat safe halfway up the stairs because he took a second to breathe. He wasn't a fighter and it was really showing right now. It didn't take much to slip past him and then suddenly, Runa was blocking the way up to safety. His face lost all colour, his pristine clothes were dusty and had rips, he was even bleeding from a cut on the face. It was the first time she'd ever seen him bleed.

"Runa," he almost stammered and gave a quick glance behind himself, no one else was paying attention to them, yet.

Runa raised her hand and pointed her knife at him.

"Seems like you've reached the end of the line, old man," Runa said with a smirk.

"Just step aside, we can both make it out of here!" Mr Parker said and took a single step closer to her.

Without moving much, Runa's blade was pressed against his throat. He wasn't even armed, the stupid bastard. He'd gotten everything handed to him on a silver platter so why would he need to arm himself? He had his soldiers for that.

"I almost killed the person I loved for you," Runa said through gritted teeth. "I can't believe I ever thought you were worth it."

Mr Parker swallowed hard and she could see sweat on his brow.

"Beg," Runa said.

"What?" Mr Parker said.

"I said, beg," Runa said and pushed her blade a little harder into his throat. "If you want to live, that's it."

"Please. Please, Runa," he begged. It hadn't even taken him a second to think it through. Runa could finally see his true self. Not the calm, sharing boss and not the angry, aggressive man but the pathetic creature he really was.

"We can make it out of here. We can make a plan! We can..." Mr Parker rambled.

"No," Runa said shortly.

Mr Parker's eyes widened in fear.

"You don't deserve to make it out of here," Runa said.

"You're going to kill me?" He asked with a shiver.

Runa moved her head closer, so she could whisper and he would still hear her perfectly. "You're not worth the effort I'd have to do to clean your blood off these knives," Runa said and leaned back.

"R..." Mr Parker started.

"He's here! Mr Parker is right here!" Runa suddenly yelled down the stairs where the fighting was still going.

Mr Parker looked like he was going to pass out and looked behind him, and it had barely been a couple of seconds but two people were at the bottom of the stairs, making their way towards them. Runa knew that the Rusty Coffins wanted Mr Parker. If they got rid of him, they got rid of the gang and would gain all their turf and anything in the Keg. Runa wouldn't have Mr Parker's blood on her hands, but she truly would not let him leave either.

Mr Parker looked back at Runa and there was a desperation in his eyes, and he moved to try and force his way past her up the stairs. Runa raised her leg and slammed it right into his chest, knocking the breath out of him and causing him to tumble backwards, right into the arms of the people that wanted him dead.

Runa stayed long enough to see the first sword go into Mr Parker's stomach before she quickly ran back to her room and climbed out of her window.

Runa took a quick glance back at the Keg, the place that had been where she'd stayed for the past five years. She hoped some of the better people of the Silver Swans made it out, like Irena, Tamara or Egil. Though when she thought of it, she hadn't seen Egil there at all. Perhaps they were somewhere else and safe already.

Runa had lost places she'd lived plenty of times, but she'd only lost her home once, and she was going to do whatever it took to bring Anya back to her.

Chapter 33

INARA

Malik spent a good portion of the afternoon showing Inara around the Castle, pointing out the most important places in his opinion and where she could ask for help, take a shower or train if she felt the need. Inara was incredibly appreciative but something felt off, perhaps it was the fact that the War Counsellor himself was showing her around when he had to have a lot of other things to do. He was in charge of every guard in the city after all but she said nothing about it.

Perhaps this was his way of keeping an eye on her for the first couple of days, to check how she reacted, how she adapted and if she was trustworthy. Inara could find Malik staring at her sometimes, like he was reading her every move and facial expression but the moment she caught him, he'd simply smile and look away.

Inara had a terrible memory when it came to places and this place was still an absolute mystery to her, everything looked the same everywhere. It was like the Castle was made to keep intruders confused and stuck until they could be apprehended by the people who knew this place like the back of their hands. Right now and for the last few days, Inara had felt like that intruder, just waiting to be caught.

The one place Malik did not show her was where Anya was kept and even though Inara wanted to ask about it, she knew patience here was the best way to go forward. She couldn't seem too eager, that would cause suspicion. Though Inara wasn't sure why she felt like this, it wasn't like she was planning on breaking Anya out of here or doing anything against them, she simply wanted to see her and make sure she was okay.

Maybe even make sure she was being treated kindly if she had any say in it, which she seemed to have got some all of a sudden. Finally, they stopped in front of another large ornamental door covered in gold and purple and with the sigil of the Royal family painted on it. Malik turned to Inara, his hands behind his back.

"It's time," he simply said.

Inara frowned slightly, feeling her throat get dry.

"The Royal family is beyond this door, they are expecting you. We are standing in front of the main Throne Room of the Castle," Malik said. "Remember it."

Inara glanced at the door and at a second look, this door was slightly different from the others. The painting of the sigil was larger and more detail oriented than the other she'd seen and this was a double door that reached up to the roof. It was a grand entrance to be sure. Malik must have seen the slight panic on her face because he spoke again.

"How old are you?" He asked with a gentle smile.

"What?" Inara said, slightly surprised by the sudden and seemingly random question.

"How old are you? You can't be very old from the look of you," Malik said.

"I'm 20," Inara said low. She was barely out of her teenage years and often tried to hold herself to a higher standard, pretending to look and act older than she really was. With age came some amount of respect and people usually lost it the moment she said she was 20. It was like people couldn't possibly fathom a young person being responsible and goal-oriented.

"Well, then you are in the same age range as the Princess, she turns 20 soon as I told you," Malik said. "She doesn't have a lot of people her age around the Castle, I'm sure she would appreciate some company."

Inara simply stared at Malik for a short moment.

"She's the princess," Inara said shortly, not really knowing what else to say.

"Yes, but she is also a young girl without a lot of friends," Malik said.

Malik glanced around the place they were standing and it hit Inara how spacious and lonely these corridors really were. So impersonal and so empty of life.

"It can get quite lonely here," Malik said. "For all of us. So it's good to have friends and people you trust. Otherwise, it could go days without you speaking to someone properly and that isn't good for anyone."

Inara simply nodded but she couldn't quite take in what he'd said entirely, it was similar to what Fatima had said. It's good to have friends. Inara had grown up without friends and had always been alone and she'd turned out fine, she didn't need others in the way other people seemed to need someone. Inara was happy to be alone.

"Do you know their names?" Malik asked.

"Of course. It's King Widald, the Fourth, his Queen, Pritha, and their one surviving child, the princess, Vesper," Inara said, her voice almost sounding like she was reading from a book, which wasn't too far from the truth. Her father had made sure she knew the history of this city and its rulers, it had been important for him. He'd always said that without knowledge she'd get nowhere, no matter how hard she worked.

Malik looked slightly impressed.

"I wouldn't say 'one surviving child' in anyone else's presence," Malik said with a wink. "It might upset them."

Inara nodded rapidly. Of course that was a sensitive subject, she'd have to keep that in mind for future conversations.

"Now get in with you," Malik said and nodded towards the door.

"You're not coming?" Inara asked, trying to sound calm.

"I can't hold your hand through all of this," Malik said, the same gentle smile playing on his lips as always. "You'll do fine, don't worry. Come find me once you're done."

Inara turned to the door and unsurely pulled up her hand to knock on it, then turned to Malik for confirmation and he simply nodded. Inara knocked, feeling the thick and hard wood against her knuckles. Her knocks were barely audible and sounded pathetic in this large place but the door immediately started to open. Inara gave Malik one last glance but he'd already turned his back on her and was walking down the corridor.

Inara was going into the dragon's nest head first.

Inara walked inside and immediately heard the doors behind her close but she kept her head looking forward. She focused solely on keeping her face neutral and from hopefully keeping her body from shaking. She was stepping on a long deep purple carpet, leading straight to the three thrones at the end of the room. The rest of the large room was quite empty, leaving large holes of nothing between pillars and the few occasional flowers.

The thrones were placed on different heights, the King's was the highest, closest to the ceiling and probably closest to the Gods in their thoughts. To his right and slightly below him, sat his Queen and to his left, even further down, sat his princess. They all loomed over her nonetheless, all looking down on her. It seemed that there was no one else in the room except the four of them, which both reassured Inara but also made her more afraid.

The King was an older man, clean shaven and with dirty blond hair. He had small beady eyes and thin lips. The Queen looked considerably more approachable and she looked to be approximately the same age as her husband. She wore a thin, almost see-through scarf lazily wrapped around her head, slightly showing her deep black hair beneath it. Her light brown skin was covered in reddish tattoos in intricate patterns. They seemed to cover most parts of her body but most prominent were the thin lines and curves decorating the sides of her face.

The princess was a fat, young girl with large brown eyes and dark blond hair with a tinge of reddish hue to it. She seemed to take after more from her mother, her skin a healthy light tan and a kind face.

Inara stopped at an appropriate distance from them and immediately bowed deeply. Her father had taught her manners, now was the time to really test them.

"So you're the one who caught the girl?" The King spoke, his voice filled with an unpleasant raspiness.

Inara nodded.

"My name is Inara Justifa," she simply said.

"Come closer, let's have a proper look at you, girl," the King spoke again.

Feeling her heart beat hard in her chest, Inara slowly moved closer, making sure to keep her eyes towards the floor.

"Please look at us, child," the Queen spoke in a soft voice.

Inara reluctantly raised her head and looked at them, now a lot closer than before. The Queen and princess were smiling lightly but the King had a neutral look on his face.

"You don't look like much, how did you find her?" The King asked.

"Widald! Don't be rude, she has done us a great favour," the Queen spoke.

The King huffed in response.

"Call it intuition or luck I suppose," Inara said and tried to smile but failed miserably to make it look natural.

"You're very pretty for a guard," the Queen said with a pleasant tone.

Inara frowned slightly but quickly relaxed her face. She wasn't sure what the Queen had meant by that. Had it been a compliment on her features or an insult to her competence as a guard?

"How are you finding life here then?" The King asked.

"Good," Inara quickly answered. "It's fantastic. I appreciate it greatl…"

"Skip the compliments," the King said, interrupting her. "I've heard them all at this point."

Inara just stared at him for a short moment.

"It's…confusing and slightly overwhelming," Inara said honestly. "But I am very appreciative of the position I've been given and I will do everything in my power to do my best for this city."

"You seem like an honest and hardworking woman," the Queen said. "From what I've heard and from what I can see in front of me."

"Looks can be deceiving," the King said.

"You said that the day before you married me as well," the Queen said with a teasing tone and Inara thought she could almost see a smile cracking on the King's face.

The King turned his head towards the princess, who hadn't taken her gaze off Inara this entire time.

"Vesper, leave us," the King said.

"You said I'd get to see her!" Vesper protested.

"You've seen her," the King retorted. "Now we have business to discuss that you don't have to worry about right now."

"I'm your heir! I need to know…" Vesper started.

"You need to do as you're told," the King snapped. "Until you are the ruler, you are beneath me and shall do as I say, understood?"

Vesper turned her gaze towards the floor, slowly nodded and then got up from her seat and started to walk out of the room. As the princess passed Inara, she had to resist the urge to take a few steps aside to give her extra room, even though there was more than enough room to pass. The doors closed behind the princess.

"You're being too hard on her," the Queen said, her gaze had followed her daughter the entire time. The King didn't answer her, simply stared at Inara.

"Tell me what you saw," the King said.

Inara could have asked what he wanted to know but she knew exactly what he wanted.

"The girl, she conjured flame out of nothing and shot it in an arch towards us," Inara said. "We were lucky the fire wasn't as intense as it could have been."

Inara paused for a moment, thinking back at the exact moment she'd seen the flames coming towards her.

"For a moment, I thought the flames were going to cut us down in half," Inara almost muttered. "Or consume us all."

The King leaned forward, showing any sort of emotion on his face for the first time. Excitement.

"The flames went out the moment she fell unconscious," Inara continued. "That was all."

The King and Queen exchanged glances that Inara couldn't interpret.

"Anything else?" The King asked.

Inara hesitated for a moment.

"She was warm to the touch, almost unbearably so and…" Inara said. "And the Mark on her hand seemed to glow for a short moment after she'd fallen unconscious."

"Incredible," the Queen whispered. The only reason Inara heard it was because it was completely silent in the room.

"Indeed," the King said. "I hope Malik has prepared you for what is to come."

Inara nodded but wasn't entirely sure if he really had, but she was sure he was going to. "Good," the King said. "We are going to need all the manpower we can gather with trustworthy people to keep searching." Inara frowned slightly.

"Searching?" She asked low.

"For the other Marks of course," the King said, a small and unpleasant smile playing on his lips.

Chapter 34

JAMES

The sound of an explosion in the distance woke James from his slumber, his heart racing and flashes of memories he'd rather forget. It hadn't been a loud bang but the morning was silent and James had become sensitive to sudden loud noises like that from his youth. It was an explosion and deathly silence that followed and he almost thought for a moment that he might have imagined it.

James was tired. He hadn't been able to fall asleep for many hours after his and Runa's talk but he wasn't just bodily tired, it felt like his soul was exhausted as well. Perhaps he had been a little too harsh on Runa. After all, she knew better than him how to break into places, break people out of places and anything regarding thievery. He really couldn't fathom that Runa wouldn't want to rescue Anya unless it was entirely futile; he saw how her eyes glimmered each time Runa said her name.

How Anya's name almost sounded sacred when spoken by Runa. James was a proud man, but nothing compared to how he had been in his youth and he now knew the strength in being able to apologise and recognise one's own faults. If he hadn't been so pushy and harsh on Runa, maybe they could have talked properly and without all that venom.

After all, it was obvious that they wanted the same thing, Anya to come home and be safe.

James made his way up the stairs, leaning heavily on his cane and slowly knocked on the door.

When no answer came, he opened it and found it empty and as if no one had been there at all. James smiled vaguely; after all, Runa had said she'd be gone before sunrise but still. It had been nice to hear her very careful and silent steps above him. They were almost undetectable but he'd lived with Anya for so long, he could hear them anyway. Besides, Runa wasn't as stealthy as Anya, almost but not quite.

James closed the door and went back downstairs and sat by his table. He glanced around his home. It suddenly looked so empty and he felt a surge of loneliness almost overwhelm him. James closed his eyes and forced himself to take deep breaths.

James wanted to help Anya more than anything else. He owed it to her even if she didn't realise it. But he was just a doctor who flinched at loud noises and would get nauseous when being violent. He was also getting old and his bad leg made him slow and a potential liability. He felt helpless and like any control he had managed to gather over the years had slipped through his hands in a matter of seconds.

The sound of soft feet landing on the floor above him was suddenly heard, and James frowned and looked towards the stairs leading up. If he wasn't mistaken, it had to be Runa again but he also couldn't really imagine her showing up again so soon after their little talk. The face that greeted him coming down the stairs was indeed Runa, but she was dirty and had multiple cuts on her face and pieces of her clothes had rips in them. Otherwise, she looked relatively unharmed.

James was stunned. He didn't know what to say but luckily Runa ended the silence.

"What are you looking at?" Runa said and sat down in a chair, obviously exhausted.

"What happened to you?" James asked.

Runa rubbed her neck.

"Nothing much. Just my gang killed five of our own, then tried to kill me and then another gang attacked and coincidentally saved my life," Runa said in a monotone voice.

James stared at her, trying to take in what she'd just said.

"So what's the plan, old man?" Runa said.

"What?" James said, blinking towards her.

Runa rolled her eyes and coughed slightly.

"You wanted to break Anya out of the Castle. What's the plan?" Runa said and wiped the sweat from her forehead but noticed her hand coming back tinged with red. "Also, can I get something to wipe my face with?"

James quickly handed her a handkerchief and she wiped away the blood and dirt from her face.

There was a renewed fire lit in Runa's eyes but her body was as relaxed as ever.

"What changed?" James asked with a slight frown.

James was almost certain it had to do with what had happened with her gang but still, he couldn't help but to ask.

"Does it matter?" Runa said. "Breaking into the Castle is a suicide mission and I have nothing left to lose, so why not."

James just stared at her. She noticed and sighed heavily.

"I guess I realised that some dreams are worth pursuing," Runa said low and looked away from James. "Even if they seem impossible."

That James could understand. Some things truly were worth pursuing no matter the consequences. Nothing good, nothing truly amazing came from standing on the side-line, doing nothing. What was the point in living if they didn't try and make it worth every second?

James poured two glasses of water and put one in front of Runa before he sat down beside her.

Runa downed the water in a matter of seconds.

"Thank you," James said sincerely.

Runa scoffed.

"Don't get it twisted. I'm not doing this for you, I still hate your guts," Runa said.

"But you love Anya," James said.

Runa looked away with a frown on her face.

"I don't know. I only know one thing," Runa said seriously.

"What's that?" James asked.

Runa looked back and straight into his eyes.

"That Anya was there for me when no one else was, without her I would have died on the street," Runa said and leaned back in her chair. "And even though she left me, I can't leave her."

Runa sighed deeply.

"If you never see her again, would you regret not telling her?" Runa asked.

"I'm planning on seeing her again," James answered quickly.

Runa took a deep breath and clenched her jaw.

"But if you don't. Would all of this have been worth it? Or would it just be another failure as a father on your part?" Runa said, her voice was concerningly empty.

James quickly averted his gaze and he felt sick to his stomach, and he truly didn't have an answer to Runa's question.

"I know all about shitty dads," Runa continued. "And believe me when I say this."

Runa took a pause and James glanced over at her.

"She'll hate you forever but at least she'll know," Runa said. "You could at least give her that after everything you've put her through."

"I've only tried to keep her sa…" James started, his voice shaking.

"Yeah, but you failed, didn't you? Who cares about 'tried' or 'good intentions'? Anya has suffered so much because you weren't here. Because you couldn't be a good father," Runa said.

"You don't know what you're talking about, you know such a little piece of this story," James said, trying to keep the anger from rising inside of him.

"I don't need to know more," Runa simply said. "When you've met one shitty dad, you've met them all."

"I'm sorry your father wasn't good to you," James said. "But we're not all the same."

"Oh really?" Runa said with scoff. "Yet here we are."

"I wanted to be a good father to her. Things…just became complicated," James said low.

"That's what they all say," Runa said.

"Her mother took her and left. I didn't leave them," James said, honesty flooding his voice. "I searched for years across Taurin and my home country, I never stopped searching. Until I found her here and I've been trying to be anything she's needed ever since."

"She needed her father," Runa said. "Not a random dude with suspicious intentions."

Silence flooded the room.

"If we get her out, if you don't tell her, I will," Runa said, meeting James' eyes. "I don't care about you and your guilty conscience, I just care about Anya. That's the deal if you want my help in trying to get her out."

James closed his eyes to keep the room from spinning. How had it all come to this? All because he'd once been careless with the few pictures he had of his wife and Anya as a child and the letters they'd exchanged before they left him. All because Runa managed to put two and two together because James couldn't help but do anything for Anya. Runa had seen his eyes, she had seen the truth in them because of the pictures and letters. It didn't matter than Runa couldn't actually read the letters, she was far from stupid.

He had always planned on telling Anya, of course he had, but days had turned to weeks and then to months and finally, into years. Anya had looked at him with such gratitude and trust, he knew all of that would disappear if he told her the truth and he couldn't bear it. He'd lost her as a small child and now he'd been reunited with her; perhaps it was for the best to just start anew?

Pretend his past life had never happened and repent by doing anything and everything for his daughter? Perhaps it could have worked, in another life. But here they were and nothing was simple.

"Do you ever think back?" Runa suddenly said, a tinge of sadness in her voice. "Do you ever wish you could go back to happier days?"

"Every waking moment," James said without hesitation. "But I've realised that the past is beyond our control and all we can do is look to the future. Though I can't help but glance back and wish with all my might that I could have made different choices and wonder how my life would have been then. Those kinds of thoughts wounds you in a way no weapon ever could."

Runa turned her face away from James and wiped her face again with the handkerchief James had given her. He was pretty sure she wasn't wiping away dirt or blood this time.

"I agree," James finally said.

Runa turned back towards him.

"If we get her out, I will tell her," James said and swallowed hard.

Runa simply nodded in response.

Chapter 35

INARA

Inara left the Throne Room and took a deep breath, it felt like she'd been holding it ever since she'd entered. Though she returned to her more stoic poise once she saw that the princess was standing just a few feet away from her, clearly staring right at her. Inara tried to smile and the princess' face lit up.

"It's nice to meet you, Inara," the princess said and held out a hand for Inara to shake.

For a second, Inara just stared. She didn't know if this was some sort of test, this was something her father had not prepared her for. It seemed wrong to be so casual with royalty, like they were equals. Finally, Inara decided and slowly took the princess' hand. She smiled and her skin was smooth and soft, hands that had never worked a day in their lives.

"It's nice to meet you too, princess," Inara said courteously.

"Please, call me Vesper," she said and they let go of each other's hands.

Inara looked around the now almost suspiciously empty corridor, where had all the other guards gone?

"I…Is that proper?" Inara asked with uncertainty clear in her voice.

"Well, I'm giving you permission to call me Vesper. I'm even asking you to!" Vesper said with a gentle smile. "It won't get you in trouble if that's what you're worrying about, and if you want, you can call me princess when we're around my mother and father."

Inara simply nodded as an answer. She felt incredibly awkward and held her hands clasped behind her back tightly, otherwise she wouldn't have known what to do with them.

"I'd like an escort to my room," Vesper said.

Inara looked around the empty corridor once again.

"I can fetch someone…" Inara started.

"I'm asking you," Vesper said.

"I unfortunately don't know where your room is," Inara said slowly.

"I didn't ask you to lead me there, simply to escort me. Otherwise known as having company," Vesper said with a smile.

"As you wish," Inara said.

It felt wrong. Vesper was being so approachable and open, she was nothing like the stories Inara had heard about the Royal family. Though she was pretty sure she hadn't heard much about the princess now when she was thinking about it. As they started walking, Inara found that she had to slow down her steps quite a bit to not out walk Vesper immediately.

Inara was more than a head taller than the princess but even for her height, she walked slowly, perhaps it was from never having been rushed or stressed to get somewhere but Inara didn't know. They walked into a wing of the Castle that Inara hadn't been in yet and she wondered if Malik would have shown her it later this evening. She hoped she wasn't making him wait for her. Though Inara couldn't imagine him being cross with her for following Vesper's wish; she was royalty after all and they all served them.

"Tell me about yourself," Vesper said as they continued to walk.

"I'm sorry?" Inara said, slightly confused.

Vesper glanced over at her.

"Things you value, people you love, favourite food?" Vesper said, throwing out things for Inara to answer.

Inara stared forward, not looking at Vesper.

"I suppose I value justice," Inara said slowly. The words almost felt like heavy lead on her tongue.

Silence and Inara could feel Vesper's eyes on her and the expectation to say something more.

"I...I really like tea," Inara finally said and glanced over at the shorter woman.

"Tea?" Vesper said, almost surprised.

Inara nodded.

"I wouldn't have taken you for a tea lover," Vesper said. "We have quite the stock of tea in the Castle. A lot of imported and expensive things you can't get a hold of in Taurin. I could show you it later if you'd like?"

Inara frowned slightly but quickly stopped, she didn't want the princess to think she was being suspicious or not thankful. Though this entire situation was slightly suspicious.

"That's very kind of you," Inara said, then added. "Vesper." Vesper's face once again lit up once Inara had spoken her name.

"What about you?" Inara asked slowly.

Inara knew it wasn't her place to ask that question even if Vesper had just asked her, she had no right to pry in her personal life. Though Inara supposed that she already had a head start on knowledge on the princess as most of her life was public knowledge.

"Me?" Vesper said, almost shocked to have been asked.

Vesper laughed low.

"I suppose I like people," Vesper said. "Always have, ever since I was a small child. My mother and father would have to constantly have me surveilled or I would go and speak with the closest stranger."

Vesper took a deep breath and looked forward.

"Nowadays the Castle is rather empty," Vesper said and turned back to her.

"It is a large place," Inara said, not sure what to say.

"You get used to it," Vesper said. "And it is a tremendous place to play hide and seek. I think I sat in one place for three hours before they were even close to finding me when I was a child." Then they finally came to a rather decorated but less so than a lot of the other doors and Vesper stopped in front of it.

"Would you like to come inside?" Vesper asked politely.

Inara looked behind herself. She really should go and find Malik and continue whatever he wanted to show her. She still had no idea where they kept Anya and it kept nagging in the back of her head.

"I think the War Counsellor is requiring my presence," Inara said as politely as possible.

Vesper smiled but it didn't really reach her eyes.

"Of course. We all have our duties," Vesper said. "Well, feel free to come by if you want to have a look at our tea stocks."

"I will, thank you," Inara said and did a little bow.

Vesper entered her room and gave Inara a quick glance before she closed the door behind herself. For a short moment, Inara just stood and took several deep breaths and tried to collect her thoughts and wrap her head around what had just happened. So the princess was friendly, that was good to know but it seemed that

Vesper was either completely naive or was playing a game with Inara and she didn't know which one was preferable.

***

Inara found Malik back at the War Room and she felt quite proud, she'd only taken a wrong turn twice. Malik nodded in greeting as she entered and he quickly placed a few documents in a drawer that he then locked.

"How was the meeting?" Malik asked. "I hope the King wasn't too intimidating."

"It was intense," Inara said honestly. "But it went well."

"Good," Malik said. "Then let's not waste more time. Let's go, shall we?"

Inara nodded and followed the War Counsellor. She wanted to ask him about what the King had said, about there being other Marks but she didn't feel like this was the time. Malik would probably bring it up sooner or later, they seemed to want her help in locating them after all. Malik started to lead them down, further down than Inara had ever been before. They stopped in front of a large steel door and Inara felt a chill going down her spine just looking at it. She had a good guess what was behind it.

"I suppose you've never been down in The Grove?" Malik asked seriously.

Inara shook her head, not entirely trusting her voice to be steady. The door almost emanated a cold and desperation that she couldn't explain and her whole body just wanted to turn around and leave and never come back to this door.

"Would you like to see it?" Malik asked.

"Not really," Inara answered before she'd even realised it.

Inara glanced over at Malik, slightly worried he'd be cross about her answer. Worried he'd find her answer that one of a coward but he just nodded and there was an understanding clear in his eyes. Malik took up a large steel key from his pocket and inserted it into the large steel door and Inara felt her heart drop.

"Don't worry, we're not going to The Grove but we need to get past this door to get to where we are going," Malik said and shot her a reassuring smile, he must have seen how tense she'd gotten all of a sudden.

Malik turned the key and opened the door. It was a steep stairway down into complete darkness and Inara could feel cold creep towards her. She thought she could almost see it, slowly climbing up from the depth towards any light and life it could find. Inara involuntarily took a step back. "Are you alright?" Malik asked.

Inara looked over at him, swallowed hard and then nodded but she knew she'd lost all colour in her face and she felt cold sweat run down her back. Malik picked up a lantern that had stood just to the right behind the door and lit it, illuminating a small part of the space. He started to make his way down the stairs and it took all of Inara's will power to go after him. The lantern only surrounded them in a vague glow of light and it made the shadows around them play tricks on her eyes, making her almost jump every other second.

It felt like the way down was impossible long and when she glanced behind her, she could no longer see the door leading out and she could certainly not see any end to the darkness when she glanced down. Then all of a sudden, Malik stopped on a little plateau and Inara saw another, smaller, steel door in the rock wall. With another, smaller key, Malik unlocked this door as well and they were met with a well-lit corridor. Inara took a deep breath but couldn't help but to glance down the staircase one last time, still no end in sight, and she prayed that she would never have to visit The Grove. This was enough for her.

Malik closed the door behind them and started walking down the corridor. Once again she was struck with the fascination that there were no torches, there were only small orbs hanging from the walls that emanated light.

"What are those?" Inara asked and pointed at the light orbs.

Malik raised an eyebrow before he looked over to what she was pointing at. He smiled gently.

"Our scientists call it electricity," Malik said. "A wonderful alternative to torches and fire. It lights up an entire room with just the click of a button."

"How?" Inara asked, not understanding how that could be possible.

Malik laughed low.

"That is beyond me unfortunately, all I know is that it works," Malik answered. "It's very new and experimental but it's been installed in the entire Castle. Hopefully it can be installed in the entire city at one point."

Inara simply nodded in response, if he didn't understand how it worked there was no point in her trying to ask more questions. It was fascinating but nothing Inara needed to concern herself with.

The corridor was clearly carved from the rock beneath the Castle but it was smooth and had been painted white, making it a stark difference from the tunnel down to The Grove.

"Where are we going exactly?" Inara asked after a few seconds of silence. Malik glanced back at her.

"We are going to do what we are really doing here," Malik answered. "What the King has put all his focus on."

Inara instantly knew that he was taking her to see Anya and whatever cold had tried to take a grip of her down in the dark, it dissipated and determination took its place.

"The Mark," Inara simply said.

Malik didn't answer but they finally came upon another door, leading into what looked like a large workroom or laboratory. It was filled with people in simple clothing, seemingly doing paperwork, discussing things and mixing what looked like chemicals. "You'll be working here a lot," Malik said. "You'll be at their disposal."

Inara looked at him.

"To look for other Marks?" Inara finally asked. "The King told me."

Malik frowned lightly but then just nodded.

"And as you actually captured and saw what the girl could do, you are invaluable here," Malik said.

A fat woman with deep brown eyes and curly hair approached Malik with purpose and Inara couldn't help but to straighten her back.

"Esther," Malik said with a slight bow.

The woman called Esther smiled lightly back at him before turning towards Inara.

"So this is her?" Esther said.

Inara didn't like that she spoke as if she wasn't here or could talk for herself but kept her mouth shut.

"This is Inara," Malik said.

Esther looked Inara up and down with a neutral face before turning back to Malik.

"She's woken up," Esther said.

"Has she said anything?" Malik asked.

Esther was silent for a moment and shot Inara a glance she couldn't read before she answered. It was most likely distrust.

"She claims and swears that she did not steal the Mark but that…" Esther seemed to struggle with finishing her sentence. "That Andrew had it and forced it on her."

"And what do you think?" Malik asked.

"I would say that it was a complete lie but..." Esther said. "That might just be my personal feelings getting in the way. We have nothing that shows that she is lying and Andrew did disappear at the same time as the Mark so it's not impossible. I just don't want to think that of him."

Inara's head was spinning. Anya hadn't stolen the Mark? She hadn't broken into the Castle and stolen anything but the Mark had been forced upon her? Anya's words came rushing back at her. They had confused her back then but now it all made sense.

I will not be punished for something I had no choice in.

Anya had told her but Inara had just not understood. Inara closed her eyes and forced herself to take a deep breath. She wished Anya had just told her that, she wished she'd listened better. There were a lot of things Inara wished for right now. She felt slightly sick as she opened her eyes again and found that Malik and Esther had continued talking but she couldn't hear a single word they spoke. Inara had turned in a completely innocent person, someone who was technically a victim in this. A victim to this damn Mark that everyone obsessed over.

"How long will you keep her?" Inara spoke, the words leaving her mouth before she had any power to stop it.

Both Esther and Malik went quiet and turned to face Inara and she tried with all her might to keep a neutral face.

"What do you mean?" Esther asked with a frown.

Inara cleared her throat.

"We were told to look for a thief with the Mark but this girl is not a thief as you just said, so how long will you keep her?" Inara asked.

Esther and Malik exchanged glances.

"The Mark is royal property," Malik said. "As long as she has it, so is she."

"Can't you just take the Mark from her?" Inara asked.

"We haven't found a way to remove it without immediately killing the host," Esther said. "It is an unfortunate situation we've found ourselves in but also one of opportunity. She is the first person we've encountered that has survived merging with the Mark. She will be of immense help in our research."

Inara just stared, not saying another word and when the silence had gone on for slightly too long.

Malik cleared his throat.

"Will you excuse me, Esther, I would like a word with Inara," Malik said.

Esther nodded and gave Inara a last look before she went back to work. Malik put a calm hand on Inara's shoulder and guided her into a corner.

"What's wrong?" Malik said. "It's clear as day on your face."

Inara glanced down into the floor.

"I…I thought I brought in a criminal," Inara said truthfully, her heart aching. "I thought…"

"You haven't done anything wrong," Malik said. "You have done the Royal family a great service and this entire city for that matter by bringing her in."

"But she's innocent," Inara said and looked straight into Malik's eyes.

Malik's face hardened slightly and his reassuring hand slipped from her shoulder.

"It's good to have morals," Malik said seriously. "But you owe no allegiance to this street girl. You saw what she could do. It would be impossible to release her into the city even if we didn't need her for research."

Inara didn't answer.

"Is this going to be a problem, Inara?" Malik asked. She'd never heard his voice this cold before.

Inara quickly looked up and straight into his eyes.

"No," Inara said. "As you said, things work differently here. I was simply not mentally prepared for it but now I am."

Malik scanned her face, but she kept a mask of stone.

"I will do whatever I can to help," Inara said. "I apologise for my reaction."

Malik's face softened slightly.

"We are only human," Malik said. "Just be careful. That kind of reaction can get you in a lot of trouble here. It could even be seen as treason if you're not careful."

"Thank you," Inara said. "I can't ever repay you for what you've done for me here."

"Don't thank me," Malik said and turned his gaze towards where Esther was. "Things might be getting a lot worse soon."

Malik turned back to her.

"Which is why I need people like you. People who are willing to do what has to be done but still have some humanity left in their body. We might have to bend the law sometimes but it doesn't mean we have to be cruel. Do you understand?" Malik said.

Inara nodded and she did truly understand. In her state of panic, something had snapped and a calm had overtaken her instead.

Anya had spared her life, even though it had caused her nothing but trouble. Inara had to repay that by getting her out of here. There were things Inara could bend the law for but the imprisonment of an innocent person for one's own personal gain was not one of them.

Anya might be dangerous with the Mark, but it wasn't her fault and she was still human. Inara wasn't sure on how much humanity would be left in her if she didn't try and help Anya. After all, helping people had always been her first priority.

Chapter 36

ANYA

"Why are you sulking?" It said with its monotone voice.

Anya had sat down in one of the corners of her little box as soon as Esther had left her and she hadn't moved since. She wasn't sure of what she was feeling. It was a storm inside of her—anger, despair, desperation.

"You lied to me," Anya said low.

"About what?" It answered.

"You never told me I'd die if I tried to remove you," Anya said.

Something close to a laugh came from it and the sound sent a shiver down Anya's spine, it was a bad imitation.

"You knew," it said. *"You knew since the moment we merged."*

Anya was silent.

"You sang a different tune to that woman than what you said to me last time," it continued. *"You told me you'd do whatever it took. You told me you wanted my help. Now you say you want nothing to do with me? Pick a side, Anya."*

"Shut up," Anya hissed.

"If you have no intention of using me or taking advantage of the gifts I am willing to give you, why are you still here? Give me to a host worthy of my time," it said.

"You think I should kill myself?" Anya said, her voice teeming with anger.

"What's the difference from how you've been living? You're a spectator of your own life. You've been living a dead life this entire time," it said.

Anya looked out into the once again dark room that surrounded her. The moment Esther had left, the light had turned off again.

"You're alone. Your friends are most likely dead by this point. No one is coming to save you. Do you wish to spend the rest of your life in this cage? Or worse, on a leash?" It said.

Anya glanced down at the mark on her hand.

"You're just a parasite," Anya said low.

"What you call me does not change me. I do not care about how you perceive me, you will never truly understand me," it said.

"As you will never understand me," Anya retorted.

Anya didn't know how, but she could feel it smiling inside of her.

"Now you're starting to get it," it said. *"We are separate beings merged together. My best interests are yours as yours are mine. I want to live at my fullest capacity, as much as you do and together, Anya, we can achieve that."*

"I just want to go back," Anya said, feeling her eyes burn. "I don't want this."

"You do want it though. You crave power, that is nothing to be ashamed of, especially not when you've been deprived of it your entire life," it said.

Silence.

"If you truly do not want this, then say so. I will leave you be, you will disappoint these people holding you hostage. They will grow tired of your failures and they will transfer me to someone else and you will die," it said. *"Or we wait, we bide our time and when the right opportunity comes, we strike. We escape. We run far away from here or we stay and get revenge. It will be your choice."*

"My choice…" Anya whispered.

Her choice, it almost sounded unbelievable in her own head. What if it was right, what if Runa and James were dead because of her? The mere thought almost sent her spiralling into a panic attack and she willed herself to think of anything else to make it stop. It would drive her insane. Her choice.

Anya had spoken the truth when she'd said that she didn't want this, that she wished she could just go back to before all of this but it was an impossibility and it was childish to even consider. The only way was forward or to lay down and die. The second choice had never felt as tempting as it did right now because if Runa and James were indeed dead, then what did she have? She had nothing.

"We can build something for ourselves," it said, almost as an answer. *"There is nothing more cleansing than fire."*

The flicker of fire inside of Anya ignited and took flame faster than ever before. If they had killed or even hurt the people she cared about, she would burn this entire city to the ground. It was true, without them she had nothing. This city was nothing without the people she loved. If they took everything from her, she would erase it and build something better in its place. Or just leave it in ashes.

Perhaps this place was cursed and nothing new should be built here. Perhaps if she burnt it to the ground, she'd burn with it even; she knew in her heart that would bring some form of peace.

"You humans crumble all the time, you burn yourselves out until you're nothing but ashes. It takes something special to use that fire without letting it consume you. Give into the fire, Anya, but don't let it consume you. You are in control, remember that," it said, it's voice was almost comforting.

Anya closed her eyes and took a deep breath, the small fire inside of her chest expanding with every gulp of air she took. Feeling it spread to the tips of her fingers and down her legs, it was a warm, comforting feeling of energy. Dormant but ready to be used when the correct kindling was added. It felt like nothing she'd felt before, not the intense spurt of energy and strength she'd felt when she'd managed to shed some of Inara's blood, this was calm and collected.

This was her own fire she finally let flow through her body, just with the added push of the Mark. Anya realised she'd always had the fire, the Mark had just ignited it again after it had gone dormant after all these years.

Anya opened her eyes and she felt her breath catch in her throat at what she was seeing. It was a short, chubby older woman, her short hair completely white and her porcelain skin was riddled with wrinkles from old age. Her small crystal blue eyes found Anya's, and for a short second, they just stared at each other.

"Who are you?" The woman asked and tilted her head slightly.

"Am I hallucinating?" Anya said low, almost more to herself.

"No," the woman said. "What is your name?"

"Anya," she finally said, still not being able to really understand what was happening.

The woman quickly nodded and looked over Anya.

"Could you stand up?" The woman asked.

Without saying anything, Anya rose from where she'd been sitting and walked closer to the woman but keeping a fair distance.

"Who are you?" Anya asked. "What are you?"

"I'm Merope," the woman said, clearing looking Anya up and down. "What Mark do you have?"

Anya just stared at her.

"Are you with the scientists?" Anya asked.

Merope frowned slightly.

"What Mark?" She asked again.

"Fire, I suppose?" Anya answered.

"You haven't had it long, have you?" Merope said. "I haven't seen you before."

"What are you talking about?" Anya said, confused. "What is happening?"

Merope cleared her throat.

"Are you safe?" Merope asked.

Anya looked around the little box she was currently in, in certain ways she was safe she supposed.

"I'm in the Castle," Anya answered.

"Which country?" Merope asked.

"What?" Anya said.

"Which country?" Merope pressed.

"Taurin," Anya answered.

Merope seemed to be thinking slightly before she turned her attention back to her.

"You said you were in the Castle, does that mean that you've been captured?" Merope asked.

Anya nodded slowly.

"Because of the Mark?" Merope asked, her voice slightly more sorrowful.

Anya nodded again.

"I am sorry," Merope said.

"Who are you? How are you here? What is happening?" Anya said, just letting the words spill from her mouth. She was beyond confused and was almost certain she was having a mental breakdown at this point.

The woman held up her left hand and showed a similar but entirely different Mark on her hand. "I have the Mind Mark," Merope said. "In short terms, I can communicate with everyone who has a Mark, through the magic that connects us all. Amongst other things."

"You have a Mark," Anya said and she wasn't sure on why she almost felt like crying out of relief. There were others in the same position as her; it wasn't just a hypothesis, it was a reality.

She wasn't completely alone.

"We are a group of people, though we are far from where you are currently and cannot offer our assistance at this time," Merope said.

"How many?" Anya asked quickly, ignoring the other parts.

"We are twelve at this point," Merope said. "We would like you to join us, if that is something you'd like."

Something between a mix of a sob and a laugh escaped Anya's lips.

"Yes. Please," Anya said.

"As long as you have your Mark, I can find you. I have been held captive myself, Anya, stay strong. The power at your disposal is nothing like they will ever have seen. Make them realise their fault in caging a free and dangerous thing," Merope said, her eyes intense and venom clear in her voice.

There was a moment of silence.

"We will make them regret the day they lifted a finger against us. They will see what true power can do, unlike their Kings with the pretence of it. We will show them," Merope said.

Merope reached out her hand towards Anya and she felt a smile creep onto her face. Anya took her hand and it was a strange sensation as Merope was not actually here but she could feel the handshake in her soul.

They would show them all what they could do.

Chapter 37

RUNA

Some time had passed. Runa had cleaned up and tried to dust off her clothes as much as possible. James had told her that Anya had a couple of spare clothes in her room but Runa hadn't even bothered looking, they weren't even close to the same size so she just had to get by with the clothes on her right now. Getting the dust and blood properly off her face felt nice and almost like she was wiping away some of that past with it.

Mr Parker was dead which meant the Silver Swans were no more and Runa had no idea how many of them had died or made it out of there. There weren't a lot of them that she cared about enough to worry about, but she did worry slightly about Tamara, Irena and most of all Egil. Perhaps she would try and look for them later; after all right now, they had no plan on how to get Anya out of the Castle and it was always a good idea to have some alliances.

When Runa came back down the stairs, she saw that James had placed two plates on the table with what seemed like simple sandwiches and a glass of water next to it. James had already sat down and started eating and Runa slowly sat down next to him and stared at the plate. Was this how Anya had been greeted every time she'd come home? Had James always made sure she was fed and clothed?

Runa glanced over at James. Any time Anya had come home with the slightest wound, James must have seen to it immediately. Runa stared down into the sandwich in front of her again and she felt something she hadn't properly felt in a long time. It was jealousy. Jealousy for a simpler life, jealousy for someone waiting for you to get home with a meal on the table and worry for your health.

Runa couldn't remember the amount of times she'd gone to bed hungry or how many times she'd sewn her own wounds together because they were minor and she'd rather suffer than go to James for something simple. How many times that had led to an infection that had forced her to go straight to James' door anyway.

"You alright?" James' voice spoke softly.

Runa snapped out of it and looked at him. She hated that soft and caring look on his face, it made her irrationally angry for some reason. Perhaps because she couldn't find it in herself to believe that it was directed towards her and that it wasn't a trick. Runa didn't answer, just picked up the sandwich and aggressively took a bite out of it. It was just bread with some simple meat and cheese on it but it tasted divine after everything that had happened.

They sat in silence, the only sound filling the room was the sound of the chewing and occasional clinking of glasses as they were lifted and put down on the table again. Then suddenly, there came multiple rapid knocks on the door. Runa stiffened and James shot her a glance before they both moved, almost in sync, almost like they knew exactly how to act in this situation.

Runa hid behind the wall leading into his makeshift office and peaked out her head slightly, just so she could see the door and James. James walked up to the door with calm steps and slowly opened the door. Runa heard James almost gasp but she couldn't see who was at the door until he stepped aside and she saw the familiar face of Irena. She was pale and her greying hair had streaks of red in it.

Her entire right side of her face was covered in blood but she didn't look to have any wound there. The most alarming thing was the makeshift bandage around her left shoulder that was completely soaked through with blood. Runa immediately came out of her hiding spot and walked up to Irena, without really thinking she simply pulled the older woman into a hug. Irena laughed low then winced in pain and Runa quickly let go of her and guided her to a chair. James had already gone to fetch his medical kit.

Runa knelt in front of Irena.

"You have no idea how happy I am that you're alive," Runa said honestly.

Irena looked into her eyes. She looked tired and haggard and there was an emptiness in her eyes that Runa had never seen before. Irena tried to smile but her bottom lip couldn't stop shivering.

"T-Tamara," Irena stuttered. "I tried. I tried to…"

Irena took a deep breath and she didn't have to finish the sentence for Runa to understand. It wasn't a surprise that Tamara hadn't made it. She hadn't been with them for too long and she was basically still a child with little experience.

"I really tried," Irena said with a sniffle.

Runa looked at the blood on her cheek and only now did she realise it was from a hand resting there, most likely Tamara's as she'd been dying. Runa quickly fetched a wet rag and first she showed Irena it, before she carefully started to wipe the blood from her face.

"I know you did," Runa said. "I'm sorry I didn't stay to help."

Irena shook her head.

"We all betrayed you, I don't blame you for leaving," Irena said, tears starting to form in her eyes.

"Hey," Runa said and grabbed Irena's good hand with a hard grasp. "You did not betray me. Okay? I don't blame you."

Runa felt Irena squeeze back and even though Runa couldn't bring herself to even try a comforting smile, it felt enough. James finally returned and shoved Runa out of the way. He immediately took off the makeshift bandage to really see the damage. It had almost completely stopped bleeding which was good, but it looked fairly deep and it was far from a clean cut.

"I recognise you," James said with a soft voice. "It's been a while since you were here so I apologise that I don't remember your name."

"It's Irena," she answered low.

James nodded.

"This is going to hurt," James said as he picked up all the things he needed.

Irena took a shaky breath.

"Who else made it?" Runa asked.

"A lot of the worst," Irena said. "A lot of them joined the Rusty Coffins as well."

"Do you know anything about Egil?" Runa asked.

Irena managed a true smile and nodded.

"They're okay. After the attack, I went to their home, they're the one that patched me up," Irena said. "But we both realised someone with more knowledge should have a look at it, so I came here."

Runa sighed in relief. Two friends alive at least, that was more than she could have hoped for. "Whoever Egil is, they did a decent job at patching you up," James said. "Without them, I doubt you would even have made it all the way here."

"I'll thank them next time I see them," Irena said with a weak smile.

Irena's eyes were getting heavy, the adrenaline must finally be leaving her body and pain had a tendency to knock a person out.

"Runa, could you help me get Irena to a bed?" James asked.

Runa nodded, helped Irena stand and then put her good shoulder over her own and slowly walked over to the two patient beds James owned. Irena laid down in the bed with a hiss of pain as she accidentally moved her bad shoulder. Irena looked over at Runa, her eyes slowly glossing over.

"I'm sorry," Irena whispered.

Runa shushed her gently and softly pulled some of Irena's hair out from her face before she turned to leave but was met with James staring at her with a look in his eyes she'd never really seen before. It was almost a little unnerving.

"What?" Runa hissed.

"I've just never seen you like this," James said honestly.

You have no heart, James' words echoed in her head. It hit Runa that that was really how he saw her, someone with no heart, no allegiance, no kindness.

"Because this is not who I am to you. To you, I am Runa without a heart, Runa who does nothing if it doesn't profit herself. You never even entertained the idea that I could be someone else to other people," Runa said coldly and shoved her way past James.

Runa walked up the stairs and threw herself into the bed. Anya's bed. It felt cold and empty but Runa fell asleep in a matter of seconds, something she hadn't done in years.

***

Two days passed. Irena was up on her feet on the second day and some colour had returned to her face and she was almost back to her cheerful self. Almost. Runa had been going out every day to scout potential options but also to just see how the city was going. She had noticed an irregular amount of fancy carriages driving through the west district and directly towards the Castle, it wasn't until Irena reminded her that the princess' birthday was in a few days that she remembered.

They were having a party, celebrating, when Runa's entire life was falling apart at the seams. Runa had also noticed that the two Blue Birds that had been stationed outside of James were gone, perhaps the party at the Castle had them all working in different places. Runa had also been and visited Egil, who had given her a tight and warm hug when they'd seen her. She had simply told them that she was staying at James and they could find her and Irena there. A look of relief came across their face when Runa mentioned that Irena was alive and doing fine.

Runa had multiple times considered going to Mara to talk but always decided against it at the last moment, she didn't want to involve her in all of this.

Now Runa was patrolling the east side, keeping her eyes open for any Rusty Coffins members or any surviving Silver Swan members or anything that could be of use to her when she spotted something. Or rather someone. It was that guard woman with the scarf who had interrogated them and most importantly, she'd been the one to bring in Anya.

Runa saw red but kept her wits enough to stay in the shadows and follow the woman for a short while. It seemed like she was alone and she was walking close to all the alley openings instead of more towards the middle of the road. Runa ran ahead of her into an alley and when the woman passed, Runa quickly and silently pulled her into the darkness and pushed up the much larger woman against the brick wall. A sharp knife was against the woman's throat, almost like it had almost always been there.

"Do you have a death wish?" Runa hissed.

"Runa," the woman said calmly.

"You take *her*. You put us through interrogations. You almost cost us everything. And you think you can walk through the east side by yourself? Is that a death wish or are you really that fucking stupid?" Runa said.

The woman just looked straight into Runa's eyes and the raw focus in them almost made Runa want to look away but she forced herself to keep eye contact.

"I told you I'd show you my justice," Runa said and pressed the knife closer to the woman's throat.

"You can drop the act, Runa. You are not going to kill me," the woman said.

"Oh yeah?" Runa said with a laugh. "And why not?"

"Because I know where they're keeping Anya and I can help you," the woman said. "You have no reason to kill me but every reason to keep me alive."

"Of course you know where they're keeping her, you put her there," Runa hissed.

"I would like to help you," the woman simply said.

"I can't trust a word coming out of your mouth," Runa said. "You're insane."

"I'm the reason you and James are walking these streets," the woman said. "I know both of you saw what happened."

Runa narrowed her eyes.

"I didn't tell anyone. I lied for you," the woman said.

"How fucking noble of you," Runa said. "Once again, why should I believe that?"

"I only brought in Anya because I thought she was guilty of a crime, I swear it," the woman said, her eyes furrowed in sadness. "The moment I found out she was a victim I…"

"You changed your mind? Just like that?" Runa said.

The woman looked at Runa, her stone face showing cracks in the facade.

"Anya could have killed me. She could have ended this before it even began but instead she spared my life," the woman said. "Anya ended up in the Castle because she spared my life." Runa couldn't help but let out a sad laugh because if that wasn't Anya in a nutshell.

Runa had told her, she had told her over and over again that sometimes some things were necessary. That you had to act on instinct so someone else's instinct didn't get you. Yet, here they were. Anya had spared this woman and it had led to this hell.

"I know you don't trust me. I know you don't believe me. That is fine," the woman said. "But I just want justice to be done."

"Your justice," Runa spat out.

The woman almost flinched a little at that.

"I want to do good," the woman said. "And locking up an innocent person for something they can't help, because someone else wants to take advantage of that person? I can't stand by that."

"How noble," Runa said, her words laced with venom.

There was a short moment of silence.

"They think you're dead," the woman said.

"What?" Runa said, surprised.

"The guards who were supposed to shadow you said that the Keg was attacked and that you were killed in that incident," the woman said. "I managed to convince them to tell me that they weren't sure, that they had left before it began and when they'd returned, so many of the bodies were beyond recognisable that it was impossible to tell. They were lazy, they didn't want to spend time looking for you, so they said you were dead. So that is what everyone else at the Castle thinks."

Pause.

"I came here, walking through the east side, alone, in hopes that you would find me if you were alive. I couldn't seek you out, that would be too obvious," the woman said. "I barely managed to get out of the Castle, I told them I would see my parents to tell them about my promotion and then come straight back."

"You came here with the intention of me finding you and shoving a knife at your throat?" Runa said with slight disbelief.

"I knew the knife part was a risk but yes," the woman said.

Runa carefully studied the woman but she was close to a statue and hard to read, except for the fact that she had exceptionally emotional eyes.

"Where are they keeping Anya?" Runa asked.

"Behind the locked door leading down to The Grove. Then halfway down the stairs behind another locked door. You'd have to go through a lot of scientists but she is being kept there," the woman said, almost like she was reading the weather.

"Two locked doors. Two different keys I assume?" Runa asked.

The woman nodded. Runa sighed and felt all the anger leave her body, now she just felt weak and filled with despair.

"It's impossible," Runa said low.

"Normally yes," the woman said. "But the princess celebrates her birthday in one day. All attendees are required to wear masks, guards, guests and servants."

Runa frowned.

"Why?" Runa asked.

"The princess wants to have a night of being like everyone else. Being able to dance and talk to anyone without most people knowing who she is. She will be revealed at the end of the night."

The woman said, "Everyone is required to wear masks."

"Easy to blend in and get close to someone, close enough to pick a pocket," Runa muttered.

"Or easy enough to slip away from the party and get into other rooms otherwise occupied," the woman said. "Almost every guard is being stationed in the Throne Room where the majority of the party is going to be celebrated, the rest of the Castle is going to be relatively empty."

Short pause.

"You just have to get a mask and the clothes of a servant," the woman said. "Which I can't help with unfortunately."

"That won't be easy," Runa said low.

"The masks are being handed out at the Castle. I heard someone mentioning that all the servant outfits are being sent to be cleaned at multiple places on the west side. It was simply too much laundry for the Castle staff to handle on short notice," the woman said.

Runa slowly lowered her knife.

"If you're lying, I'll kill you," Runa said.

The woman nodded.

"What's your name?" Runa asked. "I didn't listen last time we met."

"It's Inara," she said low.

"And you're doing this for Anya?" Runa asked.

"Aren't we all?" Inara said.

Chapter 38

INARA

Inara walked out of the alley, not glancing behind herself but making sure her scarf sat tightly around her head and that her uniform didn't look like someone had just pushed her up against a wall. She could almost still feel the cold blade against her throat, and even though she had been sure that Runa wouldn't kill her, she wouldn't have blamed her too much if she had. Inara continued down the street, towards her parents' home.

She had asked for leave to go see her parents and even though she had ulterior motives, she intended to do this as well. Inara hadn't seen her parents in a while, not since the last time she'd visited and they'd had a fight. Or rather, her father had shouted and scolded her while her mother looked on with an apologetic look.

Ever since Inara had found out that Mara was her half-sister, she had held a certain resentment towards her father but it had just grown with the years and the closer Inara had tried to get with Mara, the more she realised that she perhaps could never forgive him for abandoning her. Inara had grown up an only child, isolated and without friends and then to have found out in her teenage years that she'd had an older sister this entire time had been world shattering.

Inara had always been the good child, the obedient child. She had never once spoken back at her father, not until she found out the truth. Her father didn't want to acknowledge Mara as his child and pretended she hadn't existed and he hadn't wanted Inara to ever find out. When he found out that Inara had been to visit Mara's shop on the regular, he had almost exploded.

In his eyes, Mara was the failed prototype and Inara was the child worthy of his last name and legacy. Not that it was much of a legacy; they'd lived on the east side as long as she could remember and he worked at the brewery. He was nothing special but acted like his last name and legacy was some sort of trophy, something to be proud of. Inara had idolised him her entire childhood.

It wasn't until she'd gotten older that she'd realised that he only ever showed any kindness towards her when she did what he wanted. So Inara had sought that kindness like a dying man in the desert had sought for water. He was a cold man that didn't care about anything if it didn't involve his reputation or his legacy.

Inara didn't realise that she'd been standing in front of her parents' house for what had to have been a good ten minutes before she came back to her full senses and knocked on the door. Her mother, Sophia, opened the door and her large dark eyes shone with happiness as she saw Inara. Sophia's skin was dark brown and she had a healthy flush on her face. She smiled kindly and put her hands softly on Inara's face before letting her in.

"My dove," Sophia said with a smile. "I'm so happy to see you."

Inara looked around but found no trace of her father and part of her felt a tinge of relief at that.

"Hello, Mother," Inara said.

Inara looked at her mother. She knew she looked more like her than her father. The same way Mara had to look more like her mother. Neither of them seemed to have inherited any sort of physical trait from their father.

"Is father at work?" Inara asked.

Sophia nodded.

"Would you like a cup of tea? Are you staying long?" Her mother asked, her voice filled with joy at seeing her only child.

Inara smiled gently.

"I can't stay, unfortunately," Inara said.

Sophia's face dropped slightly but quickly tried to cover it up with another smile. She swept some dust off Inara's shoulders and made sure the collar was straight.

"So handsome," Sophia said. "My little dove."

Inara took her mother's hands in hers to stop her from fiddling.

"I've gotten a promotion," Inara said. "I'm working in the Castle now."

"The Castle?" Sophia said, shocked. "How?"

"I...caught someone important," Inara said vaguely.

Sophia placed a gentle hand on Inara's face again.

"I'm so proud of you," Sophia said. "And your father will burst with pride when I tell him." Inara only cared that her mother was proud of her, or that was what she kept telling herself. Her mother who had always been kind but shy, timid and quiet. That approval was worth so much more. Yet, it had been ingrained in her from a young age to seek her father's approval, so even if she told herself she didn't care, it did make her happy in some way to know that he would be proud of her. It confused her.

"Is he treating you well?" Inara asked.

"Don't worry about me, my dove," Sophia said with a kind smile. "I am okay. We are okay." There was a pause of silence and Sophia looked around herself, probably more out of habit than anything else.

"How is your sister?" Sophia asked. "I hope everything is alright with her."

"She's…fine, I think," Inara said. "Thank you for caring."

Sophia sighed.

"If it had been up to me, you know I would have…" Sophia said low.

"I know, Mother," Inara said. "But it wasn't up to you."

Sophia nodded and a sad expression came over her face.

"A child shouldn't be without parents," Sophia said. "I can't imagine if he'd done that to you, I simply…"

"It's not your fault," Inara said. "You didn't know when you married him."

Sophia took a deep breath and then tried to smile again.

"I am so proud of you, I truly am," Sophia said. "Please come and visit when you can, I know your father…But I miss seeing your face."

Inara pulled her mother into a tight hug, it wasn't something she did with a lot of people. Having that kind of body contact with another person felt so incredibly intimate; it made Inara uncomfortable and sometimes even made her skin crawl but this was her mother. Inara placed her face in the crook of her mother's neck and just felt the warmth and comfort. Inara released her mother even though she felt a slight resistance, almost like Sophia didn't want the hug to end.

"I have to get back," Inara said.

Sophia nodded.

"Be good, my little dove," Sophia said. "Do good."

***

The way back to the Castle was a haze. Inara just let her legs lead the way and before she knew it Malik stood in front of her and she was in the War Room.

"Everything alright with your parents?" Malik asked pleasantly.

Inara simply nodded.

"Good," Malik said. "We have a lot of preparations for tomorrow night. You'll find the clothing you'll be wearing in your quarter."

Inara nodded again and Malik frowned slightly.

"Is everything alright with you?" Malik asked.

"Sorry," Inara said. "Just a lot on my head."

"Well, clear your head, at least until after the party," Malik said with a slightly joking tone. "We're going to need everyone at their best."

"Of course," Inara said.

"But also, you are allowed to enjoy yourself," Malik said. "At the party I mean. You are there to do your job, yes, but the princess has been very clear that this is a celebration for everyone to enjoy."

Everyone in the Castle, Inara thought.

"Before I forget!" Malik said and picked up a note from his pocket. "I'm quite busy, but on your way to your quarters, could you walk past the princess and give her this?"

Inara wanted to ask what it was but knew she should just say yes and do as he told her.

"It's nothing important. Just a little reminder for her," Malik said.

Inara nodded and took the note and put it in her pocket.

"Fatima will come get you in the morning to make sure you're up to speed with everyone else," Malik said. "Look your best, act your best, nobility from all over the country will be watching."

Inara couldn't stop thinking about Runa and James and what they might be attempting tomorrow with the information she gave them. It would give her no rest until all of it was over, of that she was sure. Inara started to make her way towards the door when she stopped and pretended like she'd just remembered something, she hoped it was convincing enough.

"Right, could I ask one thing?" Inara said. "It has nothing to do with the party."

"Of course," Malik said with a raised eyebrow.

"How will I get to Esther and the lab later if I'm needed?" Inara asked. "I assume you can't accompany me every time."

Malik stared at her. It wasn't completely out of the blue. The lab and the Mark and all of that had almost been the only thing Malik and Inara had talked about when they hadn't been talking about the party. Every time, Malik had accompanied her, opened the door down to The Grove and then the secondary door as well. Inara had wondered for some time if she'd be given a key of her own at some point.

"You won't be needed until after the party," Malik said.

Then he frowned slightly and sighed.

"Well, with Esther you can never know," Malik said. "She does not particularly care for parties and will probably not attend at all."

Malik stared at Inara with an intense gaze.

"You can get the key to The Grove by any of my personal guards if needed, just tell them I gave you permission," Malik said slowly. "Then knock three times fast, then two times slowly on the lab door and someone should come and open it for you."

"Thank you," Inara said. "I'm not a party person either so to be honest, I wouldn't be upset if Esther called for me."

Inara tried to smile slightly.

"Be careful, Inara," Malik said. "Not everyone in this Castle has your best intentions in mind."

Inara swallowed hard.

"Well, I'm lucky I have you on my side then," Inara said.

Malik smiled one of his warm smiles but the intensity stayed in his eyes.

"Lucky indeed," Malik said.

Inara gave a short bow before she tried to calmly leave the room, her heart beating hard in her chest. Inara couldn't lie, she felt bad lying to Malik and using him for what she was planning. He had treated her almost more like a daughter than her own father had done. He had been nothing but accepting and kind and this was how she was repaying him.

Inara knew it had to be done, so her conscience could be clean but she started to realise more and more that the deeper she got, the more people she had to betray, the more people she had to go behind their backs, to try and do something good. It seemed in her quest for a clean conscience, she was constantly making it worse at the same time.

Inara stopped in front of the princess' door and found another King's guard, one of Malik's personal guards, in front of it.

"The princess isn't in shape to see anyone right now," the guard simply said.

Inara nodded slightly.

"I have a note from the War Counsellor to give to her," Inara said.

The guard was silent for a moment.

"Give it to me and I will make sure she gets it," the guard said.

"Is something wrong?" Inara asked.

The guard was silent for a moment and glanced around the empty corridor.

"The princess is having…a rough day," the guard said. "She will be better by tomorrow."

"She's sick?" Inara asked.

"The princess' state is none of your business," the guard said. "Give me the note and then leave."

Reluctantly, Inara handed over the note to the guard and part of her kicked herself for not reading it earlier. It just didn't come naturally for her to do things like that. The guard nodded and made it clear that Inara should leave, so she did.

Inara glanced back at the princess' door, she couldn't help but wonder what was wrong. Perhaps just a simple cold that would be gone by the morning, it was just the fact that Inara had seen the princess before she'd left the Castle this morning and she'd seen fine.

Chapter 39

RUNA

Runa quickly made her way back towards James' house. This new information could change everything. They would probably still get caught and get executed or thrown into The Grove for the rest of their lives, but now they had a sliver of a chance at least. There was this voice in Runa's head that kept saying, *who cares if you die, you have nothing now, you might as well go out doing something impossible.*

But Runa had found out something about herself very early in her life—a thought that would change and lead her in her life forever.

Runa wanted to live.

She wanted to live so badly that sometimes the mere thought of the seconds passing felt like sand running through her fingers, leaving her helpless. It wasn't something she often let herself actually think about, how much she wanted to live because she knew it could be taken away from her at any point. If she pretended it didn't matter that much. Having it end wouldn't be that bad but if she admitted to herself how terrified she truly was of dying?

She wasn't sure she would be able to do anything. It would paralyse her; make her never step foot outside again for the fear of anyone hurting her. If she feared death, she wouldn't be able to live.

Runa slammed open the door to James' house and quickly closed it behind herself. It took her a few seconds to realise that the room was almost full. Irena, Egil, James and Mara stood around the small table and Runa wasn't sure she'd ever seen this many people in here before, at least not healthy people. Runa was just about to speak when Mara almost jumped on her and gave her a tight hug. After a few seconds of shock, Runa hugged her back.

"James told me what happened," Mara signed with furrowed brows. "I'm so sorry."

"My signing is rusty at best but I tried," James spoke and signed at the same time.

"How much did he tell you?" Runa signed.

Egil spoke up with a gentle voice.

"Neither Irena nor I know sign language," Egil said.

"Right. I'll sign and talk at the same time and I'll translate anything Mara says, good?" Runa said, her signing was still pretty good.

Egil nodded in appreciation and that was what Runa did from then on in their conversation. It was hard to keep track of everything and she knew she miss signed at times and misunderstood some things as well but everyone was understanding and they seemed to understand the meaning of the message at least.

"I know that Anya was taken and the two of you as well," Mara signed. "I was questioned for a short period but Inara got me out."

Runa raised an eyebrow. She'd had no idea that Mara had been alongside them inside the Castle. "I also know that it was Inara that arrested you all," Mara signed and a flash of anger and confusion mixed went across her face.

Runa nodded.

"I want to help," Mara signed and lifted her chin.

"So do we," Egil and Irena chimed in.

Runa glanced at all their faces, scanning for any doubt, any weakness but found none and she didn't know why her eyes suddenly started to sting. Runa's eyes finally met James and they locked, they were filled with the same amount of resolution that he must have seen in her eyes. "Good," Runa finally said. "Because I have a lead on how to do this."

"How?" James asked.

Runa looked over at Mara.

"I met Inara," Runa said.

"What?" Mara signed, slightly confused.

"Well, I put a knife to her throat and threatened her," Runa said. "She gave me some information we could use but we don't have much time, it's going to be sloppy and a lot of it will have to rely on pure luck."

"Then let's not waste any time," Irena said with a smirk.

Runa nodded.

"The princess has a birthday party tomorrow," Runa said.

"Yeah, right I told you that!" Irena said. "Wait, are we going to use that to our advantage?"

"Yes," Runa said.

A rush of excitement went over Irena's face.

"So I was on the right track back then," Irena said. "Using the party for our own gain."

"Technically yes," Runa said and tried to not smile. "Everyone will be wearing masks, everyone will be staying anonymous until the end of the party."

"Sounds like a recipe for chaos," James said slowly. "The guard number in there will be astronomical to make sure no one who isn't supposed to be there gets in, like us."

"But they'll be focusing on keeping the Royal family safe," Runa said. "They're not our target. The rest of the Castle should be emptier than usual. I even know where they're holding Anya."

"How do you know all of this isn't a lie?" Mara signed slowly.

"I don't," Runa said honestly. "But it's the best chance we got."

"Why would Inara tell you all of this?" James asked. "Just because you put a knife to her throat? She seemed tougher than that."

"Apparently, she had a change of heart," Runa simply said. "And I kind of believe her, call me naive. We have nothing else to go on, this is our best chance. We either use the information she gave us and if she's setting us up, we get caught, it's not very different from us going in blind and without any distraction and immediately getting caught. I'd rather take my chances with this."

"So what has to be done?" Egil asked, crossing their arms.

"The servants' party outfits have been distributed around the west side to be cleaned. If we can get a couple of uniforms from them, that's a good start," Runa said.

"But if we take say three uniforms, there are going to be three servants at the Castle without any and three extra people?" Irena said.

"We'll have to take out the amount of people of uniforms we take," Runa said.

James flashed her a glance of warning.

"Not kill them," Runa added. "Just tie them up and keep them away until after the party. You realise that if all of you get involved in this. There is a high chance that you will have to leave the city and be on the run."

"Understood," Mara signed.

"It'll be exciting," Irena said with a smile.

"My bar got blown up so I might as well go to a new town and set up shop there," Egil said with a nod.

Runa looked over at James, who quickly looked down at the floor.

"I have no home here. Anya is all that matters," James finally said.

"Just one problem," Irena said and rubbed the back of her head. "Isn't everyone always saying that the Castle is practically a labyrinth; how are we going to find our way?"

"I know where Anya is being kept," Runa said.

"Okay, but do you know where in the Castle it actually is?" Irena asked. "Or did she just say 'Anya is kept in The Grove?' because we don't actually know how to get to The Grove."

"Fair point," Runa said with a sigh.

There was a heavy silence for a short moment before Mara started to sign almost frantically.

"I might be able to help!" Mara said, her eyes sparkling. "I think I have some old maps of the Castle, from when it was built, so it won't be perfect but it'll be something? I remember selling one a year ago but I made sure to make copies because I knew how valuable it could be!"

Runa put her hands on Mara's arms and actually smiled.

"You're amazing," Runa signed as she let go.

"Me and Egil can easily fix the uniforms and the servants. They're going to have to go get the uniforms at some point and then we'll dispose of them. Hopefully, we can separate them into smaller groups," Irena said and stood up.

"You're not fully healed from your wound, Irena. It could be very dangerous," Runa said.

"Everything is going to be dangerous from now on," Irena said with a wink. "We'll be fine."

Irena looked up at Egil who nodded in agreement.

"We won't fail you," Egil said.

"I'll come with you then," Runa said to Mara. "Just to make sure."

Mara nodded, then everyone looked over at James.

"I'll prepare some food for later. We're going to need all the energy for this," James said with a sigh. "All of you, come back in one piece. The real mission hasn't even started yet." Irena and Egil nodded before they headed towards the door. Egil stopped beside Runa and smiled gently.

"You make a good boss," Egil said.

"They're right, you know," Irena added quickly.

Runa didn't say anything but her entire body felt a shudder and a warm feeling slowly worked itself through her. Egil and Irena were out the door before Runa could manage a single word out of her mouth.

It was both the best feeling in the world but it wasn't until now that Runa really realised that they all looked to her for guidance in this. They were all relying on her to get them through this. If they succeeded or failed was on her shoulders. When it had just been herself, making decisions had been easy but she remembered the last time she'd have to make a decision to get a group through something. She'd killed someone.

Failure or success, Runa knew the chance of all of them coming out of this alive was slim. Even the thought of any of them coming out alive seemed like a miracle at this point.

Chapter 40

ANYA

Anya opened her eyes, standing in the same darkness she'd now started to become accustomed to. In front of her was a flame, stronger than ever before and she could feel it warm her cold skin. It felt like safety and salvation. Anya closed her eyes for a short second, just taking in the calm, the warmth and the safety of the space she was currently in.

She knew that when she woke, there would be none of that for her. As Anya opened her eyes, the flame in front of her grew even larger and took a humanoid shape before it went out in a flash and in front of her stood Andrew. He was staring at her with a calm all shapes of Fire seemed to share. It seemed like Andrew seemed to be Fire's favourite form to use, perhaps because he'd been the latest host.

"Anya," Andrew said, almost like he wasn't sure he was going to make a sound as he spoke.

The voice coming from Andrew's mouth wasn't Fire's, it didn't sound the same and for a moment. Anya just stared at the form in front of her until she realised that this was the closest she'd been to the actual Andrew since she'd found him that stormy night. Or at least the closest thing left of Andrew.

"You're Andrew, right?" Anya asked slowly.

The man nodded slowly and looked down at his hands, almost like he was inspecting his body. "Strange," he muttered to himself.

Anya just stared at him, this had never happened before. She'd only talked to Fire directly and seen a flash of some of the previous hosts to the Mark, but that had been it. Andrew's dark eyes shot back up to Anya.

"I've been trying to talk to you for a while now," Andrew said, his voice monotone. "To explain myself."

"That would be nice," Anya said low.

"I am sorry," Andrew said with a frown. "I didn't mean to put this burden on you, I just had to get it away from them."

"I don't want your apologies," Anya said with a soft tone. "We're well past that. I just want some answers."

There was a brief moment of silence before Andrew spoke again.

"I think this will be the only time I will be able to speak to you," Andrew said. "Every host is part of the Mark but...the more time that goes, the less me I'm becoming. That's what it feels like anyway. I'll just be another face for it to use."

A shudder shot down Anya's back at his words. Andrew seemed to collect his thoughts. "It wasn't just me and Esther that started this project," Andrew said. "We had a colleague with us. Moira Stone."

"The woman you wanted me to find," Anya whispered.

"When we found the Mark, Moira begged me to let it be, to bury it and forget about it. She told me that it was dangerous and she didn't trust it in the hands of the King," Andrew said. "I didn't listen. I was too curious. Too young and full of myself to listen."

Andrew cleared his throat.

"She left us once she realised we were going to continue with the project. It was laid on ice for a couple of years until we realised the Mark needed a host to activate," Andrew said. "We found test subjects. They told us they were volunteers but it was evident all subjects were people no one would miss. People willing to do almost anything for a roof over their head and a hot meal. They had no idea what they were agreeing to."

Anya didn't say anything, she just listened. It was almost like he was trying to get through everything as quickly but precise as possible.

"None of them survived," Andrew said and glanced down at his own hands for a short moment.

"Neither did I, I suppose."

"What happened?" Anya finally asked low.

Andrew looked up, his facial expression hadn't changed this entire time.

"I wanted to do this project to see what uses the Mark could have for us, if it could help us or..." Andrew started. "How well do you know your history?"

Anya frowned. She hadn't expected to be quizzed right now.

"Not very well," Anya admitted.

"50 years ago, the last time our country was at war, we lost a portion of the country to Tradeius. To most of us, this was a victory because the war ended, no more people had to die and everyone could come home. People were upset about losing their homes but they preferred that in front of getting killed. Many of the people living in the lost portion simply stayed there, officially living in Tradeius instead," Andrew said.

"The King at the time, our King's grandfather, saw it as a great shame. Something our King has inherited and only let fester in himself."

Andrew took a short pause.

"When I found out that the King wanted to use the Mark to make soldiers, to have us try and replicate it to make an army of unstoppable people, to bring war back to our nation, I was shocked. It wasn't what I had signed up for. It wasn't what I wanted my legacy to be," Andrew said. "I panicked. I remembered Moira's words and for the first time in my life, I acted without thinking. I just knew I had to get the Mark out of here, to get it away from the King."

Andrew closed his eyes.

"We have lived 50 years in peace. The King doesn't concern himself with the state of his capitol or his country, all he cares about is making a name for himself in the history books as the King that took back Taurin from Tradeius," Andrew said. "So when it was my turn to watch the newest subject who had been unconscious and burning up from the inside for hours, I couldn't stop myself."

Andrew opened his eyes and in the blank face, his eyes sparked of intensity for just a moment.

"I took the Mark. It hurt, like something I've never felt before. The panic I'd felt doubled and all I could think about was getting out of the Castle, to get out of here," Andrew said. "It must have heard me, or felt my emotional state because the next thing I saw was a flash of white in front of me and then all of a sudden I was laying on cold wet dirt."

"That's when I found you," Anya said.

"Yes," Andrew said. "I think I could have survived the merge with the Mark, if I hadn't expended all my life energy getting out of the Castle. I knew I was going to die as I laid in the rain, not even sure how far away I'd gotten when you approached me."

A flash of sadness came over his face, but it was gone in the blink of an eye.

"It was like the Gods had heard my dying prayer," Andrew said. "To find someone out in this storm, in the middle of the woods, it seemed beyond *improbable, yet there you were. You were the chance to get this Mark away from the capitol. I was afraid that they were going to find my body and just retrieve the Mark and all of it had been for nothing."*

"But your body turned to ash, how would they have retrieved the Mark?" Anya found herself asking. "Wouldn't it have disappeared with you?"

Andrew shook his head.

"The Mark will preserve it's host body until it can be transferred to a new one. Only then does the body turn to ash," Andrew said slowly. "It will do everything to ensure its survival."

Andrew sighed.

"I am truly sorry," Andrew said.

Anya took a deep breath and for some reason, sadness came over her in an overwhelming wave. "Now my soul is part of this Mark," Andrew said. "As are hundreds of souls before me. Our souls can never pass on, we are doomed to stay in this entity. I don't know if it's to fuel it in a way, or simply the price one pays for being its host."

Anya glanced down on the Mark on her hand, her cheeks were suddenly wet. When had she started crying?

"Power like this, comes with a price," Andrew said. "Don't let them take it from you. Don't let the King get his way. Don't let them start a war, Anya. You have to get out of here."

"I don't know how to," Anya said with a sniffle.

"Use the Mark," Andrew said. "It isn't an evil thing in itself. Listen to your heart and to your instincts. Do whatever it takes. The cost if you don't, could be millions of lives." Anya quickly dried the tears on her face but already found her cheeks dry again. Andrew frowned and looked down at his body.

"Goodbye, Anya," Andrew said. "I believe in you."

In a flash of fire, Andrew's body disappeared and in front of her again was just a large and flickering flame. A hollow laugh echoed around her.

"That has never happened before," the Mark said, almost amused. "Perhaps his soul was stronger than I gave credit for."

"We're getting out of here," Anya said, her eyes filled with intensity. "One way or another."

"You know what to do, Anya," it said. "Feed the fire."

Chapter 41

JAMES

James made some simple food while he was waiting for the rest to come back, just some bread and warm soup but it would do. Runa and Mara were the first ones back, which wasn't surprising. Egil and Irena could be back at any moment or just before they had to enter the Castle, it was all a huge gamble and in the worst case scenario, they got arrested and everything would fall apart. James shook his head, that couldn't be his focus right now.

Mara threw five large scrolls on the table, getting James' attention as he had to carefully move the soup and bread to the side so nothing got ruined.

"This is what I have," Mara signed.

Without saying anything else, they all started to unfold the scrolls. Some of them seemed to match up together while some seemed to be their own pieces. It was like a puzzle they were desperately trying to finish in a short amount of time.

"This place really is a maze," Mara signed and released a deep sigh.

"This should be the Throne Room," James said after having looked through the five scrolls frantically and pointed to a large room on the map. "Some of the markings on the other scrolls match up and it's a large central room, which makes the most sense."

"Which means that's where the party will be held," Runa added.

"So where is Anya held?" Mara asked.

Runa bit her lower lip and tried to scan the maps. James could tell by the look on her face that she was struggling to make sense of anything she was seeing and he couldn't blame her. "Inara said to enter The Grove, then halfway down the stairs there is another door. Behind that is where Anya is supposedly held," Runa said with a heavy voice.

"The Grove?" Mara signed with a nervous expression on her face.

"Two keys to get I assume?" James said with a sigh.

"Correct," Runa said. "I told you it wouldn't be easy."

"I think your exact words were that it was a suicide mission," James said.

"Same thing," Runa muttered. "We'll just have to hope the Gods are on our side and give us some luck."

"Will Inara help us on the inside?" Mara asked.

Runa shrugged.

"I don't know. I wouldn't count on it," Runa said. "She will probably be more monitored as a guard than any of the servants."

A short silence fell before James spoke again.

"This has to be the entrance to The Grove," James said and pointed to a place far on the left of the Castle on the bottom floor. "It's an entrance to something but there is no room behind it and all the maps have it. It has to lead down to The Grove."

"So we have to get from here," Runa said and pointed to the second floor Throne Room. "To this." Her fingers slowly weaved through the many corridors and staircases until she finally stopped at the point where they thought The Grove was.

Silence.

"Easy," Runa added.

"Now what?" Mara asked.

"Now we get ready and wait for Irena and Egil to get back," Runa said.

"And we eat," James said and pushed the soup and bread forward.

***

Night fell and they all took turns sleeping, making sure two people were awake at all times. They didn't want to be surprised by anything and if Egil and Irena came back, they wanted to be ready to go but they knew that they all needed sleep for the day to come. James had picked up some playing cards and spent most of his guard, either with Mara or Runa, to just play some cards.

They were all tense and on edge but it made James smile to see the frustration in Mara's face when she was losing or even Runa's mocking when she won, because he knew that even for a second, he'd help them think of something else. James had also checked on Runa's arm, to see how it was healing. It was far from healed at this point and all the struggle and moving she'd done while it had been fresh had made sure that the scar would be large, visible and jagged.

Runa had simply shrugged when he'd told her that.

At one point in their watch, while Runa and James were playing a game of cards, he looked up at her and found her staring at him as well.

"What?" He asked.

Runa continued to stare at him, that intense glare she could muster that managed to convince almost anyone that she was capable of doing anything.

"How far will you go to get Anya out of there?" Runa asked.

James was stunned for a short moment before he answered.

"I'd die for it," James answered.

Runa looked away in frustration and huffed, James frowned at her reaction. He'd thought that answer would have pleased Runa but apparently he'd been wrong.

"You?" James asked instead.

Runa looked back at him, her eyes softer, the same softness she always had when she spoke Anya's name.

"I guess we'll find out," Runa muttered and turned her attention back to her cards.

They continued playing for a while until James woke up Mara and he placed his head on his pillow, trying his best to sleep. To his surprise, sleep came easier than he would have thought.

James woke up by a pair of sturdy arms gripping him and shaking him slightly. At first, he was confused until he saw Runa's excited face.

"They're back," was all she said before she left him.

James quickly rose, grabbed his cane and went out into the larger room and found Egil and Irena amongst the others. They looked unharmed and almost rested which made him frown slightly. On the table lay two what looked like fancy servants outfits alongside two full face silver masks that looked slightly unnerving.

"Only two?" James finally said.

"It was all we could get with the time we had," Egil said.

"It's good enough," Runa said and gave Egil a pat on the shoulder.

"What did you do with the two servants?" James asked hesitantly.

Irena smiled mischievously at that, she looked up at Egil before she looked back at him.

"We paid them off," Irena said.

"With what money?" Runa asked with a frown.

"Well, you know Mr Parker had a secret safe where he kept his money, right?" Irena said.

Runa nodded.

"It was ransacked after the attack of course," Irena said. "But I happened to know he stashed a lot of money at a different place at the Keg. I saw him once, a few months back. He pulled out a wooden plank in the wall and behind it I saw stacks of cash. The plank slid back into place, like it never had been removed."

A smile started to spread on Runa's face.

"Well, we went to check if it was still there," Irena said and gave Egil a little nudge.

"All the money in the wall was still there and Irena had been right, it was quite a large amount of money," Egil said.

"So when we found two servants getting their outfits and saw that they weren't returning to the Castle, but that they lived outside in houses in the west district, we followed them," Irena said. "Apparently, some servants who have families can choose to live outside the Castle, as long as they are there on time for their jobs."

"So we simply gave them enough money for a month's worth of work to just skip work tomorrow and give us their uniforms, and to tell no one of course," Egil said.

"Let's just say that they were more than happy to comply as we also promised that we were not intending to do anything harmful with the costumes, somehow they believed us. Or wanted to believe us enough so they could take the money," Irena said. "And they'd already gotten their masks apparently because they lived outside of the Castle."

"How much money is left?" Runa asked.

Irena smiled.

"Enough to get out of this town when shit hits the fan and get us through at least a month," Irena said. "If we use it sparingly."

Runa put her hand on the back of Egil's neck and did the same with Irena before they all bowed slightly until their foreheads were touching. James almost wanted to look away, it seemed to almost be an intimate gesture. Runa then turned back to the two outfits. They were a very generic size, all of them except Egil, would probably fit into these uniforms. It wouldn't be perfect but at least it would be good enough.

"I'm going," Runa said. "I'd like to see anyone try and argue that."

No one said anything.

"I'm also going," James said.

Runa frowned slightly and he could see her gaze shift from him to his cane.

"We're already going to be suspicious, but if they've never had a servant with a cane and then suddenly have one. They're going to ask questions and that's the last thing we want," Runa said. James glanced down at the cane and it was almost like his bad leg had a sudden spike of pain, almost to mock him.

"If anyone asks, I'll say that I fell and wounded my knee and a doctor gave me a cane for a short amount of time," James said.

"We can't have them asking questions. We don't actually work there. If some random guard asks, that should be fine, I doubt they know every servant but what if the person in charge of all the servants asks and they ask for your name? What if someone who actually knows the employees asks you anything. Then you're screwed," Runa said.

"I'm going," James said.

"You would risk everything for your pride?" Runa asked with a frown. "It's not wrong to admit one's shortcomings, James."

James thought that that must have been one of the first times she'd ever said his name, instead of old man or something else.

"I wouldn't bring you for a marathon race as you wouldn't take me to…" Runa didn't finish her sentence but James could see the meaning in her eyes. He wouldn't bring her to a library to do research. James found it funny that she'd just said that it wasn't wrong to admit one's shortcomings but she wouldn't even admit her own.

"What if your shortcoming hinders you in this?" James said, his voice steel. "There will be a lot of listening, a lot of scouting and possibly some *reading* to get to the right place with the right keys."

Runa clenched her jaw. James could feel everyone else's stares at them. They didn't really understand the power struggle they were fighting right now but he could also tell that none of them wanted to interfere.

"Fine," Runa said, her voice cold. "But if you get caught because of your cane, I'm not coming to help you."

"I expect nothing else from you," James said.

Chapter 42

INARA

Inara had crashed that night. She'd seen her uniform for the next day but she'd simply put it away carefully and then fell asleep. In the morning, she felt refreshed but the anxiety was still there deep in the pit of her stomach. Today was the day. Inara had to admit that she hadn't thought further than today.

If Runa and James succeed in getting Anya and themselves out, where would that leave her? The chance that they found out she'd aided them was low unless they were captured but could she just go back to work like nothing had happened? Inara forced herself to take a deep breath, she'd just have to wait and see. Normally, Inara liked to plan and know the future at least to a certain extent but these last weeks had been anything but that.

Anything could happen today and Inara just prayed that no one would get hurt because of her.

There was a sudden knock on the door that startled Inara.

"Good morning! Are you ready?" Fatima's cheerful voice came through the door.

"Give me a second!" Inara answered and she quickly threw on the outfit she'd been provided. It was quite simple but soft and comfortable. It was a simple shirt with pants and suspenders; she'd also been provided with a deep purple tie and a little golden pin attached to said tie with the emblem of the Royal family.

Inara opened the door and found Fatima in the same outfit. She smiled and handed over a mask that fully covered one's face, the only truly visible part was the eyes but there was also a small hole for the mouth.

"I know they're a little creepy but you know," Fatima said jokingly. "All the nobles only have to wear half masks of course, otherwise how are they supposed to consume copious amounts of alcohol?"

Inara took one of the masks and smiled lightly.

"You don't have to put it on yet, you'll know when it's time," Fatima said. "Now, breakfast?"

"Actually, I wanted to check on the princess really quickly," Inara said.

Fatima raised an eyebrow.

"On the day of her party? I'm sure she's very busy," Fatima said.

Inara was silent for a moment.

"I tried to check on her yesterday and the guard outside said that she was sick, so I just want to make sure she is okay," Inara said.

"Oh," Fatima said and her face dropped slightly.

Inara immediately saw the change in her tone of voice, in her body and face language. Whatever was going on with the princess, Fatima knew about it.

"You know what's wrong with her?" Inara said.

Fatima glanced around them for a short moment, the corridor they were in was completely abandoned.

"It's not my place," Fatima said with a weak smile.

Inara recognised that phrase all too well, hadn't it been exactly what she'd told Anya when she'd asked about herself and Mara?

"Then I will just go and speak with her myself really quickly, I promise it won't be long," Inara said.

"Then I'll come with you," Fatima said quickly. "I'll walk you there and then we can have breakfast afterwards?"

Inara nodded slowly. It was obvious that Fatima didn't want to leave Inara's side, or perhaps she'd been ordered to not leave her side. Malik had said that Fatima would come and get her in the morning and make sure she was ready for the day. Inara couldn't put her finger on it but something had been off about Fatima since the first time she'd met her.

Fatima working down in the holding cells and then suddenly almost being Inara's chaperon. Fatima had told her that she did whatever was required of her at the Castle, which wasn't a position Inara was aware really existed because it was obvious that Fatima was more than a normal servant.

They walked in relative silence for a moment before Inara couldn't help but to ask.

"How did you come to work here?" Inara asked.

Fatima's face lost colour and she swallowed hard before she put on her smile again.

"It's a long and uninteresting story," Fatima said with a short laugh.

Inara knew she had said the wrong thing when she saw Fatima's face. The emotion on Fatima's face hadn't been one that Inara had expected to see. It was sadness or despair.

"I'm sorry," Inara said, honesty flooding her voice.

Fatima looked at her with a slight surprised look.

"For what?" Fatima asked, the smile still plastered on her face.

"Whatever brought you here must have been painful," Inara said. "I didn't mean to pry." Fatima turned her gaze forward and she cleared her throat. The smile now slightly wavering but not leaving her face.

"We all have our burdens, don't we?" Fatima said. "Scars that continue to hurt years after they have healed."

Fatima's hand instinctively went up to the scar that went from her cheek down onto her throat before she noticed herself doing it and dropped her hand. Inara simply nodded and decided to not say anything else about it.

"I like you," Fatima said. "I truly do like you, Inara."

Inara looked over at her; her turn to be slightly surprised. Those words weren't any that she often heard, especially not directed towards herself. Inara knew she could be seen as cold and imposing. She was clumsy in her speech and could get easily flustered and her whole body language was stiff.

Fatima laughed low.

"It's public knowledge I suppose," Fatima said. "Anyone in the Castle could tell you about me, so for once I can tell it first-hand. Everyone usually just finds out and then avoids me."

There was a short pause before Fatima continued.

"My father was wealthy and close to the King. He lost it all and got in deep debt with the Crown. A debt he knew he could never pay off," Fatima said, her gaze fixed forward. "He simply made a deal and it placed me here, until his debt is paid off."

Inara frowned.

"Where is your father?" Inara asked.

"Dead," Fatima simply said.

Fatima cleared her throat and smiled gently.

"I told you it was uninteresting," Fatima said.

"You also said it was long," Inara said.

"You got the short version," Fatima said. "I don't want to bore you with any details." They finally saw the princess' door, two guards were standing in front of it. "I'd like to hear the full story sometime," Inara said. "If you want to tell it that is."

Fatima frowned slightly.

"What about you?" Fatima said. "What's your story?" Inara glanced over at the door.

"We can talk after the party if you want?" Inara asked.

"I'd like that," Fatima said.

Inara walked closer to the door while Fatima stayed put.

"Be quick okay!" Fatima said.

***

Just as Inara reached the door and was about to speak with the guards, the door opened and a tall man exited the room. He was carrying what looked to be some sort of large bag, similar to doctor's bags.

"What's your purpose here?" One of the guards asked.

"I wish to speak with the princess, if only for a moment," Inara said.

The two guards exchanged glances.

"The princess is very busy today to get ready for the festivities," the other guard said.

"I know, it won't take more than a moment," Inara said. "Please tell her Inara wants a word with her. If she dismisses me, I will leave."

The first guard rolled his eyes but creaked open the door and talked with a low tone. His face when he turned back to her was rather shocked and he simply opened the door to Inara. She took that as an invitation to enter so she did and the door closed behind her.

This room was almost as gaudy as the rest of the Castle, purple and gold decorations everywhere. A bed large enough to fit comfortably at least four people and impeccably carved chairs and desks. The princess was standing at one of the large windows only in her morning robe, she had her back to Inara but quickly turned around as the door closed.

Vesper smiled as she saw Inara.

"I'm pleasantly surprised to see you," Vesper said.

Inara bowed.

"I am sorry to disturb you, princess..." Inara started.

"Vesper," she added. "And you're not interrupting at all. You're actually right on time to help me get into my dress, if you'd be so kind as to help me?"

Inara just stared at her, thinking she'd misheard her.

"I'm sorry?" Inara said.

"I have a party to attend in a few hours and I would like your help to put on my dress. It has more layers than are necessary and don't start me on the corset, it takes more than two hands to put it all on," Vesper said.

Vesper started to walk over to her large wardrobe and picked out a magnificent purple and gold dress and she continued to pick out underskirts and a corset and more things then Inara had ever seen could belong to a single dress.

"I…I don't know how to put on any of that," Inara confessed.

"I'll instruct you," Vesper said and flashed her a smile.

Inara only nodded, not sure on what else she could do in this situation. Vesper turned her back to Inara and let the morning robe drop to the floor, wearing nothing underneath. Inara immediately averted her gaze and she could feel her face burning.

"The slip goes on first," Vesper said. "It's the white short dress."

Inara quickly retrieved the slip and pulled it over Vesper's head, she tried to keep as much distance as possible but it was impossible in this situation. Inara's hand brushed against Vesper's bronze skin and it was smooth and warm and Inara retracted her hand immediately.

"Now the corset," Vesper said and glanced over her shoulder with a smile.

Inara followed all of Vesper's instructions but it took a lot longer than she would have thought and she felt bad for Fatima waiting outside.

"Why did you come here by the way?" Vesper asked.

Right, Inara had come here for an actual reason.

"I tried to come by yesterday night but the guard said you were sick," Inara said. "I just wanted to make sure you were alright."

"That's kind of you," Vesper said. "I am quite alright."

"Who was the man leaving your room?" Inara asked.

"Just my masseuse," Vesper said.

Inara said nothing more and continued to dress Vesper until she spoke again.

"Can I ask you something?" Vesper said.

"Of course," Inara said.

"What did you and my parents speak of when I left the Throne Room?" Vesper asked.

Inara stopped lacing the dress for a brief moment before she remembered what she'd been doing.

"If your parents won't tell you, then I don't think I'm in a position to do so," Inara said slowly.

Vesper huffed irritatedly.

"Could you tell me about the girl you brought in then?" Vesper asked.

Inara was silent for a moment.

"Have the King and Queen told you nothing?" Inara asked.

Vesper suddenly turned and faced Inara, half dressed.

"I am the crown princess. I will be Queen one day. Are you saying you refuse to answer my questions?" Vesper asked but there was no malice in her voice, almost desperation.

"You're the crown princess, so why haven't they told you anything?" Inara asked.

Vesper glanced over at the right wall and Inara followed her gaze until she saw a large family portrait. It was of the King, Queen, three younger boys and what had to be a toddler Vesper.

"Do you know what happened to my brothers?" Vesper asked.

Inara slowly nodded. She'd been advised by Malik to not mention it because it could be a sensitive subject so she wasn't entirely sure on how to respond in this situation.

"Of course you do," Vesper muttered. "Everyone knows everything or at least they think they do. Then you know that they all died before I reached my fifth birthday. One by one they fell, like flies, leaving only me."

Vesper laughed low.

"I was never supposed to be a ruler. I was supposed to live an unremarkable life, perhaps marry some duke or prince. I never wanted to be Queen," Vesper said.

Vesper turned back to Inara.

"I barely remember any of them. I have a vague memory of my oldest brother kissing me goodnight but that could have been any servant and I just replaced it with my brother in my memory," Vesper said. "Is it bad to say that I don't really mourn them as much as I mourn the life I should have had that they took with them to the grave?"

Inara just stared at Vesper, having no idea what to say or why she was telling her all of this.

"I was never supposed to be Queen yet here I am," Vesper said and glanced out the window. "By Artios' fifteenth birthday, he had been on more than a dussin council meetings. He never left my father's side when it came to anything political, or so Malik tells me. Then he died. Then the rest of them died."

Vesper smiled gently.

"I haven't been to a single council meeting," Vesper said. "I am always ushered out of the room when anything of importance is discussed. How am I supposed to be a just ruler if I don't know what to do? My father treats me like a child, tells me that I can learn later, that I should focus on other things now. So I read, so I sit in this room, day after day, dreading the inevitable moment I will be crowned Queen and everyone will look at me with expectation and I will have no idea what to do."

Vesper walked closer to Inara, her eyes almost pleading.

"I ask for your help," Vesper said. "Malik has tried for years to let me be at council meetings but my father refuses, he tries to give me information whenever he can."

Inara remembered the note she'd handed over to the guard from Malik yesterday.

"I need people on my side. People that are willing to help me," Vesper said. "I just want to know what is going on in my own Castle. I just want to be somewhat ready for the throne, despite my father's efforts."

Inara didn't say anything. This entire thing was overwhelming and this was the last thing she'd needed today. With everything else going on in the background and now Vesper asked her to practically act as a spy for her?

"I will protect you," Vesper added. "If you help me, I will give you my protection."

"What protection can you provide against the King?" Inara asked, her voice hoarse.

Vesper straightened her back and her sweet face turned serious.

"He might be King, but I am his only surviving child," Vesper said. "If he wants his lineage to continue, he will listen to me, sooner or later. I refuse to play spoiled princess anymore. I want to be in the game, not a disposable player on the side."

Inara stared at Vesper and the conviction she had in her voice, the want she had to do something and not just sit idly by. Vesper's words resonated deep within Inara's soul. Perhaps Vesper could be the change to this city? And perhaps

Inara could stand close by and make sure she was going down the right path. Perhaps Vesper could break the chain of lazy rulers. It was a lot of perhaps, but it was better than what Inara had heard in years.

"As long as you strive to do good, I will help you," Inara said and bowed.

Inara heard Vesper take a deep raspy breath, like she'd been holding it this entire time unsure of what Inara was going to say. Vesper gently put her hand beneath Inara's chin and made her look up at her. The sun shining from behind Vesper almost made her shine and she looked angelic.

"I will do good. You have my word," Vesper said.

Chapter 43

RUNA

The walk towards the Castle was silent. It was right before sunrise so there were barely any people outside and the streets were eerily quiet. Runa had been out at night before but something felt different today, the only real sound that was heard was James' cane hitting the cobblestone over and over again.

Runa glanced over at him, they were both wearing the festive servants outfits and they had both decided to immediately put on their masks, there was no need for anyone to see their faces beforehand. Runa felt her heart pounding in her chest. The costume was a little tight over her chest and arms, nothing noticeable but it made everything more uncomfortable. James' body language looked calm every time she looked over at him but he was walking slowly even for him, he was leaning heavily on his cane and was in obvious pain but trying to hide it.

Runa clenched her jaw and focused her gaze upon the Castle. She couldn't be thinking about James right now, they had more important things to think about. If she worried he'd be caught because of his cane, it would jeopardise herself as well and if they both got caught, it was game over. Even if Runa wanted them all to come out of this alive and well, she knew deep down that she would throw James to the wolves if necessary and she was sure he would do the same.

They didn't care about the other. They were only here because of a common goal that meant more to the two of them than anything else in the world.

When they finally reached the gate to the Castle, there were almost a dozen guards standing outside, all of them on high alert. Runa forced herself to take a deep breath and relax her body. This was what she did, she talked, she lied and she pretended to be someone far more confident and capable than she actually was. One of the guards put up his hand, a sign for them to stop and they immediately stopped moving.

"You're a little early," the guard said with a slight frown. "Do you have a special reason to go through the main gate and not the servant's entrance?"

They hadn't known about a servant's entrance but it made complete sense now when he said it. Would they really fail this mission without it even really getting started?

"I wounded my leg yesterday, I got permission to enter the main gate with assistance from our superior, they didn't mention that?" James spoke, his voice steady and calm.

The guard sighed deeply and looked a little annoyed.

"They did not but I'm not surprised really, the communication these past few days have been awful," the guard said.

There was a pause before he spoke again.

"Are you sure you can work like that?" The guard asked.

James nodded.

"I am sure, it's just a simple sprained knee. I can walk without the cane but doctor Marsh down the road insisted," James said with a slightly playful tone.

The guard chuckled slightly.

"Ah, that old fox," the guard said. "Did he make you drink his new 'miracle' elixir?" The guard said, the tone of his voice completely changed.

"He did!" James said. "It did nothing and tasted vile but he seems certain it will be a miracle at some point."

The guard laughed and James joined in, like they were having some inside joke with each other. Runa just stood in silence, quite shocked by the whole situation. She'd had no idea that James was capable of being this charming and good at lying.

This wasn't who he was to her and this really showed how little they did know about each other.

"Go on inside," the guard said and made a hand wave to open the large gate. "Have a good day and if you see my nephew, Clark Grilsh, tell him I still expect to get paid back what he owes me!"

"Will do," James said with a little bow.

The large gate opened and James started walking inside. It took a beat for Runa to start moving and catch up, she was still slightly in shock from that whole conversation. The moment the gate closed behind them and they came into a large hall, which for this moment was empty, Runa leaned closer to James and spoke.

"What the hell was that?" Runa whispered.

"You mean me saving our entire mission?" James said. "You're welcome."

"But how did you know what to say?" Runa asked.

"I used my leg to my advantage and I know of every other doctor in this city. A lot of their people come by my place and are more than happy to talk. I knew that if I talked about something they knew off, something that felt recognisable and safe to them, they would let down their guard," James said.

Even through the full face masks, they locked eyes with each other. Runa opened and closed her mouth at least three times, almost saying something but finally decided to keep her mouth shut.

"So where do we go from here?" James asked and looked around the room.

Runa took a deep breath just as a door to the right opened and another guard came into their line of sight. The guard frowned slightly and walked straight up to them.

"What are you guys doing here? You're supposed to be in the kitchen helping out!" She said, slightly annoyed.

Runa was just about to say something but was interrupted.

"Gods, everything's a mess already," the guard said with a sigh. "You're one of the newly hired ones, aren't you?"

Runa immediately nodded.

"Of course you are," the guard said. "Just follow me but I'm going to tell your superior about this later, so don't screw up any more today or this will be your last day working here."

"Understood," James answered.

The guard rolled her eyes and quickly started moving, not really caring that James was using a cane and walking slower, she simply glanced back at them from time to time and then gave a deep, annoyed sigh. This would surely be their last day working in the Castle but then again, that worked perfectly for them. If everything worked out, they wouldn't set foot in this city for a good while.

As they walked, Runa and James exchanged one last glance. They both knew there was no turning back now. They would either succeed or spend the rest of their time in The Grove. If they were lucky.

Chapter 44

INARA

Inara couldn't help but feel uncomfortable as the Throne Room had quickly started to fill with people in clothes she barely could believe were real. The dresses were large and with intricate embroideries that glittered when the light hit it just right. The suits were tailored to perfection and were made with fabrics in the most extraordinary colours.

Inara had thought that the princess' dress had been extravagant but now she knew that the princess had probably gone for a more toned down version so she could blend in better. No one knew what she was going to wear, except the guards and the King and Queen so they could keep an eye on her during the night. Inara also doubted that a lot of the people there had actually seen the princess in recent years.

This was a huge celebration and she knew that people even from outside Taurin had come to celebrate her birthday. So blending in probably wouldn't be that hard and it would make the reveal at the end so much more extravagant.

It was hard to recognise any of the people Inara knew in the costumes and masks they all wore that made them look almost identical. The hair and body type was the only thing that could distinguish someone but it was still almost impossible to know who was who. The room had also started to fill with servants walking around with trays that contained both alcohol in tall glasses but also small pieces of food. Inara couldn't help but wonder if any of the servants walking around was Runa or someone else from that group.

The band in the corner started to pick up the pace with the music, showing that the celebration truly had begun. Inara looked over at the King and Queen, they were both dressed beautifully and they were sitting closer to each other than they had before. Both had a glass in their hand and it would seem they thought they were unobserved because they were whispering to each other and the King even seemed to laugh a little. If it hadn't been for the throne and the extravagant clothes, they could have looked like any other couple enjoying each other's time.

Then suddenly someone moved right beside Inara. She glanced to her side and saw the same outfit and mask that she was wearing staring back at her.

"Are you enjoying things so far?" Malik's voice came out from beneath the mask.

Inara sighed slightly in relief that it was someone she knew and trusted and not some stranger.

"It's a lot," Inara said honestly. "This isn't anything I'm used to."

Malik chuckled and turned to look out through the crowd.

"It is something special alright," Malik said.

Inara stared at the costume he was wearing. It was the exact same as the one she was wearing which seemed strange to her. He was the War Counsellor after all, the one in charge of every guard in the city, shouldn't his outfit be different to show his status?

"What's going on in that head of yours?" Malik asked.

"I thought you'd have a different outfit from the rest of us," Inara simply said.

Malik chuckled once again.

"I am technically just a guard like the rest of you," Malik said. "No reason for me to stand out, especially not on the princess' birthday."

"You're the War Counsellor, you're not…" Inara started.

"Well, perhaps the princess isn't the only one who enjoys a little anonymity from time to time," Malik said, his voice soft. "It's nice to just melt into the background for a moment and forget all the burdens put on you, even if only for a couple of hours."

"I'm sorry, I didn't mean…" Inara started.

"Enjoy yourself tonight," Malik said, his voice a little more serious. "I have a feeling this celebration will change things."

A chill went down Inara's spine at those words. He wasn't talking about her betrayal or the plan to break out Anya, he couldn't be. It was impossible but somehow that didn't calm her down.

"For the good of course," Malik said with the same cheerful tone as he usually had. "I think the princess will have the strength to stand up to her father after tonight. For her to finally take some control."

Inara swallowed and just nodded. Of course that's what he was talking about, the princess had mentioned that Malik had tried to help her gain some control and gather knowledge within the Castle. Inara hoped he was right. She would follow the princess if she held true to her word that she wanted to actually make some changes for the good in this city and country.

"Now, you're allowed to have one drink tonight, make it worth it," Malik said with an obvious smile beneath the mask. "And enjoy yourself, dance, talk but continue to do your job."

"This really isn't my thing," Inara said. "I don't dance, I don't really talk…"

"Well, I think I see someone who might want a dance with you," Malik said, his gaze fixed forward.

Inara turned forward and saw a shorter woman in the same dress that Inara had helped the princess get into. Her face was covered in a beautiful golden mask and she was wearing a ruby red lipstick. She walked up to the two of them and gave Malik a slight nod before she turned to Inara.

"Could I have a dance?" It was obviously the princess' soft voice that spoke to her and Inara thought her heart might stop dead in her chest.

Inara looked over at Malik but he'd already left his spot and had disappeared amongst the other guards. The princess held out a hand towards Inara.

"I'm sure there are other people you'd rather dance with," Inara said softly.

"If that was the case, then I'd be standing in front of them," Vesper said with a smile. "Are you going to refuse me this dance?"

The smile lingered on Vesper's lips and her hand was still outreached towards her. Inara couldn't help but glance over to the King and Queen. Vesper followed her gaze.

"Don't worry about my parents, they're not paying attention to me right now. Some of the other guards might talk though," Vesper said. "They might be jealous."

Inara swallowed hard before she slowly nodded.

"One dance," Inara said. "Though I have to warn you, I'm an awful dancer."

"Then just follow my lead," Vesper said.

Inara took a hold of her hand and Vesper led them out onto the dance floor. Inara didn't know where to place her hands but to her relief Vesper guided her where to put them. Though when her hands touched Vesper's waist, Inara could feel herself getting red in the face and she thanked the Gods that she was wearing this stupid mask right now.

As they started to slowly dance, Inara felt incredibly self-conscious and looked around herself at all times, worrying that people were looking at them but found that no one paid any attention to them at all. Vesper's grasp on her shoulder and her hand was comforting and steady. Before Inara had really noticed it, she'd let out a small laugh when Vesper let go of her shoulder and did a small twirl before they went back to the same slow dance they'd done before.

"You're not that awful of a dancer," Vesper said. "I've danced with worse."

Inara smiled gently and found that she actually enjoyed this and wasn't it her job to keep an eye on the princess after all? This way she made sure that her eyes never strayed from her side.

Inara found that she didn't want to look away from Vesper anyway, she didn't want to let go of her or go back to where she'd been standing. Inara wanted to stay right where she was, with Vesper in front of her.

Then from out of the corner of her eye, she spotted something she immediately recognised and brought her back to reality. Inara saw a man dressed in the servants' outfit, using a cane, the same cane she'd given back to James Braelish just a few days ago.

Chapter 45

JAMES

The Throne Room was packed to the brim with people and it took James a moment to realise that the guards were wearing the same outfits as the servants with the exception of a golden sigil with the royal emblem on their tie. He tried to stay away from them as much as possible as he slowly made his way across the room with the tray of alcohol in one hand and his cane in the other.

As soon as he and Runa had entered the Throne Room, he'd lost sight of her, there was just a sea of identical outfits amongst the obviously noble people. James just had to hope that because he was using a cane that she would be able to find him but with every minute passing, he started to get more worried about their plan. Barely anyone was leaving the Throne Room, except the few servants who were responsible for getting more alcohol and food, and unfortunately, neither him nor Runa had been assigned that position.

They were stuck walking around, serving all the guests. If they left the room it would be obvious, at least at this point. They would have to wait for something to distract everyone enough for them to be able to sneak out and he had to trust that Runa could get the keys needed for them to get where they needed to go.

As James scanned the crowd, he wondered if Inara was behind any of those masks. They'd gotten this far so it seemed she was a woman of her word and it wasn't just a trap, which in itself was a relief but this was far from over.

The music suddenly changed and the crowd in the middle of the room went from quietly mingling or dancing to suddenly forming two rows and dancing rapidly with each other while laughing. The volume in the room had increased in a few seconds and it was a much livelier affair than it had been a couple of moments ago. James' leg hurt as he kept walking around offering drinks, he couldn't sit down and do nothing.

Multiple people had already asked about his cane and what had happened and he didn't need more attention directed towards him or worse get thrown out for not being able to do his job.

He could rest once this whole ordeal was done or when he was dead, whatever came first at this point.

Another hour passed and now he could really start feeling his leg start throbbing in pain and he was leaning more heavily on his cane as he made his way around. James took another step and felt how his leg buckled from the pain and he felt himself starting to fall forward with the tray of glasses still being held up in his other hand. He was going to fall and drop all the glasses on the floor and probably get the liquid on multiple noble dresses when he quickly felt a strong hand catch him and steady his tray.

For a second, James could barely breathe and he looked up at whoever had saved him from tripping, expecting it to be a guard. It was a servant and when his eyes met theirs, he instantly recognised Runa's intense gaze behind the mask.

Runa said nothing but took the tray from his hands, she must have just put down hers to be refilled and then passed him, like nothing had happened. James thought that no one must have even noticed their interaction, it had happened so fast. He couldn't help but follow Runa with his gaze as she walked away.

That girl kept surprising him and every time she did, he felt shame flood his body.

James knew he couldn't continue like this, he had to take a break or he would only be a hindrance for the rest of the night. He managed to find a small crook behind a pillar in one of the corners of the room where no one should be able to find him if they weren't looking. With a heavy sigh of relief, James leaned against the wall and took some pressure off his leg.

His heart was beating fast from that close incident and if they got out of there, he would tell Runa that he was grateful for her assistance. She probably wouldn't take it or say something sarcastic back or tell him it was only for the mission but he had started to see past her facade. It was a small crack but it was there, it was obvious the more time he spent time with her.

Another hour passed when James went from serving people and hiding in his corner to letting his leg rest and even though his leg was still killing him, those small breaks did help to keep him going but if this kept up, he knew he wouldn't last the entire night. There had been multiple speeches made by a dussin nobles directed at the disguised princess in the crowd. Mostly to wish her a happy birthday or tell some stories of when the princess had been young and similar.

James hadn't really been paying attention, they all sounded pretentious and made them sound more important to the princess than they probably were. James could also clearly tell by the speeches that the alcohol had really started to set in and he saw more and more people slightly swaying as they walked to get another glass. That was good at least, they would demand more attention from the servants and guards, taking attention away from him and Runa hopefully.

The whole atmosphere changed in a split second.

All the lights in the room turned off, leaving them all in pitch black darkness. James realized he hadn't noticed any torches or similar on the walls and he had no idea how all the lights had disappeared at the same time. But that was the least of his problems as it just took another second for panic to set it, people started to scream and shout and move around the room in chaotic patterns.

Someone knocked into James and the tray of glasses fell to the floor but he could hear that sound from multiple places in the room, he hadn't been the only one to drop things. He couldn't see anything at all, just felt people moving around and hearing their panicked talking.

This was their chance, whatever had caused the darkness had given them the perfect opportunity to sneak out of here, as long as Runa had the keys.

A pair of strong harsh hands grabbed his free arm and dragged them both to the side of the room. It was obvious to him from the length of this person that it was not Runa and he felt his heart drop. James tried to get loose from the person's grip but they had an iron clasp around his arm. Something was shoved into his hand. It was cold, small and it only took him a beat to realise it was a key.

"Knock three times fast, then two times slow, someone will let you in. The laboratory should be quite empty but there will still be people down there. Anya will be easy to spot the further in you go. Be quick," Inara's voice sounded raspy and slightly panicked as she spoke.

"Thank you," was all James managed to say back.

"Don't thank me yet, I have no idea what's going on," Inara said and then quickly left his side.

As James slowly tried to make his way through the crowd, a voice broke through the panicked shouting.

"Everyone stay calm!" It was an obvious authoritarian voice and James thought he recognised it but he couldn't place it. "Until we get the lights on again,

I will escort the King and Queen to their room! Miss Justifa, please escort the princess to her room! This is for the safety of the Royal Family but the rest of you will stay in here. The guards will make sure you are safe as well!"

More shouts and murmuring started up after he had spoken, the nobles didn't seem to be happy with that answer. James got a horrifying feeling that this was more than just some accidental darkness and that man knew it, he just didn't want to scare the rest of the guests too much. When James had been in the civil war back in his home country, he'd heard his superior speak with the same kind of cadence as that man. It never meant anything good was happening.

Was it possible that he and Runa weren't alone in trying to sneak into the Castle tonight?

The doors opened and as James' eyes had started to adjust to the darkness a little bit, he could see shapes exiting the room but all the guests were restricted from leaving. He hoped that because at first glance his outfit could be either that of a servant or a guard, he would be let through, it was hard to see a small pin with the royal sigil on it in the dark after all.

James took the chance and moved quicker than was wiser for his leg but he managed to get out before the door shut behind him again with another couple of servants and guards. They all seemed to know exactly what to do and quickly made their way either to the Royal family's rooms to help or to go and see to it so that the lights would come on again.

James just stood still a few metres from the door, he opened his fist and saw the shape of a key in his hand. The key and then three rapid knocks followed by two slow ones, he had everything he needed to get Anya. Now he just had to find his way through the labyrinth that was this Castle, in the dark.

James took a deep breath when he felt someone grab his arm for the third time that night. Luckily, when he turned to face the person, he saw the vague outline of Runa's face, the mask hanging around her throat.

"We have to find a way to get the keys, fast. This darkness won't..." Runa started.

"I have everything we need," James said, interrupting her.

James placed the key in Runa's hand and mentioned the knocks.

"You will get there faster than me," James said, his voice filled with sadness but also honesty. "I will make my way there as well and I'll meet you on the way, but we have to prioritise getting Anya out as fast as possible."

Runa stared at James, her mouth slightly open and her eyes wide.

"Please," was all that slipped through James lips, his eyes almost pleading.

"I'll get her back, I promise," Runa said.

James nodded in reply and before he'd said another thing, Runa had started sprinting down the stairs. Her steps made no sound and he lost her in the dark in seconds.

Chapter 46

ANYA

"Do you know Moira Stone?" Anya asked the shape of Merope in front of her.

Merope crossed her arms and lifted a brow.

"How do you know of her?" Merope asked instead of giving an answer.

Anya couldn't help but quickly glance down at the mark on her hand and the vision of Andrew laying on the ground, desperately trying to tell her something as he was dying flashed before her eyes.

"The previous host mentioned her before he…" Anya said, stopping mid-sentence. "He told me to find her."

Merope was silent for a moment, contemplating what to say. Her small blue eyes staring at Anya with an intense look.

"I know her," Merope said. "But I have not seen her in a long time."

"Why would Andr…the previous host tell me to find her?" Anya asked.

"Probably because she is one of the oldest Mark hosts I know of, otherwise I have no idea," Merope said.

"Moira Stone has a Mark?" Anya almost whispered. "But she worked here, in this Castle. Wouldn't that put her in danger?"

"Sometimes the best place to hide is in plain sight," Merope said. "Though I wasn't aware of that, as I said, I haven't seen her in a long time."

"What Mark does she have?" Anya couldn't help but ask.

"I…I am not certain," Merope said with some uncertainty in her voice. "I saw her use her power once or twice but she wouldn't let me see the Mark or explain which one it was. Even with my Mind Mark, I couldn't figure it out."

Anya was silent for a moment.

"Do you think she could help me?" Anya asked low.

"Help you with what?" Merope asked, confused.

"With the Mark? With explaining all of this? Telling me what I'm supposed to do?" Anya said, her voice gaining some stress.

Merope was now silent for a few seconds.

"No," Merope finally said and stared right into Anya's eyes, her own eyes as cold as steel. "You have most of the information we all share but every Mark is different and no one will know yours better than yourself. Moira has been a recluse for a number of years. Every time I try to talk to her through my Mark, she refuses to say or do anything until I leave."

Merope sighed deeply.

"I doubt she will be of much help," Merope said. "But as I said, if you desire you are more than welcome to join our little group. We are stronger in numbers and there is safety in not having to hide who you truly are."

"That…that sounds nice," Anya said. "I don't think I know who I am anymore."

"Of course not," Merope said. "The moment you received the Mark you were born anew. No normal human will ever understand how people like you and me feel. How simply hosting this Mark changes us at our very core yet we are still the same person as we were before."

"The people closest to you will never understand and they will come to fear you, because the truth is now you are much more powerful than any of them. The truth is that we are dangerous and we could destroy entire cities if we desired. It is hard being nothing besides a God."

Anya swallowed hard and lifted her left hand, staring at the Mark so clear on her pale skin. "We're not Gods," Anya said with sadness. "We're just hosts to things older and stronger than we'll ever be. Things we might never understand completely."

Merope tilted her head slightly and frowned.

"We can do things no normal human can; we can live forever, survive lethal wounds and so much more. If that is not the closest thing to a God we have on this planet, I don't know what is," Merope said. "We survived the merging of the Mark which makes it part of us. Its powers are now ours. The Marks cannot survive outside of a host; if anything they need us more than we'll ever need them."

A silence fell over the room, the tension felt so thick, Anya almost struggled to breathe at one point. Merope sighed.

"Enough philosophy talk," Merope said with a weak smile. "We are currently moving in your direction and we'll try to provide aid but it will be a while. But we cannot just storm the city and Castle, we'll have to be careful or we'll just end up right beside you."

"Didn't you just say you could destroy entire cities if you wanted to?" Anya said.

Silence once again.

"We could. But it is not our current goal to bring that much attention to ourselves," Merope said seriously.

Anya opened her mouth to speak again when everything turned dark. Her usual lit up see through cube was now as dark as the room around her. A tingling sensation, almost itching, started in her left hand and when she looked down she could see the Mark dimly glow. Anya closed her eyes and focused on that tingling sensation until it turned into a pleasant heat and when she opened her eyes, the Mark had lit up enough to envelope her in light.

"*Be careful,*" it said. "*You are using your own life energy to give yourself light, you cannot keep this up forever unless you feed the fire properly.*"

"Anya, what happened?" Merope said, confused. "I can barely see you anymore."

"The room went dark," Anya simply said. "I don't know what happened."

"Strange," Merope said slowly. "This could be a trick. Stay vigilant, stay cautious. Don't do anything stupid."

Without saying another word, the vague vision of Merope disappeared and Anya was left alone.

Though she wasn't afraid, she'd been in this exact situation a few times now in her dreams. Complete darkness with only herself and Fire providing any light, the only difference was that this was no dream. Anya almost felt as if her entire body was emitting a soft glow and the warmth and comfort it provided made her feel braver than she'd done in days.

Anya glanced down at the Mark.

It is my power, I have control, Anya thought to herself.

"*Finally, you're starting to understand,*" Fire almost whispered excitedly.

Finally, Anya did understand.

The fire raging in her body wasn't consuming her because she was the fire.

Chapter 47

RUNA

Runa ran faster than she'd ever run before. She could hear her heart pounding like a drum in her ears, deafening out every other sound that could be around her. Everything was a blur as she passed door after door, corridor after corridor, everything looked the same but it didn't stop her.

She'd studied those maps and the road she'd have to take through the Castle a thousand times and even if they weren't completely correct, it bolstered her courage and kept her legs moving. Runa wasn't thinking, she was simply letting her legs lead the way, hoping that somehow, by some miracle, they would instinctively know their way to Anya.

Before she knew it, she was standing in front of a large steel door and it was the first time since Runa had left James that she actually was paying attention. The entire time she'd run, the alarms could have been going or she could have passed people and she would have had no idea. The large steel door sent a chill down Runa's spine and she knew she had the right place.

Even though she was still in darkness, her eyes had adjusted themselves a good while back and now she could see most shapes and even some of the larger details. Runa placed the key in the door and turned it. It opened with a satisfying click and she let out a sigh of relief. Step one done.

As Runa turned to stare down the long stairs, she felt all colour drain from her face. Even if she'd been running in darkness for a while, the darkness down there seemed thicker, darker. Like no light could exist without a struggle. It was like walking down into the pits of hell and she could feel the hairs on her arms raise. There was a coldness coming from the bottom that chilled her to her core. Runa swallowed and ignored the knot in her stomach telling her to close the door and leave, she had come too far to turn back now.

Runa found a torch and matches beside the door and she sighed in relief. Walking in the darkness of the Castle hadn't been a problem but she felt as if she walked down there without a light, the darkness would swallow her whole. When she'd gotten the torch going, she slowly closed the door behind her but made sure it didn't lock. They would probably need a speedy escape and couldn't stand around unlocking every door.

Runa walked down the stairs with careful steps. Any kind of rush or need to hurry had vanished the moment she'd set foot on the first step. Runa walked as fast as she could, it felt excruciatingly slow but she couldn't force her legs to move faster. Finally, she saw another door, leading somewhere else and she couldn't wait to get away from these stairs, any place had to be better.

Without hesitating, she knocked three times fast and then two times slow and waited. The door opened after a short moment, a man holding a torch of his own that slightly lit up his face and the exasperated look on it.

"What…" he said with a slightly puzzled expression but Runa didn't let him say another word. Runa kicked him in the stomach, he fell over doubled and with her quick right hand, she slipped one of the knives she'd stored on her body and hit him hard on the side of the head with the butt of the knife. The man collapsed like a sack of laundry. The torch fell to the floor but nothing would catch fire as it was made out of stone, it would burn itself out sooner or later.

The adrenaline streaming through her body made her focus and she barely stopped moving as she'd knocked him unconscious. There was a small corridor before she came to another door. She slammed it open, moving the torch to get a look around the room. It was filled with tubes, papers and other things Runa had no idea what they were. It was certainly some kind of scientific place but she saw no one else as she entered but she did notice that two torches had been put up to shed some light.

The man she'd knocked out must have been alone down here and his first instinct had been to light torches to illuminate the room, smart man. Runa moved quickly through the room. She heard a small clink from somewhere but when she turned to look she saw no one. The place was beneath the ground, it wasn't surprising that it made some weird sounds. Runa didn't have time to look through the entire room to see if someone was hiding, that wasn't her priority. After all, they'd just be scientists like that man that had opened the door, whoever it was, Runa was sure she could handle them.

Runa finally found another door and when she opened it she almost dropped the torch in her hand. In what looked like a see through box she saw Anya, shedding more light than the torch Runa was holding. Runa's feet moved by themselves, slowly closer towards Anya who was staring at her with large eyes that quickly turned into a frown. Anya looked otherworldly and Runa couldn't take her eyes off her. It was like time stood still for a short moment before it was broken by Anya speaking.

"Runa?"

That was all it took and Runa ran up to the box and she noticed a door into it. It would surely be locked but they had to be able to get Anya out of there together somehow. Perhaps there was another key back in the other room?

"Wait," Runa said out of breath. "I'm going to look for the key."

Anya turned her head towards the door. A look of surprise came upon her face, almost like she'd never noticed the door before. Runa ran back to the other room and quickly started to rummage through every drawer, box and anything that could contain a key. In one drawer, she found an entire ring filled with keys; one of them had to be to Anya's cage, one of them just had to. They were wasting time.

Runa ran back into Anya's room and didn't stop until she stood in front of the door. Her hands were shaking slightly as she tried to find the right key for the lock and it felt as if an eternity passed until she found it. The door unlocked with a low click and Runa immediately took a couple of steps backwards. She wasn't sure why but she felt as if she had to give Anya space, as if she was getting to close to her something bad would happen. Even though every fibre of her being wanted to embrace Anya, there were warning bells ringing in her head. Something about how Anya was glowing almost scared her, even if she didn't want to admit it. Anya slowly pushed the door of the cage open and then a loud bang was heard, followed by a ringing sound echoing through the room and Runa collapsed on the ground. She glanced towards her shoulder and saw blood spurting out of a small hole in her flesh. It wasn't painful but Runa knew that was the shock and the pain would hit her soon. What had just happened?

Runa tried to glance up but moving sent a shooting pain through her entire arm like nothing she'd ever felt before but she managed to see another shape in the door opening. The woman was holding a torch in one hand and some strange device in her other, it was shaped weirdly but seemed to fit perfectly into her hand and it was certainly a crafted piece. Smoke slowly billowed out of an opening at the front of it.

"Get back into the cage, Anya," the woman spoke. She was trying to sound authoritarian but the wobble in her voice betrayed her. "Or she dies."

This again. Runa got awful flashbacks from the time they'd been captured, she could almost feel the cold steel of Inara's blade on her neck. Runa glanced over at Anya who looked petrified. Runa wasn't sure that Anya could move even if she wanted right now. She'd seen that look on people's faces before.

Runa had dropped the torch but managed to keep her knife in her other hand. If she was going to die here, she wasn't going to go out without a fight. Even though her entire body protested, Runa rose from where she'd been laying and ran straight towards the woman, her knife at the ready. A scream of every pent up emotion she'd kept deep inside of her for so long filled the room.

Runa barely got halfway to the woman when that same bang and ringing sound was heard and Runa now saw that it for certain came from that strange device in the woman's hand.

Runa managed to stay up this time, slightly more expecting it and her eyes locked with the woman for a second. There was regret in the woman's face and something close to terror. Runa saw her hands shaking so bad she was close to dropping the device and the torch. Runa glanced down at her stomach and saw a big red patch soak through her clothes. Something between a laugh and a scoff escaped Runa's lips before her legs buckled. Runa let go of her knife to try and keep herself at least on her knees.

The room suddenly filled with a bright light and the warmth of a searing fire threatened to consume them all. An inhuman scream filled the room, it was a mixture of the crackling of fire and the sound of anger that came from deep inside someone. Runa collapsed on the floor and she only saw flashes of what happened next. A shape moved past her and picked up her knife but it was moving too fast to see, then a scream of pain, then nothing.

Or almost nothing. There was a sound Runa was familiar with still hanging in the air, the sound of a knife piercing flesh over and over again.

The bright light faded slightly and Runa managed to glance over towards where the woman had stood. Runa couldn't believe what she was seeing, a part of her was refusing to acknowledge what she was seeing. It was Anya, sitting on top of the body of the woman. Anya was holding Runa's knife in her hands and blood was dripping down from it.

Anya was completely covered in crimson and the woman's body was almost unrecognisable. Anya had killed her. Runa's gaze was getting hazy and she could feel her energy slipping out of her alongside the massive amount of blood she was losing.

Anya, her chest heaving and her face turned away from Runa, slowly stood up. The sound of a knife dropping to the floor was heard and then Anya looked over at Runa. Their eyes met and Runa begged that it was the blood loss making her see things because the person standing there didn't look like Anya, not like her Anya. Anya's eyes were ablaze and the mark on her left hand almost looked like it contained the sun behind it. Her pale unhealthy complexion had disappeared.

Instead, she had rosy cheeks and she looked more alive than Runa had seen her in years. Anya glanced down at what she'd done and some of that fire in her eyes flickered for a moment before it returned in full force.

Runa could feel tears streaming down her face. If it was from what she was seeing or because she hadn't blinked in minutes she couldn't tell. Anya looked at Runa with pity and cocked her head to the side, like Runa had seen her do before she'd spewed fire towards guards. It was like someone was whispering into her ears, someone telling her something important.

Runa tried to raise her hand towards Anya but she barely managed to lift it from the ground. Her body felt more like a prison to her consciousness than anything else right now.

"Anya," Runa tried to say but it was nothing more than a mumble.

Anya closed her eyes with a frown and then there was a large flash of fire engulfing her. When the fire died down, there was no sign of Anya. Runa felt her heart shattering as her eyes started to become unbearably heavy because she realised what had just happened.

Anya had left her here to die.

Runa could feel the warm blood against her cold skin, she pressed her hand hard onto the wound on her stomach in a desperate attempt to keep some of the blood inside of her. The tears hadn't stopped streaming down her face and Runa let out a high pitch scream of agony with the last of her strength.

The last thought running through Runa's head, over and over again was:

I don't want to die here.